Praise for *Ahab's Return*

"This is an adventure ——————————— fast-paced, occasionally acerbic, c————————— ing story is an homage to *Moby-D*—————————— nclusion of Ahab's story." —————————— nal of Books

"One of the dependable pleasures of Jeffrey Ford's work, apart from his precise and lyrical prose and generally ingratiating characters, is its acute sense of place. . . . As effective as *Ahab's Return* is as a fast-paced and efficient thriller, it's also a sharply critical fiction, raising issues of addiction, homelessness, and demagoguery."
—*Locus*

"Ford knows how to tell a story, whatever the genre, and how to get out of its way and when to stop, and here that makes for a great few hours between the covers. . . . Sign on for this one; it's well worth the trip."
—Washington Independent Review of Books

"An imaginary sequel to an imaginative work, a virtual or alternate vision. . . . Primed for adventure, Harrow guides [Ahab] through New York's seething underworld on his quest and perchance to find fresh material. Of that, readers are dealt a-plenty."
—*Free Lance-Star* (Fredericksburg)

"Unusual and gripping. . . . Fans of successful reimaginings of literary classics . . . will be entertained." —*Publishers Weekly*

"It takes chutzpah to revive one of the most vivid yet most unknowable characters in all literature, let alone to place him in a story that celebrates its own essential pulpiness. . . . Jeffrey Ford has that chutzpah. . . . Marvelous." —*SciFi* magazine ("A" rating)

Ahab's Return

ALSO BY JEFFREY FORD

Vanitas

The Physiognomy

Memoranda

The Beyond

The Fantasy Writer's Assistant

The Portrait of Mrs. Charbuque

The Girl in the Glass

The Empire of Ice Cream

The Cosmology of the Wider World

The Shadow Year

The Drowned Life

Crackpot Palace

A Natural History of Hell

The Twilight Pariah

Ahab's Return

or,

THE LAST VOYAGE

JEFFREY FORD

WILLIAM MORROW
An Imprint of HarperCollins*Publishers*

P.S.™ is a trademark of HarperCollins Publishers.

AHAB'S RETURN. Copyright © 2018 by Jeffrey Ford. Excerpt from THE SHADOW YEAR © 2008 by Jeffrey Ford. All rights reserved. Printed in the United States of America. No part of this book may be used or reproduced in any manner whatsoever without written permission except in the case of brief quotations embodied in critical articles and reviews. For information, address HarperCollins Publishers, 195 Broadway, New York, NY 10007.

HarperCollins books may be purchased for educational, business, or sales promotional use. For information, please email the Special Markets Department at SPsales@harpercollins.com.

A hardcover edition of this book was published in 2018 by William Morrow, an imprint of HarperCollins Publishers.

FIRST WILLIAM MORROW PAPERBACK EDITION PUBLISHED 2019.

Designed by Leah Carlson-Stanisic

Illustration by Hein Nouwens/Shutterstock, Inc.

The Library of Congress has catalogued a previous edition as follows:

Names: Ford, Jeffrey, 1955– author.
Title: Ahab's return : or, The last voyage / Jeffrey Ford.
Other titles: Last voyage
Description: New York, NY : William Morrow, [2018] |
Identifiers: LCCN 2018006262 (print) | LCCN 2018008835 (ebook) | ISBN 9780062679031 (E-Book) | ISBN 9780062679000 (hardback) | ISBN 9780062679017 (trade pb) | ISBN 9780062849090 (audio)
Subjects: LCSH: Ahab, Captain (Fictitious character)—Fiction. | Ishmael (Fictitious character)—Fiction. | BISAC: FICTION / Mystery & Detective / Historical. | FICTION / Literary.
Classification: LCC PS3556.O6997 (ebook) | LCC PS3556.O6997 A74 2018 (print) | DDC 813/.54—dc23
LC record available at https://lccn.loc.gov/2018006262

ISBN: 978-0-06-267901-7 (pbk.)

19 20 21 22 23 LSC 10 9 8 7 6 5 4 3 2 1

For the entire crew—
Lynn, Jack, Brianna, Derek, Finn, Nellie, Peps
And all the goddamn cats

Americans so dearly love to be fooled.

—Charles Baudelaire

Ahab's Return

❧❧❧❧❧❧❧

1

November 1853, a blustery night somewhere in the middle of a long week. The infernal cuckoo clock in the offices of the *Gorgon's Mirror,* the premiere five-cent illustrated rag of hokum in the great city of Manhattan, sounded. Every hour on the hour a skeleton, scythe in hand, pursued a hapless sinner out one door and round the baroque mechanism to another all the while that blasted bird chirped away. I was trying to get warm, blowing into my cupped hands and stretching them out toward the candle's glow. I'd been out for a stroll, a dozen oysters, and a tankard, hoping it would spark my imagination.

Garrick, my editor, had warned before he'd left at sundown that I'd better come up with some choice nugget of humbug for the morrow's run or I'd feel the full blast of his wrath. The old man, like his publication, was more hot air than actual horror, but still I hated to disappoint him. He was like a father to me, or at least to my flights of fancy. "Harrow," he'd say. "You might be the finest *confabulator* on this godforsaken island." Whereas another might have taken the term to mean *liar,* I understood it to be an appellation of artistic prowess.

That late night, though, I was neither. My mind was as blank as the page in front of me. Rufus Sharde, my competitor at the *Cockaigne Times,* with whom I usually had drinks at Fraunce's Tavern on Monday evenings, once told that he'd overheard P. T. Barnum, the humbug's humbug, say, in relation to one of his critics, that there was only so much imagination in a given individual and when it was gone that person was bereft of the ability to wonder. To think, after I'd come up with the "Hell's Gate Mermaid," "The Headless Strangler of Battery Park," "Colonel Maranda's Live Burial," "The Congo Homunculus," igniting imaginations from Slate Street to Forty-Second and beyond, frightening the weak of heart and head, that I was now as empty as a politician's promise. The thought of it drew a shiver.

Just as despair was sinking its claws into me, there was a great bang, the flinging wide of the door to the street, which was down a short set of steps to my left. The wind rushed up from outside, rifling the papers on the office desks, guttering the weak flame in the fireplace, and extinguishing my candle. I heard the door slam shut as I groped for matches. There came a heavy tread upon the stairway, every other as sharp and as distinctive as a hammer blow. I'm afraid I'm only courageous in the articles I pen, and so my hands shook badly as I relit the wick and spun to encounter the intruder.

He stood in the dim light of the entranceway. His beard, his glare, his stillness put me off. He exuded a sense of tension, a spring about to snap, and stared at me imperiously as if *I* had intruded upon *him*. I could tell from his peacoat and his broadfall breeches that he was a man of the sea. Noting his silk top hat and overall countenance—the stern glare of one who seemed used to giving orders—I surmised he was more than a common sailor. He had his seabag over his shoulder and a boarding ax gripped in his right hand. Only when he shifted position and tapped the floor did I notice that his left pant leg had been cut back and the appendage had been replaced with an artificial limb made of what appeared to be whalebone. I controlled my fear and, as nonchalantly as possible, said, "Can I help you?"

He continued to stare.

"Are you aware that you've come to the offices of the *Gorgon's Mirror*?" I asked.

He stepped closer. "Yes," he said in a low voice. "I seek a fellow by the name of Ishmael."

"Is this fellow a friend?" I asked.

"A colleague of the sea. We served upon the same ship."

"If I may ask, why are you looking for him?"

"Sir, don't play games with me. Do you know him or don't you? I was told he works here."

"No need to be obstreperous," I said, aiming to defuse him with my writerly vocabulary. "Pull up a chair there." I pointed to the seat behind him at the head illustrator's desk. "You look tired, sir, as if you could use a sit-down."

"Aye," he said. "That I could. I come in this morning from Nantucket to South Street, and I've been wandering far and wide looking for this place." The weary sailor half sat, half fell into the chair. When he was settled, he dropped his bag on the floor and removed his hat to place it in his lap along with that vicious-looking ax.

"Ishmael, you say. Yes, he worked here for a spell. An ambitious fellow."

"But he works here no longer?"

"He moved on at the end of the summer, just a couple of months ago, and I'm afraid I don't know where."

"An old acquaintance in Nantucket said he'd read a book written by Ishmael concerning a certain whaling voyage."

"That's correct," I said. "I read it here when it was merely a manuscript."

"You read it?" said the sailor. "Can you tell me, does it deal with a white whale perchance? Moby Dick?"

"Yes," I said, and he sat forward.

"And do you remember the captain of that voyage . . . as far as he tells it in his book?"

"Yes," I said. "A frightful fellow. A mad Quaker from Nantucket. As I recall, he was missing a . . ." As my tongue was forming the word *limb* I looked down and beheld my visitor's whalebone contrivance.

He stared at me. "What becomes of that captain in the book?"

I swallowed hard. "He is killed."

"Aye," he said.

There were a few beats of silence. "You're Ahab?"

3

"I am."

"But you died."

"Do you not know that the world and the book are separate voyages?"

I realized I'd been clutching the pen in my hand throughout our entire transaction. I set it in the inkwell and said, "In truth, I might understand it better than you think."

Ahab subtly flinched at something unseen.

"Then you were not dragged overboard and into the depths?" I asked.

"I was. But my neck was miraculously unbroken, and when I hit the water, the noose slipped up over my head. I was taken down, but not like a fish on a line. It was the draft of the sounding leviathan that drew me. I spun like a leaf in the wind, desperate for breath, and the dark was full of stars."

"And yet here you are," I said.

"The creature turned from its course, lunged for the surface, and swallowed me whole. The surge tumbled me over its undulating tongue, the size of five beds. My last thought before blacking out was that I should be emulsified in one of the stomachs of Moby Dick and shat out from pole to pole. Instead God's monster, no doubt reviled by the taste of grievous sin, disgorged me onto the rolling surface of the Pacific."

A character from a book come to life, a regular Jonah, I thought as I eyed him. It was easy enough to be frightened by his aspect, but I was beginning to feel a sense of pity what with his abject expression—the sad fate of a character rent free from his pages. If I remembered Ishmael's words, this fellow had been to college as well as to sea.

"I've heard that in Ishmael's book, my ship, my crew, myself, all are turned flukes-up and sent to Davy Jones."

"The white whale was the culprit," I said.

"Moby Dick," he said and spat on the floor. He muttered something to himself and turned his gaze from me as if embarrassed for not having died with his crew.

4

"And what would you have with Ishmael?"

"I want him to know he's not the sole survivor. He made of me in words a walking ghost."

"You came to Manhattan for that? The book was not well received by the reading public and sold woefully. A few handfuls of people may have seen it."

He gazed down at the floor and said, "I'm also here to find my wife and boy."

"Your wife and boy?" I said. "Do you have an address?"

He shook his head and I could feel his weariness. "It took years to heal and find my way back to Nantucket. When I arrived, I learned that she'd taken the child and come to Manhattan to live with her aunt. The next day, I booked passage here."

"She believes you dead?"

"She'd heard of Ishmael's version of our voyage. He didn't know I'd lived nor did I, he, until I returned. He was picked up by the *Rachel*. I glimpsed their sails in the distance, but they didn't see me in the water waving or hear me crying out."

"How were you rescued?"

"We were closer to the equator than Ishmael writes in the book. He had us much farther north. I was dragged nearly lifeless from the sea by a pair of native fishermen in a canoe off the coast of the Gilbert Islands, northwest of the Marquesas. Supposedly, there are quite a few discrepancies in those pages. In it, he lies about my age. I'm old enough but not that old. I think the only thing in the blasted tome that isn't at least tinged with fiction is his description of my madness."

Ahab put his hat on and lifted his bag. "I'll be on my way. I seek lodging. Thanks to you for your time."

I found it hard to believe, but I didn't want him to go. It wasn't that I thought him a splendid interlocutor. He was dreadful to look at and his voice was a croaking in the wilderness. What struck me was his story and what I could do with it. There was more fodder in the truth of his tale for a feast of bunkum than you could shake a stick at. In the morning I'd catch Garrick's ear and make my case that the real biography of Captain Ahab could boost sales of the *Gorgon's Mirror*. The fantastic, the forlorn, the frightening, and the philosophical. This was a "walking ghost" we could harness.

Before he turned to the stairs, I said, "You have no clue at all as to where to find your family?"

"No, except that the street is named after a fruit." No sooner were the words out of his mouth than the muscles of his face constricted into a dark oval and he whimpered.

I carefully approached, putting my hand on his shoulder. "Are you ill, sir?" I inquired.

"No. It's only that I've forgotten how to laugh."

"You seem exhausted, Ahab. We have an old fainting couch in the back storeroom beyond the presses. The thing's as big as a whale boat. I've slept upon it many a night. Quite comfortable. Besides, it's far too late to look for lodging. The world is asleep. Come. No charge. I'll help you search for your wife tomorrow."

"And my boy," he said. I took him by the arm, relieved him of his boarding ax and bag, and led him through the various rooms of the *Gorgon's Mirror*. He followed slowly, and I felt as if I were dragging him. When he was finally situated on the couch, he closed his eyes and instantly fell asleep.

The poor fellow, I thought as I made my way back to my desk. There, I took up my pen, ready to exploit his misadventures. *Garrick had better scrape together a raise for me,* I told myself. I struck with my harpoon, and the ink began to flow.

2

I woke to the sound of the street door banging open. My head was on the desk, the pen in hand, and I was staring at a burned-down nub of a candle. I realized it was morning, and it was Garrick on the stairs. He was always the first one to work. I sat up in time to see him walk past me to his office. Through the plateglass window that looked out on the writers' room, I could see him, like a fish in a bowl. I wasn't sure if he knew I was in or not. There had been so many mornings when he'd found me right where I was, with my cheek against the smooth wood of the desk and the pen between my fingers.

I liked to say that Garrick was a farmer of a publisher in the penny press. Up and at it before dawn, he was milking stories for all they were worth, ploughing through the truth, harvesting a rich crop of whimwham. He was no intellectual, but he was intelligent. He was a man of erratic ethics, save the work ethic. He toiled from sunup to sundown, and then he went home and spent the evening, a tumbler of gin beside him, in silent communion with his wizened wife.

My view of him was obliterated by the cloud from his first cigar of the day. I stood, straightened my shirt and jacket, made a feeble attempt at taming my hair, and did something to my bow tie. I took up my copy and went to make a proposal. Standing silently for a half minute at Garrick's door, I waited to be recognized. He was marking something in his ledger, so I dared not disturb him. Finally, he finished, shut the book, and without looking up at me, said, "Harrow, come in." I stepped into the swirling smoke. "Have a seat," he said, and I took the chair across the desk from him. "What have you there?"

"A piece for the day's run, sir."

"Good, then I won't have to let you go," he said and laughed. When he caught his breath, he squinted and became serious. "I don't want to hear anything more from the great George Harrow about the well having run dry."

"Yes, sir."

"What wonder have you for the presses?"

"I must explain, sir," I said, and then I did, speaking quickly and clearly so that he not fall into boredom. Garrick smoked his cigar with the contemplative air of a philosopher. When I got to the part in my narrative where I mentioned Ahab's whalebone leg, he grunted and nodded. I took that as encouragement and sailed on with my pitch. Eventually, he held up his hand to silence me and I sputtered out.

"Am I getting here, the story of a sea captain returned from the dead or a character that steps forth from the pages of a book? Either one is fairly cliché, although I'll use your copy out of necessity. You'd better start dreaming deeper, George Harrow," he said.

"I have," I told him. "Say I follow this Ahab fellow around Manhattan for a few days while he searches for his wife and boy and tracks down the man who killed him with words. I could assist him in his search, and for that perhaps he will tell me snippets of his adventures on the journey back from death. I'll follow him and report, of course, stretching the truth and teasing actuality when necessary. It can be a serial. And we can sell the fact that we're trying to help the poor sot as we exploit him. Here's the first installment." I reached forward and set the pages on his desk.

Garrick smiled. He stubbed out his cigar, thank God, and leaned his bulk back in the chair. "Harrow, you're skating between the escapist and the esoteric. Thin ice, indeed."

"I tell you this fellow's a gold mine," I said. "We could outsell the *Police Gazette* with this series."

"Don't talk nonsense. The sound of it frightens me when I'm about to make a bold decision."

"Very good, sir. Just think, the pathos of the peculiar."

"And what might you call this series?" he asked.

The Walking Ghost."

With that, I heard the stub of Ahab's leg hammer the floor in the doorway behind me. I saw in my publisher's eyes just a moment of hesitation, and then he was up, out of his chair, and ushering the captain into the room. That's when I knew my proposal had won the day. Garrick quizzed Ahab on his story, and seeming satisfied that I hadn't lied, he said, "Ahab, we here at the *Mirror* are prepared to help you locate your wife and son."

The captain squinted. "I work alone. I've no money for the services of others."

"No, no," said Garrick, "I intend to bankroll the expedition. How badly do you long to see your family?"

Ahab shook his head as if he didn't understand the question.

"Give us three weeks. In three weeks we will find your wife and son. My associate, here, Mr. George Harrow, will accompany you every leg of the journey. I will cover the cost of hotels, meals, and travel. Please, will you agree to allow us to be of assistance?"

"I work alone."

Garrick leaned across his desk and said in a low voice, "Mr. Ahab, you don't know what you're facing in this city. Roughly five hundred thousand people. I have no doubt you're a resourceful man, but your hunt could take years without a guide. You're about to dive deep into the maw of Leviathan."

Ahab gave a nearly imperceptible nod, and that's all Garrick required. He opened his desk drawer and pulled out a clean white sheet of paper. Lifting his pen, he gave it a flourish and drew a line in the bottom right-hand corner. Next to the line, he wrote a big X and slid the page to Ahab. He then handed the captain the pen and sat back.

"Go ahead and sign, sir. We'll fill in the details later."

I knew the details were the exclusive rights to the seaman's story.

Ahab hesitated but within moments he signed. That page was swept off the desk and stowed in the top drawer. My publisher swiveled round in his chair and took a small chest from the shelf behind him. He came round again and dropped it on the desk. With a key attached to his watch fob, he opened the lock and lifted the lid with both hands. Garrick reached in and drew out three bills bearing a beehive design.

"Here's nine dollars," he said and handed the money across to me. "That should be enough to keep you gentlemen alive for a few days while you search." He turned to face me. "Spare no expense," he said and winked.

Ahab sat there like the frontispiece of a ship trapped in ice. He seemed to sense that while he might be getting taken, he had no other choice if he wanted to see his family again. We had him right where we wanted him, but my plan was proceeding too smoothly. Even Garrick was on board. I should have been ecstatic, but before me now was the prospect of ushering Ahab through the city for days, maybe weeks. The captain's personality was dismal and his conversation was scant. A peculiar aroma clung to him as well, a miasma that cut through the cigar stink in Garrick's office—decidedly low tide. That ax, ever in attendance, was more than a bit disturbing. On balance, though, I had a premonition he was a world of story, at least two weeks' worth of articles.

There was a quick round of handshakes and the next thing I knew we were out on the cobblestones. The hunt had begun. He left behind his canvas bag with a promise from Garrick to have it delivered to my home, and I slung my writing satchel over my left shoulder. The offices of the *Gorgon's Mirror* were at the bottom of John Street, facing Burling Slip. We stepped into the cold blue morning and headed northwest. Scarves, mufflers, hats, and gloves were worn by those passersby who had them, rags for those who didn't. Winter was around the corner.

The street was busy with commerce bound for the shipyard, wagons of trade headed to the wharf to be loaded. As we walked along, Ahab slipped the handle of his ax into the deep pocket of his peacoat, and with the opposite hand, retrieved a small whalebone pipe from another pocket. I took a glance at the bowl and glimpsed a scrimshaw scene of a stack of tortoises. I never saw where the tobacco came from that suddenly filled it, but the match he struck with his thumb came from the brim of his hat.

"Captain, for this venture to work, you're going to have to be forthcoming."

"Certainly," he said in a puff of smoke, but his voice lacked all conviction. He trudged along, the peg leg tapping a dreary rhythm. Every few steps, he grumbled to himself. At the sight of him, people stepped gingerly aside, and some fled his path as if he were the Flying Dutchman of the sidewalk.

I noticed, now that we were in full daylight, that the captain had a pale white scar, which had been undetectable in the candlelight of Garrick's smoke aquarium. It began, I assumed, at the top of his crown beneath his steel-colored locks and ran down the side of his face and neck to disappear below his collar. I thought better of inquiring about it.

"You said the street your wife lived on is named for a fruit?" I asked.

By the time he answered we'd walked all the way to Pearl Street, and "Aye," was all he ventured. At Pearl and Fulton, we encountered a crowd. A stoppage of fish carts and omnibuses and streetcars coincided with a packed sidewalk. A wave of humanity swept around us and ignited my claustrophobia. My glance was everywhere, knowing the dangers of crowds. As for Ahab, he moved wearily, yet deliberately forward, never making eye contact. The multitude eventually released us at Chatham. My plan was to head for Mulberry Street. We would start there and then move on to Orange Street if need be.

"How old would your boy be now?" I asked, to keep him engaged.

He tapped out the pipe and the ashes trailed behind us. "I'm not sure."

"Can you describe your wife?"

"She's beautiful."

"This'll be a cinch," I said as we drew ever closer to the Five Points.

W e walked along the edge of Mulberry Bend Park, yellow leaves rolling in waves across the field. "You see up ahead here?" I said to Ahab, nodding. He didn't glance at me. "We're in the Five Points, so be vigilant of your wallet and your way. These streets are swimming with thieves, cutthroats, and deviants. Look alive, Captain. We should be okay this time of day. The gangs usually don't stir till noon."

When we reached a cluster of shops at the elbow of the road, we each dove in and began inquiring. "Have you met a woman from Nantucket? I'm looking for a local woman who hails from the isle of Nantucket." I was reluctant to offer money in exchange for information, although I realized it might come to that eventually. Every now and then, I'd pause and look over at Ahab as his lumbering form approached some nervous passerby or merchant. We pushed on, slowly making our way up Mulberry in a northerly direction.

Most people, being like most people, took a moment to stop and listen to my question. They'd either shake their heads or give me a quick, "Sorry." Then there were those who never slowed but just kept moving. The hard cases shouted at me, "Shut your bone box," or, more directly, "Fuck off." I knew my way around the Five Points, what was possible and when to run. I also knew that it was where the stories were. One of the more miserable patches of God's earth.

Not too long before Ahab lurched into my life, I wrote an article for the *Gorgon's Mirror* about a man who set himself up on Mulberry Street as a nepenthe dealer. The elixir was supposed to erase one's painful memories: of love lost, opportunity squandered, and so on. The first few customers went mad and ran screaming from their hovels as if their hair were on fire. The police caught the salesman. The mysterious cure was tested and turned out to be eight-tenths turpentine and two-tenths shoe polish and whiskey. "Remember this," Garrick told me early on. "Ignorance is the handmaiden of Wonder."

The traffic in the street got too crowded, vendors at the curbs and carriages in the middle. It was a narrow thoroughfare with ill-kept wooden tenements on either side that formed the likes of canyon walls. Within those buildings, they packed an entire family to a room. I took to the sidewalk to keep from being run over. Once there, passing the open doors of the shops and listening to the vendors cry out their wares in the street, I must have heard a half-dozen languages. The area was like some clearinghouse of Babel—there were the Irish, the blacks, the Chinese, the Germans, the Italians, the Scots—tongues and dialects intermingling.

I stopped by the open door of a drinking house called Gulley's and inquired of a small woman sitting on a chair at a table if she might know our quarry. She stretched out her hand and invited me to sit in the chair across from hers. I felt vulnerable with my back to the street, but from her look I surmised she had something to tell me. When I was seated, she pointed to a sign leaning against the building. She was some kind of soothsayer, one of the many prophets who could predict the inevitably grim futures of her neighbors.

I began to get up, but she put her hand on my forearm and gently pushed me back into the seat. Once I was still, she poured me a cup of hot water from a teapot on the table. Steam rose out of it and I became curious as she slowly added to the cup pinches of tea leaves she picked from a small silk purse in her lap.

"Drink," she said with a brogue. The sign gave her name as Mrs. Harris, and her pinched and haggard looks hinted at an affair with the bottle. She wore circular specs and a pair of dangling earrings fashioned from knucklebones.

I lifted the cup and watched the loose tea swirl, wondering if she meant to drug me. After sniffing the brew, I drank it down. The taste was not unpleasant—a dark fruit flavor mixed with clover and thyme. She pulled on my arm to prevent me from finishing it off completely. I handed the cup to her. She swirled what was left in the bottom three times and then upended the cup and dumped its contents onto the saucer. The two of us stared at the mess. Her long fingernail hovered two inches above the leaves, tracing the outline of something unseen by me. A gasp came from the street, a familiar sound for that area, and I suddenly saw a death's head in the green remains.

I fled in search of Ahab. Mrs. Harris yelled that I'd not paid her, but I was convinced my charge was in danger. I bolted between a pair of carts into the street and headed for the other side where I'd last seen him. I was nearly clipped by a carriage, and when I made it across, the captain was nowhere to be found. Garrick wouldn't be at all pleased if I'd lost him. I moved desperately along the sidewalk. Before long I spotted his high hat at the opening to an alley.

In that part of town, alleys were the dens of monsters. You could wander into one by mistake and never be seen again. I gave their openings a wide berth. From where I stood, it looked like the seaman had attracted the attention of three members of the Forty Thieves gang. I could tell by the truncheons they carried. They were surrounding him, and he was turning on that peg leg, trying to keep them all at bay with wild swings of the boarding ax.

"Hear, hear!" I said in hopes of diffusing the situation. "Police!" I called, and those around me on the sidewalk snickered. Before I could assist Ahab, one of the Thieves made a move, rushing the captain with a crowbar held high. The man's weapon was met by the boarding ax and blocked in its descent. At the same time Ahab flung back the bottom of his coat and pulled from his waist a pistol—single shot, ball and powder—that I'd not yet seen. With the handle he smashed his attacker in the mouth. Teeth flew and the man went down. Then the captain spun as the fellow behind him lunged. The gun went off with a bang and a cloud of smoke. The ball passed directly through the thief's right thigh. Blood spurted and there was a scream. At this, the third attacker grabbed his wounded compatriot. They all fled down the alley.

"Good Lord, Ahab, let's get out of here."

"I've done nothing wrong."

"Trust me. It doesn't matter." That's when I felt the muzzle of a gun in my back.

"Where's my money?" I heard a small voice say.

Turning around, I confronted Mrs. Harris, who held her own percussion pistol on me at belt level.

"Forgive me," I said. "I had to come to my friend's assistance."

"Looked to me like your friend did just fine without you."

I reached into my vest pocket and took out a three-cent silver piece. Once she had it in her hand, she lowered the gun. "The woman you're looking for lives over on Orange Street, as far as I know."

"Did you see it in the tea leaves?" I asked.

"No, I met her once. She come to inquire as to whether her husband was lost at sea or still alive."

"That could be her," I said and turned to see where Ahab had gone off to. He was standing next to me, mouth agape and his eyes, for the first time, bright.

"How long ago, madame?" he said. She waved him off and stowed the silver piece in the pocket of her coat. "Less than a year," she replied and walked away.

We hightailed it to Grand Street and then one block east to Orange.

By evening we'd traversed the length of that street twice and spoken to a hundred citizens each. To no avail. We sat, exhausted, in Yancy's and watched out the huge front window the last rays of sun and the shadow creeping across the cobblestones. Traffic on the street thinned as people headed home for dinner. Ahab smoked his pipe and nursed a pint, and I sat with pencil in hand, poised above my notebook, sipping gin. For more than two hours, we rested our feet, and I peppered him with questions. He gave me a few grunts, a strangled reminiscence, and I took that scant, weak dough and baked it with the fire of my pen. Here's what I say he told me—

The mail boat arrived in the harbor late, beneath a half moon and with lanterns set as running lights. I disembarked, thanking the captain, and, hoisting my seabag over my shoulder, made my way along the planks of the wharf. The town was sleeping. I stood at the foot of Main Street, in the silence and the night sea wind, and looked around through the glow of the lamps that dotted the way. Some of it I remembered as if from a dream and the rest meant nothing. I knew I lived up a street in the direction of Prospect Hill. For no good reason, I hoped that when I arrived at my house and lay in my bed, it would all make sense.

My house was wrapped in shadow, and I could barely see it from the street. The front gate was unlatched and hanging by one hinge. It gave a screech as I pushed it open. I wondered if Iris was lying awake in bed, listening to the tap tap tap on the slates that led to the front door. I took the three porch steps slowly and waited a moment for my vision to adjust, but as I raised my hand to rap upon the glass, I finally saw there was no glass. It was covered over by planks of wood. In fact, it became clear that the door was boarded completely shut. Twice, thrice, I circled the house, jabbering to myself as I discovered each boarded window. I knew long before I was willing to believe it that they were gone and I was cast away.

I sat on the porch step, face in my hands, lost in the world and wishing I could remember how to weep. A voice said to me, "Who be there?"

I moved my hands and opened my eyes to a bright beacon's glare. It was Pollard, the night watchman.

"Ahab," I said.

The old man lowered his lantern and didn't speak but I heard a gasp. A moment later, he stuttered and said, "Be gone malicious spirit," and waved his walking stick at me.

"Captain Pollard, it's me, Ahab. You've known me since I was a boy."

"Oh, Ahab, don't you know you're dead?"

"I'm not dead. I've returned."

"We read in the papers that you and the *Pequod* and the crew, save that one lad rescued by the *Rachel,* all turned flukes-up in the wake of Moby Dick. It must be certain, it's been put in a book."

This was the first I'd heard of Ishmael's account. "What lad rescued by the *Rachel*?" I shouted and stood up. Pollard took a step back and held the light out before him as if in protection.

"I forget his name. A biblical name. But are you sure you're not a bereft spirit wandering the night?"

"I'm sure of nothing," I answered. "But come here and touch my arm and see if I'm not real."

Pollard inched his way forward. I perceived a sinister irony in our meeting, for not only had Captain Pollard lost one ship in his command, like myself, but he had lost two. No one was willing to put another under him after the second, and he was relegated to the position of night watch in Nantucket Town. It was said that when his ship the *Essex* went down, also like mine, destroyed by a whale, he and a small boat of survivors took to cannibalism as they drifted at the mercy of the currents.

The old man touched me with trembling fingers. "Ahab," he whispered.

"What has happened here?" I asked and motioned to my house.

"Oh, let me see. It's not been good, sir. While you've been off, the fishery has waned. Whaling, it seems, is moving to New Bedford."

"I don't give a damn about the fishery, man. I mean where are my wife and the boy?"

"Easy, spirit," said Pollard, and I got the impression he was trying to remember. "Well, when we heard you had died, she and the boy left."

"Left and gone where?" I said, wanting to seize him by the collar and shake all the answers out of him at once.

He closed his eyes and tilted his head back.

"Where?"

"They went to live with an aunt of hers on the Isle of Manhattan."

"Manhattan?"

"Yes. Perhaps now you can rest, spirit."

"But I'm not a spirit."

"I see ghosts every night," said Pollard, who closed the door of the lantern and turned away. He went down the walk and past the broken gate, leaving me in the dark. When next I looked after him, he had vanished, and I half wondered if my colleague in shipwrecks was not himself a ghost.

Locked out of my own home, I curled up on the porch like a newborn and closed my eyes, repeating my wife's name, an incantation that might conjure her image. Just as I succumbed to exhaustion and fell toward sleep, I caught a glimpse of her——heart-shaped face framed by dark curls and green eyes. Then a long shivering sleep, my stump firing off volleys of agony throughout.

4

As I was finishing my article and my gin at Yancy's, I looked over at Ahab, who was a few seats down the bar from me. The place was empty but for us and the dozing barkeep leaning half off a stool at the opposite end of the place. Night was full on by then and the door to the street was open. Nothing but quiet and the subtle rustling of a cold breeze. I blinked to clear my eyes from the strain of writing in the failing lantern light. From that wavering glow, Ahab asked, "What is our course?"

"We'll go back to my home and rest till morning. After which, we'll return to Orange Street and pick up where we left off."

"Shouldn't we put up running lights and push on through the night?"

"There's no pushing on," I told him. "If we remain in the Points overnight, we won't see morning."

By luck, we dodged the shifty characters in the doorways and skirted the errant piles of trash and hog turds. At Chatham we were able to hail a carriage to ferry us to my place on James Street. Ahab was silent for the entire ride. When we arrived, I had my maid, Misha, show the captain upstairs and indicate that he was very welcome to use the bath and my shaving gear if need be. Meanwhile, I stayed on the bottom floor in my writing parlor, facing out on the street through the large window.

I took the notebook out of my satchel and laid it open on the desk. From my pocket, I retrieved my knife. As carefully as I could, I excised the most recent pages of my prose—the piece on Ahab's return to Nantucket. Once it was free, I folded it, put it in an envelope, sealed the back with wax, and imbedded the design from the crest of the *Gorgon's*

Mirror, a snake-haired monster gazing into a looking glass, with a silver stamp Garrick had provided me.

I poured myself a gin, lit a cheap cigar, and leaned back in my chair. Misha came from the kitchen to ask if I wanted to eat and informed me that Ahab was bathing. "A salubrious development," I said, and we both laughed. I told her I wasn't hungry and, after adding a log to the fireplace, she left the room. I sat with my feet up on the desk and watched the few parishioners heading home from a late service at Saint James. They passed through the glow of the gas lamp across the street, looking like ghosts.

Ahab was much on my mind, a sort of ghost himself. All day I'd been trying to remember the impression his character had made upon me when I read Ishmael's final draft of *Moby Dick.* It struck me that in those pages the captain seemed always onstage—strutting and fretting his hour, so to speak. All his oaths were melodramatic, all his actions a performance. I couldn't get past the passion and the pity of it to see who Ahab really was.

All I could picture was Ahab ranting at his crew, sick with the bard and biblical allusion. The tip of his whalebone leg was affixed in its peg hole and his body spun like a pinwheel on that still point of the turning world, bellowing orders, exhorting souls, scanning the horizon for a monster. *Ahab, thou art shipwrecked in every way,* I thought. And what kind of a name was Ahab? I remembered Ishmael telling me while he was writing the tome that Ahab's mother was insane. She died before her son's first year was achieved and her parting gift to him had been that moniker, the namesake of a king who buried children alive in the foundations of his temples.

There was a rapping upon the front door. Misha called out from the hallway that she would get it, and I opened my eyes, sat up straight, and turned away from the window. As I did, Misha led a girl into the parlor study. She was approximately fifteen years old with red hair and freckles, dressed as a boy in trousers, coat, and cap. Garrick called her his Mercury—messenger and head of the newsboys and -girls he employed to hawk the *Gorgon's Mirror* on the street. The other children called her Mavis, and she lived secretly with her two younger brothers in the subbasement of a three-story warehouse. Orphans, they dwelt in the shadows for fear of being placed in a home for indigent children.

If the girl was anything, she was capable. At least once a week, she'd meet me somewhere at some ungodly hour in order to pick up a story that Garrick had to have a quarter hour earlier. She traveled anywhere in the city, knew the secret shortcuts through alleyways and old underground tunnels. I'd seen her deal with adults and the guttersnipes who were under her direction at the *Mirror*. She could be hard as the cobblestones and wouldn't hesitate for an instant to use the switchblade she kept in her boot or the pistol stowed in her trouser pocket.

"Please, sit," I said and held my hand out in the direction of the chair closest to me. She smiled, removed her cap. I reached back to my desk, retrieved the envelope with the story for Garrick, and handed it to her. I took a drag of the cigar. She held the envelope between her knees and rolled herself a cigarette.

"I found something out for you today," she said, lighting a wooden match with her thumb. "This woman Garrick said you're looking for, from Nantucket? I know where she is."

"How'd you find her? We looked all day."

"I just put the word out among the street kids and the answer finally wove its way back to me."

"That's quite a net," I said.

"The woman lives with her aunt on Orange Street," she said.

"We were all over Orange Street."

"Right at the corner where Orange meets Elm, there's a two-story house painted dark green. The second floor."

I applauded and asked if she wanted a drink. She turned me down as Garrick had the printers working late and they were awaiting my piece.

No sooner was the girl gone on her errand than Ahab stepped out of the darkened hallway and into the glow of the parlor's fireplace. He had taken the hint of the razor and gone were the thick sideburns and full beard. Ahab shaved was a stark sight, indeed. His bare chin and sunken cheeks gave him a more human aspect but one no less troubled. His face was furrowed with worry and wrinkles. His voluminous hair, graying at the sides, was now combed straight back. His peg leg made him stand somewhat stooped, and when he moved, he swayed slightly from side to side. His sailor clothes had been traded for another outfit he no doubt had in his bag—simple trousers, cut, of course, to accommodate the ivory leg; a long-sleeved black shirt without a collar.

He walked toward me and sat in the chair Mavis had occupied. He spoke as if he were a real person in the real world.

"Tomorrow?" he asked.

"The plan is to see your wife. A friend of mine, who visited while you were upstairs, tells me, with the greatest confidence, that the woman in question can be found at a certain address at the corner of Orange and Elm."

I thought he'd be elated to hear it, but instead he appeared nervous.

"It's been a long time, Harrow," he said quietly.

"No doubt they'll be delighted to see you. We'll have a celebration on Garrick's dime."

He shook his head. "Remember, I left them to the whims of the world for the pitiful obsession of revenge. It was all I wanted."

"Anyone can make amends," I said.

"Many died due to my pursuit. Many suffered."

I had no answer. Not another word was spoken between us that night. He kept an eye on the floor, and I kept one on the ceiling. In doing so, I finally fell asleep.

The morning found me still groggy, with a sharp pain where my neck met my back. It wasn't the first time I'd slept in that chair. Ahab had obviously retreated up to the room that Misha had prepared for him.

Even if the captain feared the day's encounter, I was thrilled to get to witness the reunion of Mr. and Mrs. Ahab after an eight-year separation. I could only imagine the number of *Mirror* pieces I'd squeeze out of it.

We ate breakfast and then went out into the cold rain. I'd asked Ahab if he wanted an umbrella, but he said he liked the feel of the weather on his face. I didn't hesitate to immediately hail an omnibus to take us as far as it would go into the Five Points. Luckily, the bad weather would keep a lot of the riffraff off the street. Our journey was silent.

We went on foot the last few blocks. The mud was thick and the Points smelled like shit tea in a tin cup. Even using an umbrella, I was drenched by the time we got there, close to 10:00 A.M. The place was a hulking, ramshackle home, its upper floor listing slightly toward the street. We found a staircase on the side of the building that led to the second floor. I went first and Ahab stepped and stumped behind, shivering slightly and dripping with the mid-November rain. I rapped on the door at the top landing. We waited quite a while, and then I rapped again. Eventually an old woman answered.

"Madame," I said, "we apologize for any inconvenience in calling upon you, but we had it from a reliable source that you have, living with you, a lady and a boy who came from the island of Nantucket."

She wore glasses that magnified the width of her eyes.

"Who are ya?" she said.

"I'm a writer for the *Gorgon's Mirror*, but this"—I stepped aside for her to get a better look at Ahab—"I believe is that woman's husband." The captain stepped forward.

"You're Ahab?" she said and leaned toward him as if preparing to pounce.

"Maisie?" he said.

She nodded as she stared at him for a long while amid the sound of the downpour and finally said, "I believe you."

I divined that this Maisie must be Ahab's wife's aunt.

"Iris? Gabriel?" he asked with the tone of a beggar.

"I'll take you to her," she said and backed into her apartment. The door shut. I looked at Ahab, he looked at me, and we waited.

Finally, she emerged, dressed in a coat, a scarf over her head and an umbrella on her arm. She said, "Follow me," and her words were steam. Maisie was slow, but we fell in behind her, Ahab and then me bringing up the rear. It took us forever to descend the stairs to the street. We walked south for two blocks until stopping by a gated entrance in a brick wall. The hinges of the rusted bars groaned as Maisie pushed them open. We stepped into a large rectangular courtyard enclosed on all sides by a brick wall. Inside that hidden enclosure were grass and trees shedding orange leaves. And gravestones.

Ahab immediately recognized where we were and what was about to be revealed. I was slow to it and watched as he dropped to his knees and then forward into the wet grass. The old woman didn't slow but continued at her honey-drip pace to a headstone beneath a towering white oak. I dropped my umbrella and my writing satchel in order to help the captain up. I put his arm over my shoulder, and with great effort—he was a bit larger than I—steered him to the headstone where Maisie stood.

He regained control and was able to stand on his own. Yes, there was sobbing. Even my eyes reddened, and I traffic in the cynical. As for the old lady, not a blink, a wink, a wince. She was stone-faced throughout the ordeal. Finally, he stopped sniveling and asked, "How?"

"Smallpox."

"The boy?" asked the captain.

"Iris left a message with me for you, should you ever return. She said she loved you and that you should rescue your son from his situation."

Maisie knelt on the muddy path next to the gravestone and rested her right hand upon its mossy top. All her stoic façade crumbled, and she wept with a sadness that stripped away life's illusions. The captain leaned over and put his hand on her shoulder.

5

W e followed Maisie back to her apartment. As we traipsed solemnly along the hallway into her kitchen, I could feel the house sway beneath our weight. There were wounds to the walls where the plaster had come away and the wind snaked in through a ribwork of lathing strips. Ahab and I took seats at a table and she moved about, gathering a dusty half bottle of something and three mugs. I imagined the two chairs in which Ahab and I now sat had not too long past been occupied by his wife and child. The place was small, the furniture was threadbare, and its threat of tumbling into the street was ever imminent, but, in the Five Points, with only three people in the apartment, the accommodations were luxurious.

She poured. I waited for my companions to drink, but no one did. Finally, I lifted the mug and dashed it off. It was neither rum nor gin. The smell was rank, the taste so horrid it literally stopped my heart for a moment. Maisie looked at me as I put the mug slowly back on the table. "How'dya like that? I made it myself in the bathtub."

"The dark color made me think it rum," I choked out.

"It's pretty rum. Another?" she asked, peering at me with those big eyes under glass.

"I'm well done," I said, yet she poured anyway. The smell of it in the mug made me swoon.

"The boy?" said Ahab.

She took a sip of her own poison and her body jerked suddenly, only once, and she said, "He's a good boy, Gabriel. But they had no money and she wasn't well before she caught the smallpox. He went out to work and worked hard at many jobs, but when she died last year, he left the apartment and didn't return. He joined one of the gangs or something. He lives on the street, steals, and who knows what else."

"How old is he?" I asked.

"Sixteen years." Ahab wanted to answer but Maisie did.

"Where can I find him?" asked the captain.

The old woman shook her head and took another quaff.

"When was the last time you saw him?" I asked.

"Maybe two months ago."

"He strayed as boys do when they have no pilot."

That said, we sat in silence and listened to the rain on the roof; the drip of it into a pail in the corner.

The old woman got up and went into the other room out of sight. I heard her call, "I have a picture of the boy and his mother, not but a year and a half old." The sound of rummaging followed her words. She eventually reappeared with something in her hands. "Gabriel paid with his wages to have it made," she said. Ahab winced and looked away as she set the portrait, five inches by seven, on the table in front of him. The woman in the daguerreotype was beautiful as her husband had said, black hair draped across her throat and then over her right shoulder. Her eyes were large and piercing. The boy was well on the way to becoming a man. He was handsome; obviously taking after his mother. He had her eyes.

The captain took his hands from his face and forced himself to look. His hands hovered above the picture. Suddenly, he found his strength and snatched the image up by the frame to press it against the side of his face. Maisie turned to me and said, "Too bad he didn't care that much about her when she was alive." I was going to speak up in the captain's defense but realized she was right. The entire scene was pathetic, and I'd had enough. I abruptly stood, thanked Maisie, and said to Ahab, "Come, it's time to find your boy." I put the picture in my bag and we left. The old woman called after that if she were to see Gabriel, she'd let us know.

The rain had stopped when we reached the street. Damp, overcast, and the wind was high, papers and leaves blowing past us as we walked. Ahab was silent.

"Now what?" I said to him.

He stopped and turned to me, "We hunt the boy with the same fierce devotion as I hunted the white whale."

"Man the harpoons?" I asked.

"For the deserving," he said.

I made a mental note to remember that exchange as it would make good copy. As the skies cleared, the streets began to fill. We made our way slowly toward the park at Mulberry Bend, showing the daguerreo-type to individuals willing to be accosted for a moment. Not a soul knew the boy nor had seen him.

We sat on a bench in the park, taking a break, when, from across the field, there came a thin, bald man with a scar that snaked from the corner of his left eye to under his ear. His coat was too large, his boots were full of holes, and a cutlass was secured in his belt.

"Ahoy, Captain Ahab," he called as he shuffled toward us.

The fellow approached, his tattered coat flapping. The captain stood to greet him. They exchanged a sort of secret handshake, each grabbing the other's forearm well above the wrist. The fellow's name was *Usual*, which struck me as rather unusual. Usual Peters. I could tell by his ac-cent that he hailed from the upper reaches of the Northeast, where they speak like cranky church people. Aye!

I tried to remain an outsider to their conversation. Though I turned slightly away, I kept an ear open. Peters was, as he put it, "landlocked." He'd gotten into the drink and it kept him ashore for two years. When he decided to go back to sea, no one would hire him.

"A harpooneer can't have shaky hands," said Ahab, who, if I remem-bered correctly from Ishmael's manuscript, had once plied that trade.

"Don't I know it, Captain," said Usual and nodded. "One of the ship-owners who used to give me steady work told me, 'I can't hire ya. You look like nine-tenths of the life's been sucked out of you. You'd spook the others and the whales wouldn't come near the ship.'"

"Cursed, like me," said Ahab.

I thought to show the man the portrait of Iris and Gabriel. Taking it out of my bag, I handed it to the captain, interrupting their conversation. The captain inquired if Usual had seen the lad. The sailor took his time eyeing the daguerreotype, but when he spoke he nodded.

"Seen him down at Peck Slip."

That was all I had to hear. I got to my feet and tapped Ahab's shoulder. "The hunt is on," I said.

Ahab didn't follow immediately. He leaned in close and grabbed Usual's forearm in that peculiar handshake again as the old lush whispered into the captain's ear.

Usual called back as he moved away, "A strong wind for ya."

"Calm seas," said Ahab.

My intention was to hail a carriage for South Street as soon as we left the park, but when we reached the cobblestones, the captain grabbed my arm to slow me down. He leaned over my shoulder and said, "The harpooneer says we're to go to the slip after midnight. There's a clipper, laden with special cargo, which, every few nights, is unloaded and sent back out to sea by daybreak."

"And what is the fellow doing on the wharf at night?"

"For a few nights he kept watch for the ship's owner."

"Kept watch against what, whom?"

"He didn't say."

Ahab wasn't very good at waiting. We sat in my parlor office after dinner, killing time till the clock struck twelve. I, of course, was drilling the captain for anything that might make a suitable article for the series. He stared intently at the picture of his wife and child, and all his answers were grumblings. It was like talking to a beast.

"For instance, what's the story behind that wicked white scar that runs down the side of your face and neck?" I asked, probing for the light of a tale. "I'll bet there's something fascinating at its origin. It's not from a blade as Usual's wound was."

"It runs all the way to the center of the world," he mumbled. "I never speak of it."

Finally, I said, "Ahab, come now, help me get your story out into the street. There's a chance your son might read it. The *Mirror* gets around, you know."

He winced, took the pipe out of his mouth, and said, "Very well. Here's something else. On the voyage home, I was stranded in the town of Sydney in Australia. I made the acquaintance of the harbormaster who got me in touch with some of the shipowners and captains. They arranged a living situation for me for three months until the next ship that would leave for Boston. I stayed with a woman on the outskirts of town. It was only me and her in the house. Her husband had within the last year gone down with a ship under the direction of a Captain Crevcoure, a fellow known to the international fishery as inept. My benefactors informed me that she was aware I'd lost my entire ship and crew and would not speak to me. Still, she would allow me to live under her roof.

"I knew her as Lisle. A pale, frightened woman. Sometimes I'd come in from a morning walk through the countryside and find her hiding, twisted up in the drapes. Every night she cooked fish, clear as glass and the consistency of jelly. We sat together and ate in utter silence. When she thought I was sleeping, she'd slip into my room. I kept one lid cracked the merest slit. She stood over me and watched me breathe. Some nights I was convinced that she would cut my throat. And then she vanished. Days went by and I didn't see her. I informed them in town that she was missing. They acted like they had no idea what I meant. Some laughed it off as a joke and others just shook their heads. By the time I boarded ship and left Sydney, I realized that they'd sent me to live with a ghost. I saw her again in the mist and spray off the Isle of Treachery as we rounded the Cape of Good Hope."

Misha stayed up and made us coffee before we went out on our mid-night ramble. Wide awake and warm inside, we ventured forth into the blustery night. We headed down to South Street and took a left. Peck Slip was only a few blocks south at the end of Ferry. We stuck to the shadows of the warehouses and shops. Across the way, we passed the docks, some empty, some occupied with majestic clippers and whalers and fishing boats. The wind blew amid the rigging, the spires creaked, empty holds groaned as the vessels rocked. A moon showed itself here and there, fast clouds passing before it. Overwhelming was the scent of low tide. The captain carried his boarding ax at the ready, and I assumed he had his gun. I had my writing satchel. I'd contemplated taking a large knife from the kitchen, but really, why?

We approached Peck Slip in silence and squinted to see in those instances when the moon broke through the clouds. Staring down the length of the dock, I thought I caught some sign of movement. I turned my head to better hear and picked up the sound of voices coming from that direction.

"Do you hear them?" whispered Ahab.

I nodded and grabbed the captain by the coat sleeve, leading him back through the shadows of the buildings, nearly all the way to my place. We crossed the road to James Slip. Halfway out on the dock there, I knew we'd find a square hole cut into the planks and a wooden ladder descending toward the waters of the East River. Lashed to a beam of the dock was a dinghy. I'd seen it bobbing there on my Sunday afternoon strolls through the neighborhood.

It was easy enough to find the boat, but getting into it was another story. First, Ahab had to survive the ladder. I closed my eyes every time the tip of that whalebone leg came to rest upon a rung. I promised myself that if he were to fall into the drink, I'd not dive in to rescue him. Miraculously, he made it and settled himself into the boat. I followed him down, slipping in my descent and nearly taking a plunge. I wondered if he'd have gone over the side for me. Once we were settled, I deferred to Ahab's seamanship and let him take the oars.

He held them at a certain attitude so that they cut the water without a sound. Neither of us spoke, and it wasn't long before his rowing had taken us to the end of the dock and around toward Peck Slip. We headed across some open water and he whispered for me to duck down. After every two hearty strokes, he'd lift the oars and the boat would glide through the shadows. We came up along the starboard side of the single boat docked on Peck Slip that night. Its port was against the dock and it was from there it was being unloaded. Now we could clearly hear the voices of the men, and I grew somewhat nervous. No one going to the trouble to unload a ship at midnight wants to be seen.

I put my hand up for Ahab to cease rowing, but he kept moving the boat as if intending to sail around the ship. We swept gently along down the starboard side, and, passing beneath the prow, those clouds traveling across the moon allowed me a split second to read the gilt letters of the craft's name—*Nemesis*. The frontispiece we drifted beneath was a maiden with wings and empty eyes, holding forth a set of scales. We sailed from the front of the clipper, along its port side. I could see shadowy figures standing above us on the dock and the gangplank. Ahab let the dinghy slip in among the pilings, under the dock, and we finally took up a position beneath where the cargo of the vessel was unloaded. There, we cautiously let out the boat's small anchor and sat as still as the river would allow.

At first the voices were muffled by the planks, the sound of the wind, and the lapping of the river against the side of the ship. Slowly, though, I was able to discern what was being said. After quite a tramping upon and bowing and squealing of the gangplank, a fellow with a deep, harsh voice yelled, "Gentle with the boss's pet. If something happens to her, he'll boil our arses."

"Damnedest thing I ever seen. Keep ya up at night just think'n about it," said another.

"Ya know. If you was to ungag her, she talks."

"Saints preserve us."

There were a few moments of silence, and then a storm of scuffling directly above us as if something was struggling to be free. That deep voice called, "Jesus, watch that tail. I told you, a kiss from that stinger, and it's off to *ifreann* for ya."

As they seemed to get whatever the boss's pet was under control, I heard someone address orders to "Gabriel," and a young voice answered. The captain obviously heard it, too, and on the second utterance of it, he sprang up, or intended to, but the river sent him a wave that dropped him back on his ass and nearly out of the boat. I grabbed him by the coat sleeve at the last second. The event made a racket and upon hitting his back against the edge of the middle bench, he groaned like a ghost.

From above, we heard, "Wait. Who heard that?" There was a sudden stillness upon the planks.

"It's just the beast. Malbaster told me she's learning to throw her voice. Cunning bitch."

Ahab tried to prevent me from weighing anchor, but I insisted. He pulled his pistol, and I somehow knew he wouldn't shoot. Finally, he acquiesced and rowed us along beneath the dock. We drifted over to the starboard side of the *Nemesis*, passing again beneath the prow. As we cut across the open water to James Slip, I took a moment in the ragged moonlight to wonder at the fact that I was sneaking around in a rowboat in the East River after midnight. I shook my head to clear the thought.

Once again back on the dock at James Slip, Ahab grabbed me by the coat sleeve and said, "That was my son. Did you hear him?"

I nodded.

"Gabriel."

"I'm going to help you get your boy, but I'd rather do it without us getting our throats cut in the process. Have some patience."

"Very well, enough for tonight. Tomorrow, we look for the Jolly Host."

"The what?" I asked.

"You didn't hear them saying that? The phrase was invoked three times."

"You're certain?"

"Aye," he said and found his pipe in his left pocket.

6

It never struck me how cold it was out till the night's action was finished and we were holed up in my writing parlor, drinking gin in the glow of the fireplace. The incident left both of us, for different reasons, too jittery for sleep. Me, I didn't like taking chances. As for Ahab, it was the sound of his son's voice, or so we believed. He sat on the couch, smoking his pipe, and studying the picture of his wife and boy.

As I lit one of my cigars, I happened to look over at him and noticed that he displayed a most hideous expression. I recalled the face he wore when he told me he'd forgotten how to laugh. I guessed this ghastly mask was the result of his having forgotten something even more necessary. Trying to keep him from foundering in the slough of despond, I said, "And, Ahab, what of the creature they had trapped. What was it?"

"I'm more interested in who Alabaster is."

"No, not Alabaster, Malbaster.'"

"Yes, that fellow."

"But the creature doesn't pique your interest?"

"I've heard of it before," he said.

"A creature that can speak and has the stinger of a scorpion at the tip of its long tail? Sounds like something I'd confabulate for the *Mirror*."

"Aye."

"And how did you hear about such a thing?"

"On my journey to Australia from the Gilberts aboard the American clipper the *Eastern State*, we put into Vanuatu for a load of coconut. We had but a short stay. One of the three nights we were in port, I spoke to a native, Olima, who had sailed on British ships and knew English. He sat down and bought me a whiskey in hopes he could practice the language. This was a hardworking, honest man. I had no reason to doubt him."

"I suppose to write the things I do, it requires being a doubter," I said.

"When you're swallowed by Leviathan and live to tell about it, you recognize the truth when you hear it."

"So let's hear it," I said and poured him another drink to loosen his tongue. Getting anything out of Ahab when he knew you were trying to get something was a project. I played it nonchalant. Smoked my cigar and waited. When nothing was forthcoming, I said, "It can't be real."

The captain nodded wistfully to indicate it was. "The fellow told me he was on a whale ship, the *Suspicion,* out of Peterhead, Britain. It was the only ship from the fleet there that sailed the vast distance to the Southern Seas. The rest of the whalers in that port all headed north into the Arctic Circle.

"On the journey back from Pacific to Atlantic, the *Suspicion* put in at one of the atolls in the Deception Islands on the tip of Cape Horn. There was a fellow there, a Spaniard by the name of Sarcosa, who had one of those beasts in captivity."

"Ahab, consider who you're trying to dupe with this cock and bull," I said.

"Olima swore to it," said the captain. "Sarcosa had excavated a large battle pit and built a tree post arena around it covered with a thatched roof. He told Olima and the other sailors that he had in captivity the most powerful beast in the world. My friend told me his fellow seamen were skeptical as Sarcosa never allowed anyone to get a look at the creature.

"While the *Suspicion* was docked in the tiny port, another ship, a large fishing boat arrived with a strange cargo. The crew of that ship had captured a giant sloth, a supposedly extinct creature, in the jungles of Brazil. It was bigger than any bear, and the whole deck of their ship was taken up by an enormous crate that held the monster. They bet Sarcosa that their sloth would be victorious in a battle against whatever he was putting up. Olima said the Brits bet on the match but he didn't. They gathered round the pit, the steamy air a bug stew. Wads of money were wagered, gallons of brandy called pisco were consumed. There was drunkenness and the firing of pistols into the thatched ceiling.

"When the giant sloth was released, it roared and my Ni-Vanuatu friend nearly ran. He forced himself to stay, so that he might catch a glimpse of Sarcosa's creature. Eventually, it made an appearance. A sleek cat, like a puma, its coat rusty brown, its ringlets dark blond. The face of an angel. She was beautiful until she opened her mouth, and kept opening it to reveal the rows of tearing canines that turned in unison like an ingenious mechanical device.

"Every time her tail lashed out and buried its stinger inches deep in the sloth, the lumbering beast had a seizure. Eyes rolling back, drool, a near human moan. All the while she spoke calm poetry in the lightest, most lovely voice. One of his fellow sailors told Olima that her verses were from Giambatista's epic *Fathomless Angel*. Olima didn't understand Spanish, but he said the sound of it was beautiful.

"What was horrible was when she ate through the sloth's neck with the speed and precision of a crosscut saw in the hands of two able lumbermen. He made a motion as if washing his hands when he spoke about the blood and gore that sprayed in all directions. 'The head fell like a rock to the ground,' he swore."

"What did they call the creature?" I asked.

"Olima told me it was a manticore."

"And you believed this?"

"Certainly."

"Ahab, Ahab, Ahab," I said. "There's an art to making things up. This Olima may have been a good sailor and fine for a chat and pipe of an afternoon, but he was a terrible liar. One needs to manipulate the language, massage the falsehood, manufacture the idiosyncratic. I can guarantee you that this story you heard was bunk. I had to stifle a laugh at the giant sloth."

The captain gave me one of those biblical stares from Ishmael's novel. "There was a time," he said, "when I believed in nothing."

Hooey, I thought, but when Ahab finally turned in, I stayed up burning the oil, relating Olima's story of the manticore. There were more than a few laughs in the task, and I did some passing fair work at drawing the creature forth into reality. When I finally laid the pen down, the birds had begun to sing. I knew I'd see Mavis somewhere the next day, and she'd be expecting a piece for Garrick.

I was still three sheets to the wind the following morning, the gin having had its way with me. I don't think Ahab was top o' the mast either. We'd decided to return to the park in hopes of finding Usual Peters, the captain's old colleague. We believed he could tell us something more about Malbaster or the Jolly Host. The day was frigid. And I must admit I was beginning to question the sanity of the entire affair. Ahab turned out not to be the epic personality I suspected but more a confused, somewhat delusional has-been of a fellow. Actually, pathetic to the point where I considered giving him the slip. Still, there was something about the state in which his encounter with the whale had left him that made him seem as if he really had come back from the dead.

That boarding ax nestled in the long pocket of the peacoat, his pipe between his lips, we headed across the lawn to the Mulberry Bend, and there wasn't a soul in sight. The wind howled across the park, and we took up positions behind oak trees to block its force. The captain told me his stump was "singing with pain."

"How well do you know Mr. Peters?" I asked, trying to take his mind off his agony. "Can we trust him?"

Ahab cupped his ear to hear me over the wind. His head was wreathed in smoke and the steam of his breath. I repeated my question.

"Not likely," was all he said before falling into a prolonged silence. He watched from behind the tree like a hunter in a blind with an expression I found disturbing. It was no doubt the look he wore on deck when scanning the horizon for a spout.

Eventually, a shabbily dressed fellow came up Mulberry and headed across the park to the Orange Street side. It wasn't Usual but still we followed. We gave him a sixty-yard lead so I don't think he knew we were on his trail. He led us off the field and up the street toward the Tombs. A block on, he made a quick right and disappeared down the alley between two abandoned warehouses. Ahab did his best to keep pace, but a whalebone leg just can't compete with the real thing when it comes to stalking.

Ahab held high the boarding ax, and I followed with my writing satchel in front of me for protection. We inched along through a narrow canyon of ancient brick that was laid back in the days when the Dutch ran Manhattan. Eventually, the captain brought the ax to his side. I took it as a sign to halt and did. He had me sidle up next to him, and the two of us stared into an enormous hole in the corroded brick of the left-hand wall.

"We need light," he whispered.

"We're going in there?" I asked.

"I'm guessing all the wastrels gather into this doggery on cold days."

"I have a box of matches," I said and set to digging them out of my bag. When I had one lit, Ahab swept his arm in front of him as an indication for me to lead the way. I wasn't happy with my position in the parade, but he looked at me with his stern glare he'd no doubt used on a thousand sailors throughout his days aboard ship.

The puny light I held out with the tips of my fingers did little against the dark, but we at least could proceed around the chaos of fallen brick and the shard piles of smashed bottles. I could swear I heard rats scampering about. It wasn't the first or the worst shit hole I'd been through in the course of my investigations, but it was bad enough. I led us to a hall, at the end of which was a burning torch set into the wall, lighting the way to a set of steps that descended into the underground.

I tossed my third match and pulled the writing satchel up in front of my chest and face. When it came to the stairs, Ahab went first. We crept as quietly as possible but the wood was as old as the bricks, and anyone listening would have known there were intruders. There were two flights of stairs. They emptied into a large underground vault, not a room with walls, not a basement, but a kind of cavern beneath the streets of the city.

Here and there, in the local vicinity of where we'd landed, there were torches burning, some more brightly than others and not enough all together to see clearly. Ahab went to the wall behind us and appropriated one. As my vision grew accustomed to the shadows and the torch, I could discern the silhouettes of human figures sitting, leaning against the rock walls. I also noticed a narrow stream running through the center of the cave and leading away in both directions.

Ahab approached the first person we came to. He leaned over and held the torchlight directly in front of the individual's face. What the glow revealed was an emaciated, pale fellow dressed in mere shreds of clothing. He was obviously starving and his Adam's apple, appearing huge in his wasted neck, bobbed up and down and gave us the only indication he was alive. His eyes, though, were the most disturbing— covered with a glassy film, staring as if into heaven beyond.

"Do you know Usual Peters?" the captain asked.

"Darling," said the man in the merest whisper, "is it you?"

"I said, do you know Usual Peters?" said Ahab, raising his voice an octave in frustration.

"Easy, old man," I told my companion. "This fellow couldn't find a hole in a ladder. Look at him, he's worse wasted than Job's turkey."

"Aye," said Ahab. "We've found the Purgatory of Sots."

"Seems more Perdition," I said.

We went from one slouching shadow to another, casting the light of the torch. Each was worse off than his predecessor, and none was the man we wanted. On our fifth inspection, the captain put the torch close to the nodding fellow in question and its light revealed a smoldering pipe held in the unfortunate's hand.

"Opium," said Ahab.

"You know it?"

"The aroma, its effects. I witnessed them in Java years ago."

When he mentioned the aroma, I suddenly became aware of it—a sweet floral scent like a Five Points perfume hanging in the dark. "He looks as if he's gone elsewhere," I said.

"He's across the Far Tortuga," said Ahab and pulled the torch back away from the man's face. "There's no use in looking further. Even if we find Usual, if he's in this befuddlement, we'll get nothing worthwhile out of him."

"I'd heard rumors of opium, small amounts, with the Chinese, and tales of the East, but nothing like this in Manhattan."

"There are quite a few fallen here from it," he said, scanning the bent shadows of the rock vault.

As we headed back toward the stairs, he swept the flame of the torch along each of the hapless forms huddled against the wall of the cave and studied their faces. I moved on ahead of him propelled by the sole desire to get the hell out of that dank pit. When I was about to set foot on the first step to salvation, the tap-tap-tap of his whalebone leg ceased. I turned and saw him leaning over one of the poor wretches.

"Come, come, Ahab," I said, and left the steps to retrieve him. "I'm not going to spend my entire day drilling the living dead for information when I can ask one of my associates in the police department who Malbaster is."

He didn't budge. The man he stood over lifted an emaciated arm to block the glow of the torch. Ahab looked stunned. I stepped up next to him, prepared to pull him along if need be, but before I could hook my arm through his, I looked down and saw what had him agape. Somewhat thinner, paler, more bereft than last I saw him, now shedding patches of his curly hair, and sporting a ragged beard and ragged blouse, was Ishmael, who whined piteously for us to let him be.

sh," I called my old copy editor as I might have back at the *Mirror*. It seemed to spark a sign of life in him. His crusted eyes fluttered open so slowly, I swore I heard a creaking noise. A moment passed, and I watched the flame of the torch dance in those glassy orbs. As he regained his sight, he brought his other arm up, moaned miserably, and said, "Leave me, spirit."

The captain leaned in closer. "It's me, Ahab."

"I'm here as well," I said, hoping it would be something of a comfort.

Ishmael turned to my voice and said, "Harrow?"

"Yes."

"Why did you bring this ghost with you?" He dared not look at Ahab.

The captain said, "I'm no ghost. I survived. It is your blasted book that makes a spirit of me. Your words have become a truth beyond truth."

"I didn't know."

"I wanted you to know."

There was silence for a few beats and then a light snoring let us know that Ishmael had dozed off. Ahab gathered my former colleague's collar in one fist and lifted him toward the flame. "Awake," he yelled. Ishmael sputtered out of sleep. "I'm real," said the captain. "You are not the only one who survived."

"Not the only one," Ishmael repeated as in a fog.

"There are two now. You and me. Don't ever forget it."

"Not two."

"Aye, two," said the captain with a ferocity in his voice.

I was about to intercede when Ishmael said, "No, three."

"What say you? Three? Is that a dream?" asked Ahab.

"Ish," I said gently and patted his cheeks. "Three?"

He nodded out of a doze and held up three fingers. "Daggoo," he said.

"What the hell is Daggoo?" I asked.

Ahab released Ishmael's collar and leaned him carefully back against the wall. He now asked softly, "You mean, the harpooneer?"

Ishmael nodded.

"The African," said Ahab.

Ishmael nodded.

"Where is he?"

Ahab removed his hat and bade me go to the stream and bring him some water. Ishmael was out cold. I did as I was asked. As I dipped the brim in the stream, I heard from off in the distance the sound of a voice. I couldn't make out where it was coming from, right or left, or what precisely it was saying. However, I could discern the rhythm and rhyme of poetry. I ran back to Ahab, hat in hand, and told him, "You've got minutes before I flee."

"Stand fast, Harrow, ye sorry land mutt. Find some backbone." That said, he tossed the dripping hat of water onto Ishmael's head. I thought for a moment the poor fellow would drown, but eventually he came barely awake again.

"Where is Daggoo?" asked Ahab.

"Seneca."

"Seneca?"

"Seneca Village?" I asked.

He nodded and shut his eyes.

"It's up north," I told the captain. "Now let's get out of here. I'm feeling the smoke." Breathing all that opium was sending *me* across the Far Tortuga.

"I'm a bit touched myself," he said. "But what do we do with Ishmael?"

That's when we heard the tramping of a dozen footfalls on the stairs. They hadn't reached the first landing before I grabbed Ahab by the sleeve and pulled him away. I knew the sound of that shoe leather like I knew my mother's own voice. It was the police, and judging from the enthusiasm in the slap of their step, I was certain they were there to crack heads. I held tight to the captain as we ran headlong into utter darkness. From behind us there erupted a sudden volley of groans and screams and the dull echo of clubs breaking bones, busting skulls, punctuated by gunshots. I snatched the torch from Ahab and tossed it in the stream.

I was frightened out of my wits, and somewhere along the way, Ahab had grabbed my sleeve and was pulling *me* along. Eventually, the sounds of agony became more distant, and then far removed. We stopped to catch our wind.

Leaning over with my hands on my knees, trying to catch my breath, I said, "Ahab, for a drab fellow you attract a lot of madness."

"Aye. Light one of ye matches. We need to find an escape to the street."

I did as he suggested. What we glimpsed during the stick's brief glow was more stream, more cavern, and more darkness ahead and behind. It was easy to decide in which direction to proceed. We moved on more slowly now, agreeing that I should light a match every few minutes. I informed the captain I had but five of them left.

"Why are the police assaulting those poor wretches?" he asked.

"The hunt for your boy has brought us into the middle of something I don't wish to be in the middle of."

It was by the light of my last match that we found a ladder running up the side of the cavern wall to a trapdoor in the floor of a dilapidated shed sitting behind an abandoned pub on Mott Street. We'd traveled quite a way underground. I had always been cocksure of my knowledge of Manhattan, that I knew it like a fifty-year lover, but never having heard of that cavern before, nor of the proliferation of opium use, made me feel left out in the cold. That plus the memory of those gunshots and beatings—the screams—made me jumpy.

Once we were out again beneath the steel-gray sky, cutting a path through the icy wind, Ahab said, "What next?"

"A drink at least," I said.

We landed in an oyster shop at the foot of Wall Street, across from the old Coffee House slip. It was quite a hike getting there, but I hoped the chill would clear my head of, among other things, the fear of death. I considered how ordinary my life had been for a fellow who wrote exclusively about the strange. Then Fate seemed to have stepped in and shouted, *I'll show you strange.*

Ahab didn't eat, but I did—a six-cent plate of raw oysters and a beer. He only drank, some warm rum and coffee concoction obviously not for landlubbers like myself.

"Why are we here and not heading for Seneca Village?" asked Ahab. "We're on to something. A school of answers runs just out of sight beneath our keel, man. I've got to act. All this sitting around in bars drinking and thinking is putting a cramp in my arse."

"Slow down," I said. "Take a deep breath. We'll go to Seneca Village tomorrow. Finding the African won't bring us any closer to your son."

"I just want to move, shake off this feeling of shipwreck."

"It's too late to start up there now. It's at the edge of the city. We're here because it's on my brother-in-law's beat."

"Beat, ya say?"

"He's a cop. I'm gonna drill him on what he knows about Malbaster or the Jolly Host."

"Sound thinking."

"I didn't fall off the turnip cart yesterday," I said. "I've got years of experience investigating stories."

"But why do you investigate them when you're just going to grind them into a spread of fiddle-faddle?"

"Don't you understand that there can be a certain truth in fiction?"

"The word *certain* in that statement carries a clipper's hold of import."

"And then some," I said. "But still it's true."

"I'm wonderstruck that there be a third survivor," said the captain. "The *Pequod* was so thoroughly smashed. It astonished me when I discovered that Ishmael had come back. Now another? Daggoo. How could I have missed him in the debris?"

"Imagine," I said, "that, in fact, you all lived. Your entire crew were all still alive and each living out his life unaware of the others, each burdened by the misconception that he was the only one to have survived. As the protagonist, you wander the world, discovering each and every one of them, as if your contact with them brings them to life. You see, that story has meaning; a certain truth. Something swims in its depths."

While Ahab pondered that with his horrid forgetting-how-to-laugh face, I inquired of the boy who brought us fresh drinks, "Max, has my brother-in-law been by yet?" The young man turned to face the bar and called to the bartender, "Tommy been in?"

"Any minute," said the bar man. I put a coin in Max's hand.

I told the captain that I'd heard someone reciting poetry in the cavern. I don't know why I admitted this to Ahab, but his silence had a strange way of drawing me out. "It was a female voice," I said.

"When?" he asked.

"As I was fetching your hat full of water."

"The manticore?"

Something hard slapped against my left shoulder. I nearly jumped out of my seat. It was Tommy. He hung his club back at his side and took a seat with us by the window.

"How's Ivy?" I asked.

"You know, hard on the balls," he replied and laughed.

"This here is Mr. Ahab," I said. "I'm helping him try to find his boy."

Tommy nodded to the captain and then removed his hat, setting it on the bench beside him.

JEFFREY FORD

"They've got you in the new blue uniforms, eh?" I said.

He nodded and mumbled, "That's fashion for ya."

I called to Max to fetch Tommy a beer.

"What brings you down here?" he asked.

"We're looking for you," I said. "We want you to tell us about Malbaster."

"The Jolly Host," said Ahab.

Max brought the beer then and Tommy waited for the boy to get out of earshot before he spoke. He leaned in toward us, and the captain and I followed suit. If we didn't look like a table of conspirators, I don't know who would.

"Malbaster is not someone you want to know," he said.

"Why?"

"He's a fella that dead bodies accumulate around. Whatever it is you want to find him for, it's not worth it."

"We think Ahab's kid is working for him."

"Christ on a crutch, George, I never took you for stupid."

"I promise we will not involve you in the least," Ahab said.

"Only when it comes time to shovel your bodies off the sidewalk."

"Just tell us who he is," I said.

"He's the walkin' Prince of Death. We don't know what he looks like. He's got a stake in a lot of crimes, but his main mission is to sow unrest among the poor, the micks, blacks, chinks, wops. He's paid off by big cheeses, anonymous bigwigs of the Order of the Star-Spangled Banner and such to practice violence against Catholics and coloreds and make their lives miserable. He's got a small army of followers all hopped up on the Chinese molasses.

"On what?" I asked.

"Opium. That's how he keeps the Jolly Host loyal. The police are at war with him. He's taking over our turf."

"We witnessed the results of that this morning in a cavern under

50

where the edge of the Collect Pond used to be, down the street from the Tombs," I said.

"You were there?" asked Tommy.

Ahab nodded as did I.

"Listen, the kid's as good as gone."

"I'll do whatever it takes to get him back," said the captain.

"Kill?"

"Yes."

"How many are you prepared to kill?"

"All of them," said Ahab.

Tommy stood up and leaned down over us. "We're done. Last I'm gonna tell you. Stay as far away from this as you can. That's it. There's nothing I can do to help you."

"Give my best to Ivy," I said as Tommy walked away.

"Get smart, Georgie," he called back over his shoulder.

8

By the time we left the oyster bar, the temperature had dipped and the wind, which had been steady all day, blew even stronger. The sun briefly appeared before setting. Those gilded seconds made even the drab buildings along the east side of Water Street beautiful. The captain was in a funk since meeting with my brother-in-law. The only thing he said to me on the walk to my house was, "So many wasted days."

The sun had set by the time we stepped through the door. Ahab and I hung our coats in the foyer closet as Misha approached up the hallway. "You have visitors, Mr. Harrow," she said.

"Mavis?" I asked.

Misha nodded. "She and her brother are in the kitchen."

"Tell her I'll be right with her."

"Yes, sir."

I went into my parlor study and Ahab followed. When I was done cutting the pages of an article from my notebook, he remained seated on the couch, filling his pipe. He seemed swamped by the predicament his son was in. I feared he'd slip into despair, so I said, "Captain, you should come and meet these young people. One of them is the girl who located Maisie's house for us." I took a risk, hoping that the sight of the boy, Mavis's younger brother, might be something of a balm to him. I was dangerously unsure as to why I thought that would be a good idea.

He followed me into the kitchen where we found Mavis, hat in her lap, holding a cigarette between her fingers. She and her brother were seated at the table beneath the window. Her brother, I forget his name, was a towheaded imp with a scrunched face full of freckles. Whenever he'd arrive at the house with his sister, Misha would make him a butter and sugar sandwich. That disgusting concoction was like manna from heaven to him. His sister never partook but sat and smoked and smiled at him as he laid waste to it.

I introduced Ahab to Mavis and her brother. The boy took a look at the captain's whalebone leg and stopped chewing, his mouth open. Finally, he spoke. "For shit sake, Mavis, he only got one leg."

She reached across the table and tried to swat him with her hat. "Words," she warned. The boy turned his attention back to the sandwich until Ahab tapped the floor.

"It's made from the bone of a monster."

"What happened to your leg?" asked the boy.

"Bit off by a spermaceti whale, white as a snow-covered hill."

"Did it hurt?"

"It still hurts," said Ahab, making his horrid trying-to-laugh face. When she beheld it, I noticed Mavis instinctively reach halfway toward her gun.

The boy finished his sandwich and sipped at his tea. Every other moment, he peered at the captain from the corner of his eye.

"Are you brave?" Ahab asked him.

The youngster looked at his sister and she made as if to think for a moment before nodding.

"Yes," said the boy.

Ahab stepped forward and placed an Indian penny next to the empty sandwich plate. He bowed and thanked Mavis for finding his wife's aunt. Before she could acknowledge it, he abruptly turned and tapped away down the hall to my study.

I asked Mavis to see what she could find out about Malbaster. I wrote the name out for her and she put the slip of paper in her pocket. I walked them to the front door. Her brother, half her size, leaned against her hip, yawning. She had one arm around him and her other hand on his head.

"I've heard the name before," she said. "But I steer clear of it. Try to put two streets between me and wherever I hear it."

"If you can do it without getting hurt, bring me some information on Malbaster and I'll pay you well for it. I want to know about the Jolly Host, where it congregates, what place is its home. I want to know the same about Malbaster. Where can I find him?"

"What do you mean by pay me well?" she asked.

"Ten dollars if you bring me the answers to those questions."

"Twelve," she said.

I acquiesced.

"We'll see what I hear," she said, leaning over to help her brother on with his coat. She shoved the hat down over his ears and they left.

I called behind her as they moved down the street, "Tell Garrick I'll need more cash soon."

Misha had a four-alarm blaze going in the study fireplace, and so I anchored there and opened a bottle of gin.

"Harrow, good God, man, you're a lush," said the captain as I handed him a drink. He waved it off, and I shrugged.

"It fortifies me against reality," I said.

"How long will it take to journey to Seneca Village tomorrow?" he asked.

"I don't understand why you want to go up there. We need to keep looking for your boy. What difference does it make to our cause if another of your crew survived?"

"I must be a whole person and not a ghost when I meet my son. I need to speak to the harpooneer. If I don't, I'll never be sure that I'm not, as the Nantucket night watchman believed, a walking spirit."

"Must be strange," I said and, with that, silence reigned for a solid hour. When the fire died down, I pushed the bottle away. I thought the captain had fallen asleep staring at the slow dancing shadows, but as I stood to head upstairs to my bedroom, he spoke.

"After I could again get up and around, one of the craftsmen of the village fitted me out with a wooden leg. My whalebone piece had been shattered in the melee of my meeting with Moby Dick. The I-Kiribati cared for me as if I were one of their own and nursed me with their island medicine back to health. I was welcome anywhere in their village, and I never wanted for a meal or companionship. They gave me use of a hut and would come, one or two at a time, to smoke a pipe, speak to me. I picked up much of their language in the years I spent among them.

"I knew from earlier whaling voyages that there were English and Dutch on the main island the natives referred to as Tungaru, and I knew that I could get my hosts to take me there. From there I intended to ship to Australia or Java, and from there, home. I had landed on one of the farther-flung atolls of the chain. Blue and green and sunlight were the colors of days and Time was drawn out to sea on a strong current. The ocean wind never stopped blowing, some days a rage, some a whisper. The I-Kiribati believed the world was created by a spider and that before people there were half people and spirits.

"One day I was invited to go on a sea journey to one of the atolls somewhat even farther out. We took a boy a year or two shy of manhood to that island, and we left him there. I learned from my cronies that the island was uninhabited, and that the boy would be expected to subsist alone for ten days. After we returned home, I would think of what the boy was doing and in my imagination, I pictured him as my son. I saw him fishing with a spear, gathering a kind of swamp taro they called babai, sitting alone on the beach in the sunset, staring toward home. At times, my dreams included my wife.

"The day finally came when we manned the large outrigger canoe and returned to that far-off island to retrieve the boy. When we arrived, we found him alive and well and standing on the shore to greet us. I'd thought it would be an exciting moment to welcome him back, but the hopes of that were dashed by the fact that standing next to him was another boy, his identical twin. I looked around from face to face to find a reaction, but everyone who'd made the journey was quiet and wore a somber expression. We all got back in the canoe and returned home.

"I wanted to know, of course, where the boy's twin came from, if he'd been on the island before we'd first arrived or if he'd been brought on a separate journey. My closest friend, the old man Abiaing, shook his head at my questions and offered not a word. Soon after, one of those two boys took ill with some grim wasting disease. His ribs began to show, his eyes grew large and sunken. I would come upon him from time to time hunched in the bushes vomiting what looked like torrents of sand.

"One afternoon about a month after returning from the island, the poor lad succumbed to whatever horrible disease had attacked him and he dropped face forward onto the ground in the center of the village. No one would move to help him, and when I went to the task, my friend held me back and again shook his head. Almost the entire village was gathered in a ten-foot circumference around the shipwrecked fellow. His healthier twin was also in the crowd. We watched, me in disbelief, as the living corpse shuddered and shivered and suddenly transformed into a dark smoke that drifted out over the ocean. That night, I dreamed of my wife and boy, and the next day I begged my I-Kiribati friends to take me to Tungaru."

With that, the captain once again closed his eyes. There was nothing for me to do but continue upstairs to my bed and an uneasy night's sleep.

Ahab was up early and impatient to shove off. Before 9:00, we were on the sidewalk, heading west on Fulton Street. At the corner of Fulton and Church, with the last of Garrick's money, I contracted a hansom cab to take us to Seneca Village, wait while we made our inquiries, and then return us to civilization. I gave the driver instructions to head north on Hudson. Once our journey was underway, I eased back into the seat and stared out at the city.

"I remember reading in Ishmael's book that this sailor, Daggoo, was a giant," I said.

Ahab, transfixed by the passing sights, said, "Fancy unto fancy linking."

"Are you saying my colleague was less than truthful in his depiction of the harpooneer?"

"Daggoo was of good height, no less than six foot, but not an inch more. He was a powerful man. Could sink the steel deep. His name wasn't Daggoo, either. I can no longer recall what it actually was."

"Why do you think Ishmael made him six foot five in the book?"

"He's a sensationalist," said the captain. "One of your brethren."

We watched the buildings thin out and the pastures begin. Cows and horses dotted the passing landscape. When we reached Fourteenth Street, I opened the hatch above us to tell the driver to head over to Eighth Avenue and continue north. The road got more rugged. It was a brisk and beautiful day, and being away from the city, the difference in the air was noticeable. The offal stench of the street had receded; the smoke burdening each breath and blotting out the sun was left in our wake.

I'd only been to Seneca Village one other time. It was to gather background detail for, perhaps, one of my most fantastic offerings— "The Utopia of Races." It told of blacks and Irish and Germans living together in harmony. That part was real. Colored farmers had bought the first parcels of land and started the community. Years later, when immigrants came from Europe, they were welcome. There was one midwife who birthed both black and white. All worshipped together at the All Angels' Church. I couched the piece in terms of female visionary utopias like *Three Hundred Years Hence* by Mary Griffith. Most of the *Gorgon's Mirror* readers took it as a flight of fancy, which is what it was. Others, like the Order of the Star-Spangled Banner, nativist groups, and even Samuel Morse, who'd once run for mayor, wrote in to the editorial page of the *Mirror* to say I should be sacked or, barring that, killed.

My detractors didn't realize that I, George Harrow, was not a do-gooder, an abolitionist, a friend to the downtrodden, a lover of Catholics or the sons and daughters of Africa, nor was I in league with the idiocy of the Know-Nothings, indiscriminate haters of anything other than themselves. No, I was merely an opportunist seizing an opportunity when I chose that topic for an article. I knew that nothing sold better than controversy.

I asked the driver to stop and let us out near All Angels' Church. The scenery was made up of slow rolling farmland dotted with thickets of pin oak, boulders, and small clutches of whitewashed buildings. Some of the homes were little more than glorified shacks and others were three stories tall, constructed of wood and brick. People were out and about, but now that it was well past harvest season the place was less busy than when I was there in summer. We headed along a dirt path to the church.

There was an old colored man, dressed in a vest and white shirt, sweeping the aisles between the pews. He welcomed us and asked if we were new to the village. I told him I'd been there a few years earlier to write a story, and he seemed to dimly recall that.

"We're looking for a gentleman who might go by the name of Daggoo," I said.

"The man's a sailor, a harpooneer," said Ahab.

The fellow remained quiet but continued sweeping, sweeping, sweeping. For a moment, I thought he'd forgotten us, but then he said, "The name's not familiar, but there's a man of the sea. Go to the African Union Church just across the way. In the basement, there's a school. The teacher is Catherine Thompson. She can tell you where to find him. He works for her with the children. I haven't seen him for some time, but I believe he still lives in a small home by the swamp."

We thanked the man and were on our way. Ahab moved like a locomotive toward our quarry. I still was unsure what he hoped to get out of a meeting with his old shipmate. The building we approached was much older than the previous church, somewhat in disrepair and sagging beneath the weight of years. We took the steps to the front entrance, pulled open the door and entered.

The place was empty and eerily still. Then we heard the sound of children's voices, muffled as if from afar. Spotting a door along a far wall, I tapped Ahab on the shoulder and we went to it. I opened the door and found a stairway. Putting my hand behind my ear to listen more intently, I heard a children's chorus give way to a single female voice. "An Evening Thought" by Jupiter Hammon. It was then I felt the tip of a sharp blade pressed against my throat.

I stole a look at the captain, and he, too, was in the same predicament as myself. A large colored man held him fast from behind, an arm around his chest and a curved blade at his jugular. This, fortunately, was not the first time I'd been in such a situation. My intuitive reflex was to start talking and not stop till my captor either killed me or released me. I rattled off my name and that I was a writer for the *Gorgon's Mirror* and that I'd visited and done an article on Seneca Village not too many years earlier, and a very positive article to boot. "Check my bag," I said. "I've only writing implements in it."

"Shut yer bleedin' hole," came a command. Another large fellow, as pale as the man holding Ahab was dark, moved into view and grabbed the bag. My captor released me as the strap passed over my head, and after my satchel was removed, now simply held the knifepoint to the base of my skull. The large Irishman went through my things and seemed satisfied, dropping the bag upon the floor.

"What's this one carrying, Fergus?" said the man holding Ahab.

The boarding ax and pistol immediately came to light and were seized. This, I knew, was not a good development. "This man is my bodyguard," I said. "We've come north on an investigation."

"What investigation?"

"We're looking for a man who was in the whaling industry, a harpooneer."

"Why?"

"We shipped together on an ill-fated whaler out of Nantucket, the *Pequod*," said the captain.

The colored man holding him slowly released his grip. He commanded my captor to back off two steps. I had the opportunity to turn and see all three of the men who had accosted us. The man who'd held me was short and stocky.

"We're merely looking for information, good sirs," I said.

"Fergus, light me a candle," said the man who'd held Ahab. The Irishman did as he was told and disappeared into the dim shadows of the dark church. The only light in the place came through the spaces between some of the beams above. He returned with a lit taper and gave it to the colored man, who immediately thrust it toward the captain's face.

9

The man holding the candle had short-cropped hair. He wore a loose blouse of a shirt, open at the neck, and a pair of wide sailor's pants. Slowly, his hand came out toward Ahab's face. The captain, for his part, didn't blink. Whereas I was on the verge of crying, I doubt the old seaman's heart skipped a beat.

"What manner of magic is this?" asked the man and touched Ahab's cheek.

"It's me," said the captain. "And don't tell me I'm dead. Until yesterday, I thought the same of you."

The man retracted his hand quickly as if Ahab's words were fire.

"I remember you, sir, but I've forgotten your name," said Ahab. "You were once my harpooneer, and an exceptional one at that."

"Follow me," he said to us. We did and he led us out of the decrepit church. Once outside, he told his friends that we were to be trusted and that our business was solely with him. They nodded, grinned at us, and begged our pardon.

"We can't be too careful for the children's sake," said the one named Fergus. He returned Ahab's weapons and the other gentleman handed me my satchel.

Then the man I believed to be Daggoo took us to a large hall a few dozen yards down a path. Inside that structure there was natural light of the clear day streaming through two large windows and a table with many chairs set around it as if for a meeting. Our host motioned for us to sit. He appeared to want to speak but he was obviously dumbfounded by the presence of Ahab.

"Not in all the world did I ever expect to see you save in my night-mares," he said to the captain.

"Ishmael told me you were also alive."

"The writer?" said the man. "He and I were rescued by the *Rachel*. In fact, he was unconscious, and I was keeping him afloat, treading water for us both."

"And he never jotted a word about you having survived in his book?" I said.

The man laughed. "That book is a farce. I've read it. Miss Thompson found a copy of it someone had thrown out for junk. It's how she collects volumes for the students. She told me about it and she helped me read it. Next to seeing you here, in the flesh, discovering a book that was about a voyage I had been on was the most disturbing thing in my life."

"But you are not Daggoo," said Ahab. "I remember that."

"No, I am Madi. I have always been Madi."

I could hear the lilt and inflection of someone from Africa as I knew it, or thought I knew it, but his English was unbroken, smooth as a gentleman's. "And from where do you hail?" I asked.

"I'm Mandinka, from Guinea. My father was a goldsmith. When I left home, I swam out to a British whaling ship anchored in a lagoon and begged the captain to take me out into the wider world. All I brought with me was my name, Madi."

"That cur Ishmael penned you as Daggoo," said Ahab.

"He also made me a monster of a man. A giant. But you see . . ." He paused and his look indicated he wanted my name.

I told him, "Harrow."

"Mr. Harrow, I grew up with the fears of white men. The French were with us long before I was born."

"Did you feel like a walking spirit since, through the book, the world knew you as dead?" asked Ahab.

"I was joyful to be alive. I could go to America a free man and make my way."

"And then you got here," I said.

"Yes, yes, it took me quite a while to understand. On the sea, I was royalty aboard ship for my talent with the harpoon. Here I was shoved aside, spit at, ignored, once beaten. When I heard about Seneca Village, I came here to live with other free Africans. I met Catherine Thompson, the schoolteacher. She taught me to read, to speak better English. She told me I should work to one day own land and to vote."

"And what now do you make of our battle with Moby Dick?" asked the captain.

"Insanity," said Madi. "You murdered a ship full of men. The book captures well your madness. Do you remember how good my eyesight was for spotting a spouter two miles off?"

"Yes, I do," said Ahab.

"After Ishmael and I were rescued, I was standing on the deck relating to Captain Gardiner of the *Rachel* about the devastation wrought by the white whale, and off in the distance, in the late-afternoon light, I spotted you in the water nearly a half mile west, waving your arms. I was sure you were crying out but the distance made it impossible for you to be heard. I didn't blink, or look away, but continued with my tale to its conclusion, and then went below to eat."

"You condemned me to death. You've a right to it."

"I've more than a right."

"If it be any solace," said Ahab, "I've wrestled with my madness, with the memories of those who were lost, and I am pushing back into the world of the living for one last chance at salvation."

"Solace?" said Madi. "Not in the least, for I imagine your good deeds as tainted with self-interest as your acts of madness."

"I mean to find my boy and raise him. Whatever parcel of that task I can accomplish is what I'll spend every second doing."

"Where's your boy?" asked the harpooneer.

Ahab couldn't answer.

I hesitated a moment and then blurted out, "He's fallen in with a gang, the Jolly Host."

Madi held up his hand. "Wait. The Jolly Host?"

I nodded. "There's a man named Malbaster involved."

"My friends and I ambushed you for this very reason. Strangers in the village now are held in great suspicion. We recently had two children from the school disappear one Sunday evening. Their bodies were found in a ravine out on the path toward the Hudson. I've promised Miss Thompson that I would find out who killed them. I've traced the crime to the Jolly Host."

"What makes you think it was them?" I asked.

"It's happened in several colored villages outside the city. Every few months they do something horrible to swamp the people with fear. The same cutting instruments seem to have been used. The same circle within a circle carved into the victims' backs. These were two children, no more than six years old."

"Are there no police out here?" I asked.

"Many of them sympathize with the Jolly Host. Nativists—they want to get rid of colored and Catholic."

"How much do you know about them?" asked Ahab.

"I've learned a few things from some of the villagers. A pair of Irish brothers worked for Malbaster for a brief time until they feared for their lives and fled here. He's known to reel in the sons and daughters of poor immigrants to help him kill and torment their parents. He draws them in with the sweet smoke and then traps them with magic, or so I've been told."

"There's a lot of stories out there," I said. "We're looking for specifics, though. Places, names, et cetera."

"I know of one place from my inquiries," said Madi.

"What is the location?" said Ahab. "I must find my boy and give this Malbaster what he deserves."

"To give him what he deserves," said Madi, "would mean only one thing."

"What?" I asked.

"He deserves death, no less. Are you ready to administer that?"

"Make no mistake, my man, when the time comes, if I find him worthy of it, I will strike him down," said the captain. "The location."

"You're used to giving orders and forget you're speaking to a free man."

"But aren't you interested in finding Malbaster?" I asked. "Perhaps we could work together."

Madi was still for a few heartbeats. I could tell he was weighing my offer. Finally, he said, "You two could offer me some help. Although I'm free, there are still places I can't go, places that might get me killed. But if I travel with you in the guise of your trusted employee, the white world would be open to me."

"Yes," said Ahab. "We'll help you find justice for these children."

"I'm not looking for justice," said Madi. "I'm after revenge. And the first time you treat me like a servant, I'll abandon you to your blind groping."

"Very well then," I said, rose, and stepped forward to shake the harpooneer's hand. His grip was strong; he was a frightfully sturdy fellow. He wasn't the giant Ish had made him out to be, but I still wouldn't want to be the object of his revenge.

"How do we proceed?" I asked.

"This evening, an hour before sunset, we meet near Kips Bay. The farthest point east on Forty-First."

"That's more or less the boundary of the city," I said.

"Are you familiar, Mr. Harrow, with the shantytown there? Some call it Dutch Hill, some Goat Hill?"

"Christ, yes. I've been there only once and once was enough. The Five Points is paradise in comparison."

"You must promise that you won't attempt to make a move without me. I'll be bringing Fergus along. His daughter was one of the slain children."

"I know the place is like a maze of shacks and lean-tos, a warren of paths winding amid hovels all set on a high rocky outcropping. Very dangerous, even in daylight."

"Yes, dangerous. Those poor people have nothing. But you'll never find the Jolly Host without me. They have a place there, larger than most, acquired for nothing by Malbaster, where they congregate before setting out on their missions of mayhem or gather after the evil has been done. They have a number of such spots all over the city. I know how to identify the place. When we meet tonight, I'll reveal the secret."

"Very well," said Ahab. "We'll be waiting for you."

"Be prepared for a fight," said Madi. He rose and led the way to the door. We stepped out into the cold, bright afternoon and made our way back to the hired hansom cab.

Once we were moving south along the rugged lane, I told Ahab that we need not travel all the way back to James Street. "We'll hold up somewhere between Forty-First and there, somewhere back within the circumference of civilization. The sun will set in four hours or so."

The captain's thoughts seemed elsewhere. He merely nodded.

"You know," I told him. "I have a friend who works at City Hall. He's an informant of mine. Not long ago, he told me that the decision has already been made to dismantle Seneca Village to make way for a park that will take up a large parcel of land in the middle of Manhattan."

"What'll become of the harpooneer and the others who live there?" he asked.

"They'll all be paid some weak sum for their dwellings and their land. Then the entire village will be leveled. It was on my mind during our meeting, but I didn't have the heart or courage to out with it. From what my associate said, the park is inevitable. The mayor is behind it. The decision is twofold. The first reason is a park that can be surrounded by wealthy communities. The second reason—and who knows, this may really be the first reason—is to rid the city of a community of free colored who own land and are gaining the right to vote."

"And I thought the sea could be cruel," said Ahab.

10

We sat on the patio of the New Rose Inn, overlooking the East River, bundled in our coats and the blankets that had been brought to us. The captain couldn't possibly have sat inside where there was a fire blazing in the hearth and we were closer to the gin. He was still mulling his conference of the walking ghosts with Madi. I couldn't fathom what the importance of the meeting was, but it turned out to be propitious in that the harpooneer fell in with our purpose and brought us closer to our goal.

"You know, Ahab," I said, interrupting his grim contemplation, "it just crossed my mind that whereas you have a pistol and ax, I've got nothing to protect me should there be a scuffle this evening."

"The pen is mightier than the sword," he said and gave a strangled gasp of not-laughter.

"What exactly are we going to do there on Dutch Hill?" I asked.

"Shake the beehive. Grab one of the Host and make him tell us all."

The vehemence with which he spoke unnerved me. "Sounds like things could get dire."

"Time bounds away, Harrow. I feel I have only weeks or months before Gabriel reaches an age where it will be impossible for me to make contact. Afterward, he won't have any use for me."

"Take a deep breath," I said. "You've got a hook in your own mouth." We then sat in silence for quite a while, drinking and watching dead leaves fly on a strong wind out over the water. Sally Cocharan, wrapped in a red cape with a hood, brought us another round. She was a friend of my sister, Ivy, a schoolmate who married into the Cocharan family that owned the inn.

She put our whiskeys on the table between us and slid the tray under her arm. "I thought of you, George Harrow," she said. "I had a gentleman in here a day or so ago, and he was cockeyed drunk."

"Is that the part that made you think of him?" said Ahab.

"No," she said with a giggle. "This fella stopped in to whiskey up before continuing his flight up to West Farms. He kept repeating that the city was secretly hell. He never knew it before but he'd seen something that convinced him. He was getting out of hand, so my husband told him if he didn't pipe down, he'd be tossed out into the road. So, he whispers to me and Will, and the tale he spits out was something I could see Georgie writing for his paper."

"Do tell," I said. "I'm always up for free fodder."

"I thought you'd be," said Sally. "He said he knew Manhattan was part of hell when the previous night, on his way home from work—he tended bar at one of the groggeries by Washington Square—he passed an alleyway that was given some light from a gas lamp perched on the sidewalk at its mouth. What was revealed in that cavern of darkness . . . ?"

"Cavern of darkness, Sally! That's downright poetic," I said.

She slapped me on the shoulder. "Listen," she said. "He saw a strange creature. 'Twas a large cat, like a puma with the face of a woman and long, curly tresses. He said it had a tail that was like the stinger of an insect. And the worst part of it was that she was boring through a man's neck, blood and muscle and tendon flying. Here's exactly what he said, 'Her terrible rows of teeth were some kind of machine with serrated blades turning in unison.'"

She laughed when she was finished and wore an expression as if she were expecting us to join her. Ahab and I were staring at each other.

"Tell me something, miss," the captain finally said. "Was there a mention of poetry being recited?"

Sally looked confused but then nodded. "The drunk kept saying the word 'Poetry, poetry,' as my husband hustled him to the door and tossed him into the road. How did you know about the poetry?"

Ahab mumbled, "Luck."

"George, what aren't you telling me?"

"Nothing, nothing. Sometimes the captain has second sight."

"George?"

I shook my head and changed the subject. "Sally, has William some kind of weapon handy I might borrow? I'm going to Dutch Hill tonight to track down a story."

"Dutch Hill? You're desperate for stories if you be going there. I thought you just made that tripe up from outta your head."

She went inside and a few minutes later William, her husband, a shambling, good-natured fellow (as much as I knew him), came out. "I can't give over my pistol, George," he said as he approached. "But I've got this old fid left in one of the upstairs rooms by a shady-looking sailor. You might bash someone on the head with it or poke 'em in the eye with the other end." He handed me the tool he'd been carrying.

"Thank you, sir," I said. "To tell the truth, I can't imagine doing either, so this is all the weapon I need."

"You look like an authentic man of the sea with that marlinespike, aye," said Ahab. He wasn't missing many opportunities to skewer me, and each time I was surprised by it. At least it was a sign he might be coming out of his melancholy. I'm sure it was the promise of impending mayhem that revived him.

Two hours later, we met Madi and Fergus about a mile north of the New Rose Inn. An orange sun was on the horizon and throwing enormous shadows over everything. We spent the first few minutes of our reunion discussing what it was exactly that we were about to do. I've already admitted, I'm a coward. The thought of battling someone hand to hand in the dark in one of those stinking hovels was the stuff of nightmare for me. My compatriots didn't seem anxious about it at all.

Madi was carrying an odd weapon that looked like a cross between a handheld scythe and a throwing knife, the blade in the form of a bird's head. When I inquired as to what it was, he told me, "A Fang bieri." He said he'd been given it by an old man from Orungu who'd lived at Seneca Village. Over his left shoulder, Fergus toted a long two-handed club with an iron spike jutting from its head.

"I thought we might take a hostage and interrogate him. See what ambergris we can drain," said Ahab.

"We'll make them talk," said Fergus.

"Take two," said Madi.

I just stood there clutching my fid until they all looked over at me and stared. After a time, Madi said to me, "You're trembling, Mr. Harrow."

I hadn't been aware of it. I was instantly self-conscious and slipped my fid back into my satchel. In that moment, I realized how dangerous it was to keep company with the characters from books. They lived book lives of fierce deeds and deep yearning. This was true not only of Ahab and Madi but Fergus, too. I could imagine a novel in which he played a significant role.

We were off in an instant and I missed the announcement of the final plan. Before I knew it, we'd strayed from the road and were moving toward the river. Dark had come on, the wind blew cold, and I stumbled more than once on the rutted ground. I smelled the water and saw the stars and distant lamplight reflected in it. Then we traipsed uphill, and halfway to the top, we came upon a pen holding two pigs, skinny like bone sausages. Beyond that, where things leveled off (me out of breath and the captain struggling), we encountered a path that ran among the shacks and hovels and run-down houses from the old days of the Dutch settlers.

There was candlelight in the windows of those few dwellings that had them and it leaked out from around the leather flaps at the entrances to lesser homes. Fires blazed outside doorways and most were set up for cooking. One large spit held a medium dog roasting above the flames. There were fires within the hovels as well, burning in crumbled chimneys or dug in the dirt floor. It was a cold night that was only going

to get even colder, that much was clear. I had to tip my hat to those people for surviving, but truth be told, I'd not give them another thought
if I could have abandoned our mission and made my way back to a gin
and cigar at James Street.

As we passed, people either melted into the shadows or came out to
their makeshift porches to slap a truncheon against an open palm and
stare at us as if in defiance, to let us know they meant to defend their
homes no matter how ramshackle. I brought up the rear of our small
parade and didn't understand our movements. It seemed that Madi was
leading us from one hovel to another, leaning in to inspect the doorway
of each. None seemed to his satisfaction until we came to one with a
brand burned deep into the wood.

It was that same circle within a larger circle design left upon the
victims of the Jolly Host. As soon as it came to me what was going on,
Madi spoke in an urgent whisper. "This is it," he said and I moved in
closer to listen.

"Board her and take prisoners," said Ahab, who pushed the door
open with his shoulder and led the charge followed by Madi and Fergus. Afraid of being left in the road alone, I screwed up my courage and
joined them. Immediately upon stepping into the dark, I could smell
that sweet aroma, like paradise in hell. I recognized it immediately
from when we'd encountered Ish in the underground. Moving down
a short hallway, we entered a large room that was lit by the guttering
flames of two candles. A dozen or so young men leaned against the
wall or lay on broken-down divans and couches. A blue-gray haze hung
thick in the air.

The four of us stood ready for battle, but there was no battle. All was
surrender. I could feel the tension emanating from Ahab's subverted
expectations of hand-to-hand combat. For a second I thought he might
shoot someone merely for good measure. Instead he called out in a
booming voice, "Who wants to talk to us?" From one shadowed corner, there came a protracted fart and following it a moment later from

another corner, a faint laugh. "Do any of you know Gabriel?" he asked. Farts resounded from all quarters.

The captain tapped two steps to the left, leaned over, and grabbed one of the opium smokers by the collar. As he hoisted the lad to his feet, he said, "Front and center." A groan came from his catch.

"I think there are more rooms in the back of this place. Let's take him back there," said Fergus.

We helped Ahab drag the hapless fellow down a hall to an empty room. After closing the door behind me, I turned around and saw that the entire back wall of the room was caved in, affording us an excellent nighttime view of the river. Someone had conveniently left behind a straight-backed chair and we dropped our prisoner in it. When the lad tried to get to his feet, the captain shoved him back into the chair, which tilted on the rotting floorboards. Fergus leaned in and slapped the fellow lightly across the cheeks and chin. "Wake up, ya ratbag."

Once the prisoner's eyes opened, Madi stepped up and laid the blade of the Fang bieri against the boy's throat. "Who killed the children at Seneca Village?"

"Harrow, have you a match in your satchel? Light this rogue's face so we can see what's going on," said Ahab.

I lit a match and moved it close to see who we were waylaying. He was younger than I had suspected, maybe fifteen years old, with a thin, pinched face, a poorly healed scar across the forehead, and a mess of sandy hair.

"The killings at Seneca Village?" repeated Madi, still holding the blade in place.

The boy gave a vague smile, missing two teeth, and Madi dropped the weapon to his side. Fergus stepped in, saying, "You think you're the cat's uncle, eh?" and he smashed the lad's face with the side of his hand. Blood trickled from his nose. The match went out, and when I lit another, there were tears in our prisoner's eyes.

"Hold off," Madi said to Fergus. "He's only a boy."

"Agreed," I said.

Ahab tapped me on the back and pulled me into the shadows. "Have you got some money, Harrow?"

"A little."

"We'll offer him a three-dollar bill and see if he'll dance for it."

I dug in my pocket and produced the suggested amount.

Ahab approached the boy in the chair and drew his pistol. "We've not got the time to play here, son. I'm going to give you one chance. You've got a choice to live or die. If you don't speak, it's the harpoon for ya. If you tell us what we want, I'll give you three dollars. Harrow?"

I lit another match and Ahab held the bill out for him to see.

"You've got one second to decide."

The boy roused from his opium stupor and cried out like a toddler from a bad dream. "Noooo."

"Where do I find Malbaster?" asked Ahab. He drew his pistol from beneath his coat and cocked the trigger.

"He's got a lair neath the street near the Tombs. I swear to you."

"We're looking for a lad in his clutches by the name of Gabriel. Do you know him?" I asked.

"Yes. The boys call him the Malbastard since he's a favorite of the Pale King Toad. Can I have my money now and leave?"

"Who killed the children at Seneca Village?" asked Madi.

"I've no clue," said the boy. "Though I know Malbaster gave the order to cause trouble and fear among the people there. He's magic."

At that moment, the sound of shouts and footsteps came from the hallway outside the room.

11

Ahab gave the boy the bill with one hand and swept him out of the chair with the other. If a man with a whalebone leg could ever have been said to pounce, he did. In less than a second the chair was leaning back, wedged beneath the knob. There was a banging on the door from the hallway. "Open," a voice outside shouted. I headed for the hole in the wall. Madi and Fergus were already through. As I passed the boy leaning in a daze against the wall, I snatched my three from his hand. Ahab's gun went off in an attempt to frighten the horde in the hall and that hastened me.

I gathered with my compatriots out behind that rotting carcass of a house, and we waited for Ahab. The wind was up, and the footing on the hill was uneasy. I wasn't so sure of myself in the dark. My blood was pumping and I was breathing fast. Swinging my satchel around, I reached inside for the fid and retrieved it. Then there were footsteps on the path and Ahab appeared, locomoting like an ailing steam engine. Behind him was a pack of the Jolly Host. I couldn't see their faces but I heard their cries. The captain got to us only an instant before they did.

Madi and Fergus stepped forward and the wave broke against them. It was immediately clear that they'd decided to avoid causing grievous bodily harm. They went at the Host with fists instead of blade and club. Fergus felled three with uppercuts before he was inundated. Madi spun and used his feet as well as his fists, and Ahab swung broadly, parting the onslaught. I stood like a statue behind them until I felt a hand tighten on my throat. I lashed out with the fid and cracked the cheekbone of my assailant, who dropped to his knees, clutching his head. More came in his place and I swung the weapon like I was swatting flies.

Three of the Host backed me up a hill that edged out over the beach along the East River. I called to the captain for help. I heard him grunt as I backed up the slope and before they were on me he called, "Give them the pen, Harrow." A pummeling, mostly of me, took place at the top of the rise. I managed to fell one of the louts by poking his eye with the end of the fid. His screams drove the other two toward me. The scrawnier one, in that instant, reminded me of Mavis's younger brother, only far more dim-witted and demonic looking. It was he who pounced and wrapped his legs around my waist and snapped at my throat. I couldn't wound him with the marlinespike, for he was too close and the momentum of his lunge put me back on my heels.

I teetered for a moment on the edge of the cliff and when I fell backward, only then did I realize what was happening. There came a fleeting instant of overwhelming disappointment as I clawed the air for purchase. I hit the ground before I knew it with a jarring jolt and although my body came to rest, I continued to descend into the blackness within my rattled head.

I couldn't have been out long as the next thing I knew I was gasping for breath. My head and ribs hurt and I had sand in my mouth. I believe the little lout who pushed me over the edge had come along for the ride and landed on me before running off. I tried mightily to move my legs. They only tingled but didn't stir, and I feared I'd been paralyzed. If that was the case, my desperate thinking went, I would borrow Ahab's pistol and shoot myself.

Slowly, feeling returned to my lower half and bit by bit I began to move my legs. Eventually I was able to bend my knees and get the soles of my feet flat on the ground. Still the pain in my back and head was fierce. It was somewhere during my attempts to get to a sitting position that I discovered that my writing satchel was gone. I found a match in the pocket of my vest, thumbnailed it into life, and looked around to see if the bag had flown off in my fall. I saw the fid sticking point down in the sand a couple of yards away, but the satchel was nowhere in sight.

"I bet that little fuck knuckle took it," I whispered as I got to my feet and dusted myself off. Where to go now was the pressing issue. Looking up, I could see only the silhouette of the top of the hill against the star-studded sky. The precipice was too steep for me to dream of climbing. Beyond that I was limping. I knew the river was close by. A few feet off I could make out the dead weeds and scrub of autumn lining the bank. The battle, if it still raged, was too distant to discern or blocked out by the whistling of the wind. I wasn't sure what to do next.

I've been robbed, beaten, and could have been killed, I told myself. With that thought stewing in the back of my mind, I headed south, back toward the New Rose Inn, sticking to the shoreline as a guide in the dark. "The Jolly Host," I said, tripping over stones and stumbling along. "Jolly Horseshit." I was certain this was good-bye to Ahab, the mawkish lunatic. I'd already collected a treasure trove of story ideas for articles. The manticore alone I could milk until spring. The captain's navigation was swiftly leading us to tragedy, the best intentions run aground. It was most certainly time to abandon ship.

As that decision was made, I heard his very voice, bellowing my name in the night. "Harrow!" And the captain's cries were followed by those of Madi. They were a hundred yards north of me, and my first inclination was to hide. I, with my limp, was moving slower than Ahab across the lumpen ground. I tried to put on some steam, but my knee ached and my shoulder was in agony. Eventually I stopped walking and called out to Ahab. In return I heard, "Ahoy!" I got a sudden chill and shook my head. Before two minutes were up the captain and Madi appeared out of the night.

The African had a welt on the side of his face as if he'd been struck by a blackjack, and Ahab's coat had been sliced by a straight razor, in three places. The two of them were out of breath.

"Did you desert us, Harrow?" said the captain.

"I battled three of them and took one over the cliff with me," I said. "I landed fifty feet down next to the river, nearly broke my ass."

"We barely escaped with our lives," said Ahab. "The scallywags had knives and clubs. It was all I could do not to shoot one."

"Where's Fergus?" I asked, looking around.

Madi said, "Fergus is dead," in a grave tone that matched the look of grief on his face.

"Shivved in the kidneys by a cute little tyke with hair the color of snow," said the captain. "When he hit the deck, another came along with a bat and cracked Fergus's skull open. We left him in his death throes, one eye hanging out by a stem."

I stared at Ahab in horror, aghast at his calm reaction to a man's demise. "Christ, Ahab, you're lethal. This evening's outing was utterly pointless," I said.

"No," said Madi. "We now know where to find Malbaster."

"Was it worth your friend's life?" I asked.

"To think of it as a trade, one for the other, is frivolous. I *will* find the guilty party."

"We're all guilty," said Ahab.

"Nonsense," said Madi.

We made our way back to the inn and caught the last coach to the city proper. By the time we docked at James Street, it was well past midnight. Ahab headed directly for his bed upstairs. Luckily, Misha was still awake, and I asked her to make up the couch in my study for Madi. After she finished the task, she ran into me in the kitchen.

"He's colored," she whispered.

"There's nothing I can do about it," I said and shrugged.

She swatted at me. "Were you in some kind of fight?" she asked.

"Don't make me think about it," I told her. "I'll need a new writing satchel. Can you go over to Liberty Street tomorrow and get me one?"

She nodded. "I'll go after breakfast."

"Take whatever money you think you'll need from the cigar box."

She made her way to her little room at the back of the house. I stole into my study and sitting in my desk chair while Madi sawed wood on the couch, I poured myself a drink, lit a cigar, and quietly rocked. My companions were both exhausted and badly beaten. Not to mention poor Fergus, whom I was just beginning to appreciate. Now his wife had one fewer child and no husband. We'd have to alert the police to his murder. This was sickeningly serious business and my mind was ablaze with ways to extricate myself from it.

Every time I moved to pour another drink my ribs ached and my shoulder screamed. I thought the best thing to do was to keep drinking until I passed out in the chair. In the meantime, I decided to record our adventure at Dutch Hill. I took a new notebook from my drawer and began straightaway to write as was my custom. As Garrick had told me, "Hesitation is the impotent father of untold stories." The movement of the pen across the page helped me to forget my aches and pains better than the drink could.

In the telling, I changed our names (save for Ahab's, of course) and monkeyed with the circumstances to engender our anonymity, but the battle with the Jolly Host was recorded blow for blow, with plenty of bloody teeth flying, fists cracking skulls, and the depiction of my fall from the cliff described in such glorious detail I might instead have been flying to the moon. I knew my usual readers would lap up those scenes of violence awash in melodrama. Oh, yes, and I changed the fact that we'd battled a horde of downy-haired children to a hardened gang of degenerate men.

I lose a sense of time when I'm writing, so I don't know how long I was at my task. It could have been an hour. It could have been three. Near the end of the piece, though, weariness worked its spell on me. I was nodding in and out, and my penmanship became erratic. I admonished myself, slapped my own face, and sat up straight to finish the article. When I was done, I cut the pages out and put them in an envelope for Mavis, who was due to arrive in the morning with more money from Garrick.

After applying the *Gorgon's Mirror* seal, I stowed the envelope in my inside jacket pocket and eased back into the chair. My injuries let me know they'd not gone anywhere, but eventually I found a comfortable enough position. The fire had burned out, and soon I'd settled into a deep sleep. It seemed that only moments had passed before I was awoken by the sound of an insistent rapping at the front door. I opened my eyes. It was still dark. I checked to make sure I had the article in my pocket. The project of getting out of the chair was full of pain, but I struggled through it.

I stopped to light a lantern we kept in the foyer, and holding it aloft, answered the door. There was no one there. I held the lantern out as far as I could but the street was empty. Looking down, I saw a lumpen thing on the second step of my porch. Before I could bring the light to it, I knew it for a dead cat. I lowered the lantern, though, and that dead cat became my satchel lost at Dutch Hill. I froze with fear and knew somehow that I was being watched.

I quickly brought the lantern up and peered out again into the street. There was someone there, dressed in dark clothes. Despite the darkness of the night, I could have sworn it was Ahab's son, Gabriel. He held himself as if he was about to speak. I left the porch and went into the street toward him. "Gabriel," I said.

He turned away and walked farther down the street toward the river. Fully understanding what a bad idea it was, I followed at a slight distance. A few paces along and I heard someone approaching from behind. I spun around to find Madi. He caught up to me and I told him I thought the figure ahead of us, just barely out of the range of the lantern's glow, was Ahab's son.

"We're inviting an ambush," he said.

"Hence my motto in these situations," I said. "'Be ready to run.'"

The words had no sooner left my lips than the figure we followed, Gabriel of the shadows, stepped off the street and through the broken-down doorway of a dilapidated wooden warehouse, near the dock, which had once stored cotton from Apalachicola, Florida, bound for the northern mills.

"Here's where I turn back," I said.

"Give me the lantern then," said Madi.

I handed it to him but did not leave. I followed into the darkness of the warehouse. The glow of the lantern was a godsend, allowing us to avoid holes in the wooden floor and fallen timbers. There was, of course, no sign of the boy. In those moments we stood still, I called out his name. In response, the pigeons in the rafters flapped their wings. We had passed from the large room at the entranceway into a smaller room that opened into a hallway. I called Gabriel and heard a voice echo as in a dream.

"Do you hear that?" I asked Madi.

He nodded.

From off in the distance but still within the ruined warehouse, a voice wended its mellifluous way to us. It rose and fell in an incantatory rhythm, and although my head succumbed to the beauty, my body sensed the danger. My heart was racing.

"Got to get out of here right away," I said. Madi knew nothing of the manticore, but he did get a good look at my face. That seemed to be enough to convince him that I was in earnest. We turned hastily to retrace our steps to the entrance. As we did, something leaped down from above and landed on the floor in front of us.

I barely got a glimpse of it before what appeared to be a snake with a face that came to a needle point swept through the air, broke the glass of the lantern, and impaled the flame at its core, nipping the wick, and plunging us into total darkness. Through my fear, I realized it had been the scorpion tail of the creature. At any second, I expected its poisonous barb to lodge in my heart.

I scrabbled frantically for the way out and saw it ahead of me. Dawn was coming on, and the rectangle of my escape was dimly lit. All else around me was black. I called out to Madi and realized what a mistake that was, giving away my location in the dark. I turned and saw the creature's light blue eyes aglow mere paces behind me. Up ahead,

I saw Madi's shadowy form slip out through the faint rectangle. I had almost reached it, when I saw another figure step through the entrance. I bounded through the opening, passing Mavis, who had her pistol in her hand.

As I hit the street, the gun went off and then Mavis was close behind me. We followed Madi back to my house. I slowed only to snatch my satchel off the step. Once we were inside, I locked the doors and we tumbled into the study.

12

H arrow, what was that? I saw it with my own eyes but I don't believe it," said Madi.

"At first, I thought it was a wolf," said Mavis. "I saw you two sneaking up the block, following someone. So I decided to follow."

"I'm glad you did," said Madi, who extended his hand toward her.

Mavis introduced herself. Good thing, as I was too busy reaching
for the gin. "Did you see the face of the monster?" I asked each in turn.

"I saw the eyes. The face was human. I think there was blood on its
lips," Madi said, shaking his head as if to deny the image in it.

"I only saw it bounding after you, George. Saw it best in the spark of
the shot," said Mavis.

I was about to offer my guests a drink, now that I'd already drained
one, when Misha stepped into the room, still in the act of putting on her
robe. "It's six in the morning," she said. "What's the ruckus?"

"We're under attack by a mythical creature," I told her.

"What are you talking about?"

"It's part of that business I'm mixed up in with Ahab. We've riled up
an unsavory element and now they know where I live thanks to my
satchel. By the way, it's returned. No need to go to Liberty Market."

Misha left the room and presently Ahab descended from upstairs.
Bleary-eyed, he looked around at us. "What have I missed?" he asked.

Madi and I exchanged a brief glance, and from it I deduced that telling Ahab we'd seen his son might be detrimental to the overall enter-
prise. For as much as Ahab was to whatever degree a devoted father, he
was equally a lunatic of the first water. Finally, Mavis, who sat rolling a
cigarette, said, "There was a beast we ran from."

"A beast?" said the captain.

"The Jolly Host knows where I live now. One of them lured us into an abandoned cotton warehouse near the water. Madi and I ventured in with a lantern. Out of the darkness came poetry."

"The manticore," said Ahab. "It's incredible the speed with which word of your address has spread."

"I think this incident was merely a warning. Mavis came to our aid at the last moment, which was wonderful, but if the creature had wanted to disembowel me and chew my head off, it could have taken me down in the dark in seconds. Its eyes are very strange."

"Blue as the ocean off Koba-Tatema," said Madi.

I was certain Ahab was about to barrage me with questions, so I was glad when Misha returned, although it was getting rather crowded in the study. She held up her right hand, clutching a pistol aimed right at my head. "I found my pepperbox," she said.

"Aim it at the ceiling," I told her.

The five of us sat staring at one another but not saying a word. I suppose once you encounter a manticore there's not much left to say. It rattled my head to try to accommodate the existence of the creature. What was worse is that it was stalking *me*. Frighteningly real yet undeniably impossible. Beneath my fear, I sensed a desire to write about the beast. As horrid as it was, there was something beautiful to it. I couldn't lose the image of those blue eyes glowing in the dark.

"I have some knowledge about Malbaster," said Mavis. "The Host call him the Pale King Toad because his flesh is like a toadstool."

That swept the pall from the room. I sat up and leaned toward her to better hear what she was about to tell. Madi and Ahab did the same. Misha patted the girl's back and said, "This is a hardworking girl," to the three of us men.

"Before you start," I said. "Did Garrick send money?"

"Yes."

"Does it cover the price of what you're about to tell me?"

She nodded.

"Proceed then," I said.

Her eyes were half closed, she took a nip of her roll-up, and her words came wrapped in smoke. "Malbaster has powers of the mind."

"What does that mean?" asked Ahab.

"I don't know, but six different people I'd spoken to who have met him used those words."

"What else?" I asked.

"He's got an assassin, whose debt he bought to have the man released from the Tombs. A thin, white-haired man with sharp elbows and a dull gaze. The fellow had been hollowed out by life and Malbaster breathed magic into him to make him kill."

"Charming," I said. "What about the manticore, anything on that?"

"Mention of it is on the street, but there is more guessing than knowing. I heard a dozen descriptions but none of them fits the glimpse I had at the warehouse."

With her mentions of the Pale King Toad, the hollowed-out assassin, and the manticore one after the other, it occurred to me that all the stories I wrote for the *Gorgon's Mirror* had polluted reality with their hokum and my efforts to deceive were now coming home to roost. There was no other explanation.

Mavis stood, reached into her pocket, and brought out a slip of paper. She took a step in my direction and handed it to me. "Go to this person and she'll tell you about Malbaster and the opium."

Exhausted, I finally fell asleep, sitting right there in my desk chair amid the quiet conversation of the others. When I woke hours later and the room was empty, I checked my jacket pocket for the article I'd meant to give Mavis. In its place was a packet of money from Garrick. There was a sizable amount, which meant that readers were responding positively to the first few stories of Ahab's plight. Every time I considered cutting the captain loose and just confabulating the remainder of his saga from thin air, I realized that without my participation in his quest, the stories wouldn't be half as good.

I found Misha and Madi in the kitchen having coffee and joined them for a cup. I asked after Ahab and Misha told me, "He's gone."

"Gone where?"

"He left about an hour ago while you were sleeping. I'm not exactly sure when; he didn't say a word. I checked upstairs for him, looked in the attic and the basement."

"I went out and looked along the street," said Madi. "He's gone somewhere."

I was momentarily stunned by this news, picturing Ahab at large in the city, swinging that boarding ax and employing his signature bad judgment. I suggested we look for him over near Mulberry Bend Park. I thought he might have gone looking for Usual Peters to wring more information from the old sot. At the same time, the address Mavis had given me was on the corner of Bayard and Elizabeth Streets, not too far from the park. We could kill two birds with one stone.

The day was cold but clear, and it was past noon when Madi and I took off on foot in the direction of the Five Points. We'd decided against a hansom in case the speed of it were to make us miss Ahab passing in the street.

As we walked along, I asked my companion, "What's your assessment of the captain?"

"He's changed from when he was my captain, and I'm not sure it's for the better. I'm telling you, Harrow, I can't get caught up in the tragedy of Ahab. I have a purpose that drives me. Beyond today, I won't be wasting time looking for him. I'll strike out on my own. Every day that passes without me avenging those murders is a mark against me in my own mind."

"You and Ahab are such men of conviction. The right and the good are somewhat more flexible in my estimation."

"You're a white man with money and a job," said Madi.

"I'm going to try to keep it that way," I said.

"That's city wisdom," he said.

"Did you bring much of your history with you when you went aboard ship to become a harpooneer?"

"I was very young and wanted the world. I spent years at sea with rarely as much as a week or two between voyages. My second captain, an American named Belliard, out of Philadelphia aboard the *Widow*, helped me obtain my protection papers to keep me out of the hands of the Fugitive Slave Act thugs and British impressment. He appreciated my aim and power with the harpoon."

"What do you remember of Africa?" I asked.

"I only dimly recall my mother and father. My homeland and Islam. All that was washed out of me by the rolling sea. I've been on a voyage to another world, suffered solid months of stillness at the equator, and been lashed by furious typhoons. At night, I have fleeting glimpses of my father's handiwork, the jewels and metals he shaped like a sprinkling of gold dust in my dreams. That and a story my grandfather told me when I was a child of the fabulous libraries of Timbuktu."

Madi fell into silence. We turned from James Street onto Chatham and headed north. In less than twenty minutes, we were standing in front of the house that bore the address Mavis had provided. It was a beautiful structure and although I'd passed it by many times, I'd never before noticed its opulence. There were tall columns surrounding the domed entrance. The path leading to the door wound around and among barren mimosa trees. The steps to the porch were inlaid with tile in green, blue, and white.

I knocked on the front door and took a step back. It opened promptly and a tall, well-built fellow with a bald head and a diamond earring answered. He was dressed in formal attire. I assumed he was the butler. I smiled, but he didn't. It was obvious from his gaze that he wasn't happy to see Madi standing on that porch.

"If you would please let your employer know that Mavis sent us," I said.

He stared at me like he was trying to knock me over with his thoughts. I simply nodded and continued to smile. Eventually, he said, "Step inside, and I'll summon the lady." We moved toward the door, but the butler said, "Not him," and pointed at Madi.

"He's my esteemed colleague. It's very important that he attend this meeting."

The butler shook his head. I looked over my shoulder at my companion and he looked at me as if to say, *This is one of those situations you're supposed to be helping me with.* When I looked back, a woman had joined the man in the morning coat. She appeared to be of my vintage, no longer a blushing maiden but by no means a shriveled shrew. She wore a dress with a design of blue flowers and a disarming smile below a pair of blue eyes; her dark hair was pulled back into a chignon.

"Yes, gentlemen?" she said.

"Mavis sent us. I'm George Harrow, writer for the *Gorgon's Mirror*, and this is my colleague, Madi."

"I'm Arabella Dromen," she said and inclined her head slightly. I did my best to return a bow. The whole thing was ridiculous, but I didn't care. Arabella Dromen had caught my fancy. "Show them both in, Otis," she said.

She led us through that remarkable house decorated with colorful carpets of Eastern design, beneath glittering chandeliers, past polished mahogany reflecting silver fixtures. As we proceeded down a long hallway hung with paintings, she spoke about how she'd first encountered Mavis at the port on South Street. "There was an indigent fellow who'd gone round the bend, brandishing a knife and threatening the stevedores and passersby. In three lightning motions, that remarkable girl subdued him, disarmed him, and stuck the knife into the left cheek of his posterior as a reminder of why going crazy had been a bad idea."

We came to a set of large doors and Otis, the consummate fart catcher that he was, moved quickly ahead to open them. Inside, the circular walls were lined with books. There were steps to the right and left that led to a second level. In the round at the room's center was a table and four chairs. Beyond that there was an enormous aquarium, the first I'd ever seen in a home. I was startled by the sight of it and its school of pale-violet fish moving with a single purpose.

"Have a seat, gentlemen," said Miss or Mrs. Dromen. I saw no ring on her finger so I assumed the former. She pulled out a chair and sat down as well. Once we were settled, she told Otis, "You may leave and on the way out dim the gas lamps to a more conspiratorial shade." He did as he was told and we sat in the gloaming.

"I'd hired Mavis, not too long ago, to accompany me to the market as my bodyguard. We had a lovely outing. On that journey, I asked her about her other employment, to see if she wanted to work solely for me. She thanked me but begged off, telling me she was partial to an old fellow she worked for who ran a penny press magazine full of the untrue and outré. To change the subject of her employment, she told me that she was hunting for information about a Mr. Malbaster.

"Now, as it so happened, I knew two things about Malbaster and I told them both to her. The first was easy enough for her to remember, but the second is more complicated with dates and personages of the past and goes back nearly forty years. My father, Edwag Dromen, was a sea captain, and he rented his ship, the *Cipher,* and his services at the helm to the late John Jacob Astor in the years around 1816 and thereafter. You know of whom I speak?"

Madi and I both nodded.

"My father, before he passed away, told me that he would sail through the Mediterranean to Anamur, a castle port on the coast of Turkey, and there would take on tons of opium. Usually, he then sailed to China and sold it illegally. It was through this method that Astor's already incredible wealth from the fur trade tripled. He carried on the illicit opium trading to China for a number of years. Eventually, when the risks became too great, Astor dropped it and delivered only to London and turned his attention to real estate. Still, my father told me of a warehouse in Hell's Kitchen that held a king's ransom of opium."

"How have I never heard this?" I said.

She continued, "Astor hid it there with plans of someday introducing it on a large scale to city residents. By my father's estimate there had to have been ten tons of it. Small globes of the tar packed fifty apiece in wooden chests stacked to the ceiling. When the old Midas died in '48, no one had thought about it in years except, of course, my father, who launched an investigation to find it. He never did, but he suspected that the man you are looking for, Mr. Malbaster, did."

"Did your father know him?" asked Madi.

"I don't know how well. But he certainly knew of him and he told me he thought the pale gentleman was using the drug to raise an army. He's in league with powerful nativists in the city. They pay him a fortune to harass and kill."

I'd seen these groups—anti-immigrant, antiblack—at work over the years. I'd stopped and listened to their rhetoric on street corners and had even, under orders, written about them in an uncomplimentary manner. That was Garrick's doing. His whole life he'd been a staunch defender of immigrants' rights. Why? I have no idea.

"We've heard he possesses magic," said Madi.

"I've heard that," she said. "What it means, I don't know."

"And what was the other thing you told Mavis?" I asked.

"Oh, she didn't tell you? I've determined by having glimpsed him there briefly once, and having Otis check for me on subsequent nights, that Malbaster eats dinner every other evening in the French restaurant Amberine at the Crystal Palace. He'll be there tomorrow night."

I was a little stunned by this revelation tossed off so nonchalantly. Malbaster was, if we played our cards right, all ours. We could ambush him somewhere along the route to the restaurant, inside the restaurant, on his way home. The Pale King Toad was within our grasp. I didn't bother considering what the hell we'd do with him once we'd caught him. Between Madi and Ahab, he had a meager chance of escaping with his life. The question for me was whether I wanted to be involved in what would surely be murder.

"And so, you offer this information to us free of charge? Surely there is something you hope to gain from this exchange," I said.

"Very perceptive, Mr. Harrow. I like a man who knows how the world works."

I was glad we were sitting in the dim room as I could feel myself blush, a condition I'd not experienced in years.

"What I want," said Arabella Dromen, "is that when you locate the warehouse with the tons of opium, I want a hundred pounds of it for my own use."

"I remember the drug," said Madi. "The British ship a lot of it to China. I signed on to a few clipper ship larks that voyaged to the Yellow Sea. The old men smoked it in the back rooms of the port at Shanghai. But I've never taken it. What does it do?"

She reached across the table and covered his hand with her own. "It allows you to see the hidden beauty of the world."

I watched Madi swallow hard and felt a twinge of jealousy at his receiving her touch, no matter how delicate it was.

So many things went through my mind, the first being that I'd encountered abusers of the poppy before but she didn't have any of the telltale signs: the sallow complexion, half-mast eyelids, and weary affect. She must have read the expression on my face and said, "I use it in my research only."

I should have asked first about her research, but instead, just like that, I promised her a hundred pounds of opium if we were to discover the trove, and Madi agreed.

13

A half hour after we made our deal with Arabella, we emerged from that dim encounter into the brightness of the afternoon sun. Our eyes were sensitive to the light, as if we'd just come from a grog shop or church, and we squinted for a block and a half before we could see clearly again.

"That last thing she spoke of before the bald one showed us out . . . ," said Madi. "Her work? The writing of a continuous story of a daydream woman, based on Miss Dromen's hallucinations?" He laughed. "Seems lunacy."

I nodded, though still enchanted by her. "What was the name of her book?"

"*One Hundred Nights of Nothing,*" he said. "I remember once being in a village just outside Fort Jesus on Mombasa Island. A Swahili craftsman had carved, in a pale wood, a figure of a man with his head disappearing into his hindquarters."

"I don't understand," I said.

"Outlandish measures are necessary for some to look within."

"Still, she's lovely," I said.

"I will see her again. I can feel it," said Madi.

I was somewhat put out by his revelation, but we had business to attend to in finding Ahab. Although Miss Dromen was quite fine, I wasn't about to challenge my "colleague" to a duel over an opium-smoking spinster we'd just met. She did touch his hand, though, and I stewed about that in silence until we reached the outskirts of Mulberry Bend Park.

Although the day was bright, like other recent days, it was freezing.

The park was nearly empty—a few stragglers heading home to their hovels in the Points, a group of young girls with sticks and beribboned hoops trying to play the Game of Graces in the daunting wind. The trees were now completely barren as opposed to when Ahab and I had traversed the plot just days earlier. Winter had settled over Manhattan and I realized it wouldn't be long before our efforts would be hampered by snow.

We strolled to the middle of the park and spun upon our heels, but there was no sign of the captain or Usual Peters. I told Madi about the underground opium den Ahab and I had discovered by following one of the local besotted ne'er-do-wells.

"We found Ishmael, paralytic on the poppy tar, down there last we'd visited," I said. "Trust me, his head *was* well in his ass."

"I hope never to see him again," said my companion.

We decided against venturing belowground into the dark without our weapons and Ahab along in case of a brawl. Madi suggested we return to my home to wait for him but that we journey by a route that took us past the docks. He wanted to make a daylight investigation of the old cotton warehouse where we'd encountered the manticore. I agreed as my bravery was at its peak in sunlight.

By the time we arrived at the place, the sun had sunk low and the shadows were lengthening. I figured we had an hour till sundown. Inside was damp and freezing cold, and a rime coated the timbers. The floor groaned and the wind whistled through holes in the walls and roof as we made our way by the grainy light.

"Why are we here?" I said.

"I want to see if they left anything behind, or if they might even still be here."

"Let it be said, I hope they're not."

Madi wasn't satisfied with touring only the bottom floor of the place and insisted we ascend to the second floor, which had in certain spots holes large enough to fall through.

Suddenly Madi pointed and said, "Look up here. There's light."

At the far end of the second floor hallway was the glow of a lantern. We carefully made our way to it. What we found were two boys sitting with their backs to the wall.

"What are you doing here?" I asked them.

"We're waiting for you, mister," they said.

I looked to Madi and when he returned my glance I noticed his eyes widening in alarm. Before he made a sound, I spun around to see what he'd seen. Stumbling into the pool of lantern light came a crooked figure in a black suit and a black string tie. He was bloodless, and his hair was so dry and light it looked like sand. It was the eyes, though, that made me want to run; dull gray orbs unbroken by iris or pupil.

The pallor of his skin was disturbing and his chin and brows seemed to come to sharp points. His limbs didn't appear to fit him, as if broken many times and healed fewer. He came at us like an old woman falling down the stairs, and we stood and watched, entranced by the inherent wrongness of his being.

The next I knew, he punched me in the jaw with a fist that felt to be all bone. As I fell backward, I saw Madi take a sharpened elbow to the side of the head. A moment later, we were both on the floor and the creaking ill-built skeleton of a man was leaning down to choke me. I brought my boot up and kicked him under the chin. He made no noise, and the sound of my heel hitting his chest was like someone beating on a drum. A cloud of dust issued from his open mouth and I saw all three of his teeth. He staggered backward, which gave me enough time to get clear.

Madi was rising to his feet and the strange man, who by this time I realized was Malbaster's assassin, turned and teetered haltingly back toward us to grab my companion by the neck. The bony hand was strong, and it squeezed Madi's throat. I stepped forward, without thinking, and planted a hard left in his right eye. The goddamned bones, it was as if I was punching a bag of nails. My knuckles were bleeding. Madi sprang free and swept the fellow's legs out from under him with a well-placed kick. Once that wreck of a man was down, the two of us fled.

Behind us we heard the two boys yelling, "Get them, Bartleby. Get up!"

I noticed as we hustled around the treacherous openings in the floor that the sun had nearly set. Looking back over my shoulder, I saw the incongruous Bartleby shuffling after us. "He's coming," I yelled to Madi. And when I said that, looking back over my shoulder, I saw him stumble into one of the holes in the floor and heard a distant thud from below. "Hold on," I said. "He's fallen through." In the distance, the children were still screaming for Bartleby. "Have at them," one called. And the younger, in a sweet voice, cried, "Break their bones!"

We went back to the opening and looked down the twenty feet to the first floor. The shadows had grown too deep by then and we were unable to see anything.

"That was Malbaster's deadly assassin?" said Madi. "Somewhat less than deadly."

"Thank God," I said.

We took the steps down to the first floor and headed for the door. Passing the spot where the broken body should have been, we discovered an old white rag lying on the floor. Madi stood next to me, staring at the rag.

"What happened to him?" he asked.

Something lurched out of the shadows around us, and an arm swiped down and cut the back of my hand with a razor blade. It was Bartleby shuffling forward with an awkward gait, one shoulder appearing to be dislocated. Still, he grunted as he limped toward me, waving that razor. My best defense was to put my arms up in front of me and yell.

My attacker wasn't paying any attention to Madi, so singular was his desire to cut me. The harpooneer caught up to him and punched him in the side of the head with the power of a hammer blow. I saw Madi shaking the pain out of his hand from having smashed it into the rock-hard head of the assassin. The blow loosened his grip on the straight razor and it clattered to the floor. My instinct was to run, but I reached into the shadows to find the weapon. Bartleby was listing to one side after Madi's punch, but he never fell and was starting toward me once more.

My foot hit the razor and it skittered across the floor to Madi, who retrieved it and brought it in an arcing motion away from himself and across the throat of our attacker. A five-inch gash opened in Bartleby's neck and his head flopped back. A fierce, steady stream of air issued from the opening followed by plumes of fine dust. As Bartleby sank to the floor, Madi threw the razor away and we ran. From above came the calls of the boys peering through the opening in the ceiling. "Get them, Bartleby," they chanted in their sweet high voices.

Around the corner and up James Street, we found Ahab sitting on my front steps, smoking a pipe, looking dejected. Once I'd stopped shaking, I told him the story of our encounter with Bartleby.

"I wish I'd been there," he said. "If ever I needed to thrash someone with the boarding ax, it was today. I followed a contingent of the Jolly Host through the Five Points this afternoon and studied them. Five boys, scurrilous louts, made oblivious to life by opium, without respect or cheer for anything. I had to weigh in when they assaulted a young girl selling hot corn on the street. If I'm to rescue my son, I fear I'll have to keep him in captivity and train him like an animal."

I let Ahab's statement go unanswered and entered my house. I'd had enough for that day and for the next year to follow. I still hadn't come to grips with the fact that we'd just killed a man—albeit a very strange and strangely put together man, but still.

Only a drink would do followed by two more. Madi even joined me. He took a sip, wiped his mouth, and said, "Where was the blood?"

I had no answers.

Eventually, Ahab came inside and joined us. He still looked dejected by the prospect of his son having been transformed into a beast. To cheer him, I told him what we'd learned from Arabella Dromen, and that we knew where Malbaster would be the next evening. Ahab got up and began pacing. He was filled with a nervous excitement at the prospect of encountering the man who'd led his boy astray.

"You must promise me, Madi, that you won't kill him until I inquire as to the whereabouts of Gabriel."

"I'll do my best, Captain, but I want you to remember that I'm not along on this spree to find your boy. I honestly don't give a fig about your boy. I have the deaths of two innocents on my conscience. If you wander away again and waste any more of my time, I'll be gone off on my own."

"Aye," said Ahab and he sat down heavily.

"All right," I began. "Tomorrow, we go to the Palace and enact surveillance before the dinner hour. We have to see where the best opportunities will be to trap Malbaster. All I ask is that you leave me out of any killing. You two have business with him. I'm along only to record the events."

Misha brought us tureens of oyster stew. After we ate, Ahab retired, obviously exhausted by thinking far too much about his son. I've noticed this with my friends who have children, even ones who have not run far afield and afoul of the law. Worry for them ages you, sometimes overnight. I like seeing my niece and nephew when I go to visit Ivy and Tommy for Christmas, but other than that I give the little bandits a wide berth. They'll sap the very life out of you. *Not unlike Ahab,* I thought.

Once Ahab was gone, Madi and I had one more drink to wash the image of Bartleby from our minds. I offered him a cigar and we sat in silence, smoke filling the room. Remembering that I had to write another Ahab piece by the end of business tomorrow, I took a chance and asked Madi if he could tell me something about Ahab that wasn't something the captain might tell me. I was surprised when he answered.

"Ahab, by all accounts of the men who'd previously shipped with him, was a good captain as captains go. Everyone on the ship, unlike on land, was treated equally. Ahab was smart enough to know that out there in the middle of the vast ocean, huddled together in an insignificant craft, we were all one another had. He expected every man to do his job and he was demanding. Even on our fateful voyage, we harpooneers, an Indian from Martha's Vineyard, Queequeg from the South Seas, myself, none of us white, dined before the others on board since no one else could do the job we did when it came to harvesting the behemoths.

"It was no doubt that the loss of his leg caused the madness to overcome Ahab. Once he sought revenge against Moby Dick, revenge against no less than the world, he was driven by a rage that would cease only with the loss of his ship and the deaths of all his crew. He was, from what I'd heard, different back in those days, different than he is even now that his world has been shattered and he is little more than a walking ghost."

"Are you, having survived it, not yourself then a walking ghost?" I asked.

Madi nodded. "I'm shattered not by Moby Dick, but by something equally as large and white and ominous. What's slain me is the treatment of the African in America. You, who've been everywhere in the city must know what I mean."

It wasn't something I wanted to spend a lot of time thinking about, but it was true. I'd seen it all around town, even though the city and the state had abolished slavery in all forms by the late 1820s. The ruling class's tendency toward cruelty was as inexplicable and undeniable as a lush's need for a drink.

"You do know, Mr. Harrow."

"Yes, Madi." It was clear he wouldn't give me a story without my admitting my complicity.

"Do you know that pale thin scar that runs the length of Ahab's body?"

"I wasn't aware it traversed his whole being."

"Yes, I have a story from an old Wampanoag Indian from Gay Head who oversaw the cutting room on the *Pequod*, an older uncle to my fellow harpooneer, Tashtego, about how the captain acquired that scar. In Ishmael's book, he gives nothing but vague notions and misdirection on the subject. This is what really happened and perhaps it's where Ahab's troubles began."

The following is what he told me.

14

The ship Ahab shepherded then was the *Quincy*, a reputable old whaler out of Nantucket. At the end of a proposed three-year voyage, they had made a killing in the Indian Ocean, their hold full of spermaceti oil. They were heading home early, passing through the Timor Sea between the island of that name and Australia. Even the lay of the greenest hand would be a fat pay packet. At the clip they were moving, they stood to reach Nantucket six months early. If Ahab could bring the ship in on that schedule, he would draw a sizable bonus as well.

On a beautiful Thanksgiving morning, the sea calm and the sun beating down, one of the men aloft called attention to a small vessel off the larboard side. The captain was notified, and eventually he appeared on deck with his spyglass. After a brief time spent studying the craft, he gave orders to bring the ship around in order to investigate. He handed the glass to his first mate and said, "Have you ever seen another ship like that?" Something like a cross between a miniature Dutch frigate of old and a Chinese junk. It was painted entirely black and bore black sails.

"It seems abandoned," said the mate.

"Aye. Tell the men to arm up in case it's a pirate's ploy," said Ahab. The seas around Timor were well known for pirates.

The *Quincy* was brought around and right up next to the odd ship with two large ribbed, fanlike sails, an exceedingly lofty stern deck, and a tiller instead of a wheel left unmanned at the mercy of the currents. Once the *Quincy* was close enough so that those on board could look down upon the other ship's deck, Ahab called, "Ahoy, there." He called out many times and then had a loaded pistol brought and fired it into the blue sky.

Eventually, a figure did stagger up onto deck, and all were surprised to see that it was a young woman. She had dark hair and a deep tan from the sun and was wrapped in a dress and shawl as black as the sails. She put her forearm across her brow to block the sun and looked up at the *Quincy* that loomed over her. Ahab called a greeting.

"Help me," she said, speaking perfect English.

"Where's your crew?" asked the captain.

"All dead," the woman replied. "The plague on board."

The captain drew breath and sighed, for in that instant he knew that this was going to test his ability to get back in time to collect his bonus. "Where are you from and where are you headed?" he called.

"We come from there," said the woman and pointed to the north. "We're going there," she said, and pointed to the south.

"What is the name of your destination?" asked Ahab.

"That way," she said and pointed.

"I think the poor woman is confused," the captain whispered to his first mate. "Get the physician."

Doctor Gasnold, the ship's surgeon, was summoned and he asked the woman the symptoms of those who'd died. When she was finished describing the bleeding through the eyes and pores, he turned to Ahab and said, "Don't take this woman on board. I've heard about these exotic exsanguinary diseases. They're virulently contagious. We'll pull into port in Nantucket a ghost ship."

Ahab called for Alfred, the half-deck boy, to bring food for the woman and lower it down to her. In the meantime, he weighed what to do. He wished he'd never approached the damned ship. As it was, he couldn't abandon her. In the end, as night came on, he gave orders for his men to secure a small boat by a long line to the aft of the ship, so that they might tow her at a safe distance behind them. He tried to explain to her what his decision was and why he'd made it, but she didn't seem to understand.

Still, when the time came, she knew enough to abandon the black ship and climb into the lifeboat. As night approached, Ahab, his first mate, and the surgeon watched the poor woman from the quarter-deck of the *Quincy*. The dark finally obscured her from view. The captain went back to his cabin and tried to calculate how much time would be added to the voyage by dint of the small boat's drag.

All that night the woman, just out of sight, wept terribly, and her moans could be heard in the forecastle, spiraling their way into the sailors' sleep like worms into wood. Ahab woke every half hour from the same dream of white enormity. After the second night, the first mate was found drunk on watch. The captain said to the surgeon, "If she had some illness, wouldn't it have presented itself by now? How long must the poor woman put up with this? How long can she?"

The days passed, it poured rain and the naked equatorial sun beat down. Her sufferings changed the tone of the nightly lament to a low echo that seemed to come from everywhere at once and make the air cold. Before long, her skin had tanned to leather. She would only eat meat and there wasn't much given as two of the barrels of salted pork left for the return voyage had gone green. She took whatever water they managed to reach to her in a skin at the end of a long cutting spade. As for the biscuit, she fed it to the fish that followed her boat.

After a night of otherworldly cries, Ahab told the doctor, "I'm going to give her three days more, and if she doesn't exhibit any signs of illness, she's coming aboard ship. This is inhuman."

"You have the safety of the *Quincy* and her crew to keep in mind, Captain," said Gasnold.

"My order stands. She's to come aboard in three days' time."

Ahab worried that the woman might not survive the three days. That afternoon he explained to her that if she could hang on for three more days, he would take her aboard. She could sleep in his bunk and he would move elsewhere, and she could eat at his table at night with him. While he spoke, he looked down upon her from the quarterdeck and he saw a wasted figure with a skeletal affect. Her black hair fell out in hanks at a time, and her stare pierced the boat and spotted at the very reaches of the horizon something enormous bearing down upon the captain.

How she managed the energy to keep up her anguished cries, he couldn't fathom. The ship's carpenter sidled up next to the captain and whispered that she must be either a witch or a demon. Ahab sent the man packing. "Save your nonsense, sir. You're not being paid to give spiritual advice." The man slunk away and no one else dared approach the captain or make a comment about the woman in the boat, although most of them had daydreamed of cutting the rope that towed her.

Before sundown that very day, she began vomiting over the side of her boat. Her body shook. It was hard to believe she was a living woman. The wailing she sent up that night seemed animal in nature. Her every utterance was an ivory needle to the spine. The night was made endless by her weeping. Another night passed, and all on board were hollow-eyed from lack of sleep. On the third afternoon, Alfred, the half-deck boy, who shared a good relationship with Ahab, came to him and told him a secret.

"It ain't right what the sawbones is having me do, sir," said the boy. The captain and the lad stood by themselves in the bow just as the ship was clearing the Solomons and heading into the Pacific proper.

"What are you saying, Alfred?"

"He had me feed the poor woman the meat from the spoiled casks for the last three days."

Ahab was stunned. He told the boy to tell no one. That night in a sea as calm as glass, amid the horrible keening, the captain walked to where the rope was attached to the aft of the ship and taking out his iron knife with the whalebone handle, cut the tether. The instant that line was severed, the livid line of a scar appeared on Ahab, smoking as if he'd been struck by lightning and stripped like a tree. More than one man witnessed this remarkable occurrence. The captain stumbled backward and was caught by two sailors, one of them being the Wampanoag Indian.

More men gathered round the captain and lifted him. They carried him to his cabin and put him in bed. Before leaving, each thanked him for having saved them from the siren. He woke from a fever two nights later to the sound of crying. He staggered forth from his cabin to see what the commotion was and witnessed a crowd gathered round the aft of the ship. He approached his men and said, "What's the meaning of this?"

"Aye, the meaning," said Gasnold. "That's what we'd like to know."

"She's out there," said Alfred. "Just beyond where we can see."

"It's not her," said Ahab. "She's gone. It's the death throes of a sperm whale." No one had the courage to disagree, but all knew exactly what it was. Across the Pacific, round Good Hope and into the Northern Atlantic, they heard her every night. The curse ended only when the *Quincy* came in sight of Nantucket. It was upon the captain's return that he discovered his wife was pregnant.

⟨⟨⟨⟨∾⟩⟩⟩⟩

By three o'clock the following afternoon, we were at the Crystal Palace. It was the first I'd seen it up close, an enormous iron skeleton supporting panels of enameled glass, all a-glimmer on a frosty afternoon. It looked like something from a fairy story. I'd read that it was built in the shape of a Greek cross, four arms radiating from a central dome that rose 123 feet above the two-story structure. Behind it loomed the Latting Observatory, a 315-foot tower from which those who braved the winding stairway could peer through telescopes and see New Jersey, Long Island, and Staten Island.

"The maw of Leviathan, indeed," said Ahab. The boarding ax was in his coat pocket, and the pistol in his belt. I had no idea what he was talking about. He crossed Forty-Second Street, his top hat slightly askew, and we followed. I'd left my satchel at home to prevent it again being snatched and felt rather naked without it.

We entered the vast structure and it was as if we'd stepped from one dream into another. Behind us was Forty-Second Street. Ahead of us was the future. The crowd around us whispered in awe of the exhibitions; displays of minerals from around the world, the Marsh Brothers' line of saws, new tools for use in medicine, the marble sculptures of Christ and his apostles, the beds of botanicals, the fossils of ancient monsters. There were so many wonders to behold, all under one roof.

The machines, large and small, whirring, sighing, blowing, grinding, put Ahab in a state. His eyes shifted rapidly side to side, tracking the actions of the unhuman. When I saw him reach for the boarding ax, I caught up to him.

"Ahoy, Captain," I said.

He turned to look at me but kept walking deliberately forward.

"Slow down. You're calling attention to us. We need to appear pleasant and unremarkable. Madi's less conspicuous than you are."

Ahab slowed. "It's a strange world they're growing in this greenhouse," he said. "The displays of energy from lifeless objects, energy without conscience, it puts me on the razor's edge."

"You mean the machines?"

"The damn machines," he nearly bellowed and I shushed him.

Madi caught up to us and we managed to divert Ahab's unease by taking a position on either side of him. Eventually, the three of us moved along trancelike, and when our sight fell upon the wonders of the world, we looked right through them as if they were merely colored lights. A half hour after entering the Palace, we found the French restaurant, Amberine. It was situated on the main floor about halfway down the eastern arm of the cross, a dark place with muted gas lighting and two mechanical fans. It was fronted by a large plateglass window through which one could see the deep blue shadows where a handful of people dined at candlelit tables.

We wandered around the exposition for hours until the sun went down. As we walked, we planned. The instant it turned dark, we were back at Amberine. Without stating the reason, we insisted on a table with a good vantage point of the rest of the dining area. I feared they might not let Madi join us, but I'd forgotten that in the confines of that establishment, American intolerance didn't reign. The new money from Garrick would come in handy as I realized we might be waiting a while before Malbaster made an appearance.

I bought us a bottle of Royer cognac and a few cigars. The waitress brought three glasses. We sat in the dim light, Madi and Ahab across the table from me. The tension was high while we waited for Malbaster to come through the door. Who knew what might happen then? The prospect of mayhem made me nervous. Madi and the captain joined me for the first round. Ahab even smoked one of the cigars and the unusual sight of him forgoing his pipe calmed me for some reason.

"I suppose we need to appear unremarkable here as well," he said.

"You're catching on," said Madi.

I lifted my glass and said, "To Fergus."

The captain clinked glasses with me, but Madi waved a hand in front of his face and said, "I can't think about that now. We never reported what happened to the poor fellow."

"If you can't manage the reality of your friend's death, you might care to ponder the reality of the manticore," I said.

"I'd prefer neither," he replied. He removed the bird head knife from his belt and placed it on the table.

"So what are your intentions when the so-called Pale King Toad hops through the door?" I whispered.

"I believe I will directly slit his throat. It might be impossible to hunt down the specific member of the Jolly Host who murdered the children, and if I were to, I might be less likely to carry out the necessary punishment seeing as it's probably some young lad with a head full of gullyfluff led astray. As for Malbaster, he's ultimately in charge. Watching him choke on his own blood will go a long way to achieving satisfaction."

"I can't argue, the fellow seems a demon," I said. "But you'll kill him without a trial?"

"Catherine Thompson's students, did they have a trial? And since when have the courts of white men sought justice for the African?"

I nodded. "Chances are, if caught you'll be hanged. It doesn't matter what a snake Malbaster is."

"I'm counting on you to help me get away."

I laughed quietly.

Ahab leaned forward and, trying to seem wholly unremarkable but failing miserably, said in rather too loud a voice, "Please don't kill him till I question him about my son. If you wait, I'll help you."

"You two won't mind if I sit this one out," I said.

"Harrow, if only you were the champion you sometimes appear to be in your writing," said Ahab.

"Do you not know the book and the world are separate voyages?" I asked.

15

W e'd drained three-quarters of the cognac and had discussed everything from the weather to the charms of Arabella Dromen. Madi and I, after having listened to her story, were still not clear as to what part she played in our quest and why we were so willing to hand over a hundred pounds of opium to her—a hundred pounds we didn't have. The amount now seemed ridiculous for one woman's consumption, even over a lifetime.

"Trust me," I said. "There's more to her than meets the eye."

"But what meets the eye is quite sufficient," said the harpooneer.

I was about to agree when a slight commotion erupted at the entrance to the restaurant. I saw Ahab snap his head around and I did the same. There was a raised, friendly voice, speaking French (I think). It appeared the maître d' and the chef were greeting someone who had just arrived for dinner. When those two parted, one in black formal attire and one in the white hat and apron of the kitchen, I caught a glimpse of the lauded guest.

Madi lifted his glass to cover his words and whispered "Pale King Toad" so that only Ahab and I could hear him.

Moving through the dim light of the place like some bloodless cave fish trolling the water for prey, Malbaster, or the man I assumed to be Malbaster, led by the maître d', headed for a large table by the window. My God, his head was huge, like a small, hairless boulder resting upon his otherwise overly generous frame. He wore an exceedingly baggy indigo suit, which contrasted with his milk-white skin, so pale he glowed in the restaurant lighting. We all looked suddenly away as he took in his surroundings. I did catch sight of his small, dark eyes, a flat nose, and the thinnest lips one might have while still claiming to have lips. He wore a boutonniere in his lapel, a white rose.

Ahab toked his cigar to cover his words, saying, "Rather brave to travel alone. I don't see any of the Host about, do you, Harrow?"

Feigning nonchalance, I shook my head.

Madi reached up to the table and wrapped his fingers around the handle of the Fang bieri. "I'll be serving that big turnip in about a minute," he said.

At that, Ahab rose and pushed his chair in beneath our table. He waited for the maître d' to leave Malbaster's side and then he walked directly to the table by the window and sat in the empty chair opposite our quarry. I was surprised Madi didn't promptly leap to the attack, but it seemed he was going to give Ahab a few minutes to interrogate the rogue.

I watched the two figures in the dim light and could easily hear Ahab's voice. The table they were at was only, at most, ten feet from us.

"Mr. Malbaster?" said the captain.

"Who's asking," said the pale one. The voice that came out of that outrage of a head was quieter than I'd imagined it might be. There was a silky smoothness to it, a mellifluous tone.

"Call me Ahab."

"I'm about to eat, and I only dine alone. What is it you want?"

"I believe my son, Gabriel, is in your employ."

"Gabriel? I do know a Gabriel. Whether he's your son or not is another thing. I rather thought that given the bond the young man and I currently share that he is *my* son," said Malbaster and snickered.

"You're mistaken. My son will not be corrupted by a miscreant like yourself."

"Oh, he won't, eh?" Malbaster moved quick as a snake and drew a pistol from his coat pocket, held it out over the table, aimed directly at the captain's face. "I'll give you three seconds to vacate the premises before I blow a hole in your empty head."

This all happened so quickly, and therefore I was useless. Numb with fright now that a gun was in the works, all I could do was stare at the scene that was about to get tragic for the prized focus of my articles. That's when Madi stood up and in one fluid motion threw his odd knife. I saw it twirling head over tail for an instant. It hit Malbaster's wrist directly and the gun went off, shooting a hole in the restaurant's front window. Glass rained to the floor and Ahab leaped to his feet, the boarding ax in hand, and lunged across the table. Madi was there in a flash. Then there was screaming and the sound of shattering crystal and china as the other patrons fled for the exit. From out of the blue, there was an explosion of smoke, and a blur of motion, as I'd witnessed at a magic show of Paschal Randolph. I stood to run but was paralyzed by fear and confusion.

A moment later the smoke cleared, and I saw the head of Ahab's ax buried in the back of the wooden chair where Malbaster had been sitting. Madi was on the floor. I looked up and saw the indigo-clad rogue lumbering away along the corridor beyond the half-smashed-out front window of Amberine.

"How?" cried Ahab.

I ran to Madi and helped him up. "He's outside," I yelled and pointed. We all caught sight of him before he disappeared past the front of the restaurant. Ahab lifted the chair he'd been sitting in and flung it through what remained of the window glass. He leaped through the new opening and landed outside, the tip of his peg leg sliding along the floor. Catching himself at the last, he regained his balance and was off, running as best he could with that distinctive alternating tap.

Madi and I had no choice but to follow him. We most certainly didn't want to be around to pick up the bill for the destruction. We leaped out into the corridor and took off after Ahab and Malbaster. Whereas the captain was slowed by his false limb, the king of the Jolly Host was slowed by his girth. The harpooneer was the most agile of all of us and he sped ahead, gaining on our prey. I was certain Madi wouldn't hesitate to kill him now. Behind me, at the opposite end of the vast hallway, I heard a police whistle and that distinctive tramping of shoe leather. I'd never before been in such a predicament, and never run as fast.

Up ahead I saw Malbaster duck out an exit of the Palace onto Sixth Avenue. Madi was close behind and followed by Ahab. In the few moments it took me to reach the doors, Madi was down on the sidewalk surrounded by a swarm of the Jolly Host. He was being pummeled and kicked. He no longer had his weapon after having tossed it to save Ahab's life. For his part, the captain was engaged in his own struggle with another half dozen of the youngsters. As they hung from his arms and back and kicked at him, he pulled the pistol from his waist and aimed at the Pale King Toad, who was, out of breath, moving toward the edge of the sidewalk where a coach-and-four had just pulled up.

The gun went off and missed its mark. Malbaster scrabbled into the conveyance. Madi and Ahab were dragged to the still-open door of the coach and thrown in. Some of the Host crowded in as well and the others leaped up onto the back of the thing. Two jumped onto the two horses, and the rest hung on and were carried straight out like flags in a strong wind as the overloaded boat of the streets quickly achieved getaway speed and disappeared into the night.

All this happened so quickly, I was stunned. My instinct of self-preservation kicked in, and I ran out into traffic, where I dodged an omnibus and a hansom cab and skirted a crowd on the opposite sidewalk. My greatest worry now was being caught by the police. I ducked down the first alley I could find and kept running. I know I stated earlier that alleys were to be avoided, but this wasn't the Five Points, and I didn't want to spend any time in the Tombs.

I headed south, keeping to the shadows and alleyways. At Twenty-Fifth Street, I cut over to Fifth Avenue and passed the burnt-out shell of the remains of the House of Refuge. Somewhere around there, I caught a hansom cab to take me down to James Street. I was hoping that my hailing the conveyance at that point was far enough away from the Palace that the police wouldn't bother interrogating cab drivers from that area who'd been working that night.

By the time I got to my place, I was exhausted. Misha informed me that a strange white-headed scarecrow of a fellow had been pacing up and down outside the house for an hour or two earlier that evening. She had the pepperbox percussion pistol in her apron pocket. I was ill at ease, worrying what would become of Madi and the captain at the hands of Malbaster. I didn't want to think they were as good as finished, but what were the alternatives? I collapsed into the chair in my office and Misha poured me a large, medicinal dose of gin.

She asked me what had happened, but I was in no mood to relate the misadventure. "Suffice it to say," I told her, "things are looking grim for my compatriots." After another two drinks and a long time staring into the fireplace where Misha had built one of her singular blazes, I fell into a nervous sleep wherein I felt often on the verge of waking but never did. In my dreams, or what I took to be dreams, I heard a purring noise outside the window beyond my desk, a constant, steady pulse of a sound like the whirring life of one of the machines on display in the Crystal Palace. In the morning, I woke just as the manticore pounced and the daylight streaming in disintegrated the creature before it could devour me. Still, I screamed.

For the next two days, I holed up in my house, occasionally peering out the windows to see if Bartleby or the Host were anywhere in sight. The streets were empty of threats. I didn't write and I didn't prepare for attack. Instead I mused upon the entire Ahab saga and the part I'd played in it. From my vantage point, I had a hard time believing the whole thing had actually happened. The most curious thing to me was Malbaster's escape at the restaurant. There definitely seemed to be some aspect of legerdemain involved—the smoke, the warping of the very atmosphere, his instantaneous disappearance from his chair and subsequent appearance, fleeing away down the corridor.

More than one person used the word *magic* to describe Malbaster's attributes, and that now appeared to be accurate. But was he using stage tricks or did he manipulate some supernatural energy? As that thought crossed my mind, I recalled Ahab speaking about "energy without conscience." It wasn't just the Pale King Toad's getaway, though. It seemed outlandish, in retrospect, that Madi and the captain were so easily drawn into that coach, as if they'd been sucked in by a strong invisible ocean current. At the time it happened, my mind hadn't questioned it, but upon solitary recollection it, too, appeared to have been an act of magic.

On the afternoon of my second day in hiding, I attempted to write a description of Malbaster. My work habits die hard, and even though I feared for the fate of my associates, I knew that I'd need an article for Garrick in the next day or so. No matter how many times I tried to describe our nemesis—even just his head, that grand, pale potato of a thing—I lost all confidence in my abilities with the pen. This was a circumstance I hadn't experienced since the very earliest days of my writing career, when I spent too much time thinking and thus too little time making deadlines. Eventually, I turned away from my desk in frustration and sought the companionship of the gin bottle.

Late in the afternoon, Misha found me staggering around the house, three sheets to the wind. She made me eat something and go to bed. I told her I couldn't sleep as Malbaster was sending strange creatures and demons to wake me up. She pushed my head back down on the pillow, and the last thing I saw before succumbing to Morpheus was her pulling her gun from her apron and nodding.

Early the next morning, jittery and somewhat queasy, having heard nothing from Ahab or Madi, I dressed and went out to the *Gorgon's Mirror* to seek advice or solace or something from Garrick. I carried that pointless fid in my writing satchel as a gesture toward self-protection and constantly looked over my shoulder for fear that the manticore or Bartleby was about to pounce at any moment. At one point, as I passed the corner of Fulton Street, I suddenly heard a storm of footsteps behind me. My heart went into my mouth, and I gave an involuntary groan as I leaped to the side. A pack of schoolchildren went rushing by, giggling and yelling.

Garrick wasn't exactly an angel of mercy. He shook his head in disbelief at the story I told him. "So, Ahab is gone," he said. "A shame, the public loved him, his adventures, and your inventions. That doesn't necessarily mean you can't write about him anymore. Make it up out of whole cloth. That's your specialty," he said and puffed on his big cigar. "If Ahab is finished, he won't mind you appropriating his name and bits and pieces of his existence. Same with the other fellow, the black."

"It doesn't feel quite right," I said.

"All these years, Harrow. All these articles, and now you're getting sensitive on me? Buck up, man. Simply think of it as back to your life as usual. Back to your *cushy* life as usual. Few earn as much money as you do for simply making stuff up. Let's stop all the crying in your beer now."

I remained quiet and nodded. Jack Coffee, the magazine's head illustrator, entered Garrick's office then to show him work for the next issue and when my boss turned his attention to the sketches, I slipped out the door and left the *Mirror*. Without Ahab and Madi along, the mystery of Malbaster, and the promise of rescuing Gabriel, I was lost. I didn't want to go home, as sitting around with no desire to write and no assignment to avoid or contemplate seemed worse than exposing myself to the vagaries of the Jolly Host on the street. I strode along the waterfront, watching the stevedores at their work, hearing the hubbub of transactions, greetings and orders, smelling the pungent low tide stink of the East River.

I walked all the way to the Battery, contemplating my options, hoping to pass some scene that might dredge up the lint of story making. As far as trying to regain our trio, I realized I was only one man against

Malbaster's pervasive evil. We were outmatched as a threesome and by myself I had no chance of rescuing my friends. That is, if they were still alive. *Besides,* I thought, *I wouldn't even know where to begin.*

Somewhere around Lent's Basin, on the way back home, I had just the merest glimmer of a notion to do a story about a modern-day witch. Six blocks later, though, it came to me that the idea was but a plate of cold turds. I'd have gladly battled Bartleby for an idea. I looked up and around but saw no threat, just the cold, insular city of the Manhattoes.

16

My fear that they would attack me in my home passed in a few days, and it slowly dawned on me that I was out of the game. The brawling sagas of Ahab and Madi had passed like a thunderstorm and left me stranded in silence. I fell back into a daily routine of walking, hoping the repetitive motion would dissolve the last of that drama's hold on me. A deadline loomed and doubt loomed larger.

Finally, late one rainy afternoon, I sat down and took up my pen. I wrote into the night, knowing Mavis would be on my steps at daybreak. I resolved to get something done before she arrived. After a hundred false starts, I latched on to the next glimmering shard of nonsense and spun it out all the way to the finish line.

I titled the piece "Death of a Ghost" and referred to Ahab by name as I had done in all the other articles about him. In this one, he was kidnapped by the Jolly Host and held captive, forced to smoke opium in an attempt by Malbaster to create another Bartleby, a mindless assassin. I could see it. The article trafficked in the agonies of Ahab, tied to a chair, in a daze, head wreathed in a miasma of yellow smoke from which the drowned crew of the *Pequod* materialized and vanished, taunting their erstwhile captain.

I took "artistic liberties" and allowed my imagination to run wild. We had papers to sell, after all. It was clear as day in my mind's eye: Two women and a man see to it that the captain smokes the tar on a regular schedule so that he is constantly wrapped in its spell. They put a mask over his head and blow clouds of the smoke into his lungs. Within days, he's a wasted shell, his utterances less than blather. There's no longer any need to tie him to the chair. He notices one day the rope is gone. Across the room, sitting on the dresser are his boarding ax and hat. He sees them there but can't get up to get them.

Little does Ahab know, but his son, Gabriel, is one of the people attending to him, feeding him opium and thin gruel in unequal measures. The boy and his father become bitter enemies. One evening, the captain's handlers, lost in their own opium-induced fog, neglect to dose the captain. In a moment of clarity, he rises from the chair, crosses the room, and picks up the boarding ax.

You can see where this was headed, I'm sure. I finished the piece with a horrifying flourish, the boarding ax blade cleaving one of his captor's pates, which I hoped would delight the bloodthirsty readership. I could not bring myself to allow Ahab to kill his own flesh and blood, and so Gabriel was spared. Ultimately, Ahab collapses, empty, too smoked-out to continue. And there, I was with him. It might have been abrupt, but I finished the Walking Ghost off and sent him packing from my life. I put the article in an envelope, sealed it, and stuffed it in my inside jacket pocket for safekeeping until Mavis arrived. My eyelids felt heavy and I found myself nodding forward and catching myself. I'd lean back in the chair and then a moment later I'd wake abruptly, leaning precipitously forward again.

To keep myself awake as I waited for Mavis, I poured a gin. Funny how drink makes you more tired and yet unable to sleep. I quaffed the crystal poison and wondered what had become of Madi. He hadn't shown up in my vision of the final days of Ahab. Did that mean he was dead? Had Malbaster killed him because he was colored? Or had he escaped and was somewhere in the city waiting to strike?

In an effort to save my mental health, I decided to contemplate what my future would be from that point forward. "Best to forget about the whole bleeding affair," I said aloud. I pictured myself on the trail of some new story, following it into the future of Manhattan. The next thing I knew, Misha was at my side shaking my shoulder. "Mr. Harrow," I heard her voice pulling me up from the bottom of the Sea of Sleep where I rested. I roused and stretched my arms.

"Mavis?" I asked, bleary and a tad confused. I slowly moved to get out of my chair.

"No, George. There's a dead man at the front door."

That brought me around in a trice. Of course, the first thing I thought was that Bartleby had come for me.

"I spied him through the front window," said Misha. "Emaciated, pale, and a shock of wild black hair."

"Black hair?" I asked perplexed. "I remembered it as white. No matter, get me the pepperbox. I'm not opening the door without that pistol."

Misha ran to get her weapon. As I stepped into the hallway and headed for the front door, she met me on the return from her errand, slapped the gun into my hand. "After every shot, you spin the barrel to the next bullet with your thumb. Percussion cap. It's ready to fire now."

I nodded and as I stepped to the door, she stood away, lighting the lantern we kept in the foyer. I pulled the door back, keeping the barrel pointed straight ahead at eye level. The sight of what stood before me very nearly made me pull the trigger. A pale, starving fellow with a pained expression, much like a skeleton who'd stubbed his toe, his black hair tangled. Those bony hands went up, and only then did I see that it wasn't Bartleby.

"Harrow, it's me," said a weak and reedy voice.

"Who?" I yelled, thinking it a trick.

"Your old copy editor," he said and Misha thrust the lantern past me and illuminated the visage of Ishmael, who if not yet dead, soon would be. His eyes seemed two huge glass marbles in the shriveled flesh of his face.

"Is Malbaster somewhere nearby with the Jolly Host, waiting to ambush me?" I asked my old colleague.

Ish managed a burst of energy and shook his head vehemently, whispering the word, "No."

"What do you want with me?"

"Please, let me come in. If they know I've come to see you, they'll kill me. I've something important to tell you."

I stepped away from the door and let him enter. While I wasn't worried about him being a threat—wrestling a pipe cleaner would have been more of a challenge—I'd learned not to trust in anything Malbaster or his associates did. I kept the gun trained on him as we made our way back to my office. We'd spent many an evening there when he worked with me at the paper, when we drank and discussed his book, or the goings-on of the city, or what an anomalous creature old Garrick was.

He sat in his usual seat, and I spun my chair around and sat, my back to the desk. Ishmael was frail and shivering with the cold he'd brought inside with him. His head was down, as if he was studying his shoes. I asked Misha to make us coffee and sandwiches.

"You seem to be quite in the thrall of the dope these days, my old friend," I said.

Ish nodded and looked up to make a glassy eye contact with me. "I'm as fond of the dream stick as I used to be of the pen."

"What happened to you?"

"After I wrote the book about Ahab and the whale, I fell apart. I initially thought I deserved some rest, having labored so assiduously to unburden myself of that mythic tragedy I witnessed."

"You were a bright lad suffused with a glow of health and morality. What in hell became of you?"

"Well, in my *convalescence,* and I use that term most appropriately, from *Moby Dick,* I fell in with a bad crowd. I attempted to expunge the image of the white monster from my memory by taking up the bottle. But I found alcohol was ineffective. I was introduced to the pipe by one of Malbaster's young assistants one night after leaving a groggery, and from that moment on the spirit of the poppy flower put its arm around my shoulders and drew me in. It's been a constant companion."

"I thought you wanted to be a famous novelist. What happened to that ambition?"

"You must know, Harrow, how using the imagination can be a sort of drug unto itself."

"I can't say that I'm immune to its joys," I told him.

"I used to marvel at the stories you concocted for your articles. Wonderful stretchings of the truth and occasional outright lies. Well, writing is work, and mining the imagination is work, and I discovered how much easier it was to smoke the tar and sit back. The daydreams flowed without lifting a metaphorical finger. They materialized out of thin air and danced before me. I didn't even have to hold a pen."

"It sounds like a trap," I said.

"Now the yellow smoke brings me visions of nothing but demons and the dead. Now I dread life. In addition, throughout my brief periods of wakefulness, I am witness to the atrocities committed by Malbaster and his horde of young criminals. I'm forced to lick his boots so as not to be cut off from the flower. Murder, torture, theft, rape. Killing children is not beneath them. And they're in league with those who'd exterminate all the Irish and Germans in Manhattan. They fear them as papists. The Catholic Church has become a bugaboo for their ilk. But the colored have it the worst. This unfounded fear of the papacy will pass in a decade, and when it does, the Irish and the Germans will, after all, be white. Not so the blacks."

I thought he was going to continue explaining his descent into the slough of despond, but he simply trailed off and again took to staring at his shoes. Afraid he might doze off before I could get from him the main reason he was in my home, I said, "Which brings us back to, 'What are you doing here?'"

"I come to tell you that I know where Malbaster is keeping Ahab."

"What do you mean, 'keeping him'?"

"He has the old lunatic held captive. I think he means to make him a puppet with sawdust brains."

"Like Bartleby," I whispered, barely able to respond. I felt bewilderment at hearing my own fictionalized scenario of Ahab's last days spoken out loud as truth.

"I've come here tonight, put my life on the line. No, far more courageous—I've put my access to the smoke on the line to tell you where Ahab is being held."

"You've seen him since his kidnapping?"

Ishmael nodded.

"And Madi? What of him?"

"Who's Madi?"

"The African harpooneer. You knew him aboard the *Pequod*."

"Oh, you mean Daggoo."

"His name isn't Daggoo. That's what you called him in your book."

"I never knew his true name. I thought 'Daggoo' a splendid character name."

"Forget it," I said. "Where is he?"

"I don't know. Malbaster kills the colored with impunity. He fears being infected by them."

"Infected with what?"

"I don't remember," said Ishmael.

"Back to Ahab then. Where is he?"

He struggled out of his chair and plunged a hand into the pocket of his greasy trousers. There were holes in the knees and the cuffs were frayed. He'd at one time been a man of scrupulous hygiene. From his pocket, he pulled a piece of paper.

"Here," he said. "The address is written here. If you are going to help him, you'd better act quickly. I've been told his mental state is tenuous."

I took the scrap of paper from him and he sat back down. Misha arrived with coffee and sandwiches. He thanked her and took a sip. But as soon as she left, he looked at the sandwich and gagged. He hunched his shoulders, his hands began to tremble, and I could hear his teeth chatter.

"You don't mind, Harrow, do you?" he said and took a long pipe—bamboo stem fitted with a clay bowl—from his stained and tattered coat. "This still has a pinch of the tar in it." He pulled a wooden match from his shirt pocket, struck it on the bottom of his chair seat, and lit the pipe. The aroma that emanated was not the floral scent of the underground I'd smelled when I'd last encountered him, but a sharp stink of vinegar.

17

꧁ꑣꕥꕥꑣꕥꑣꕥꑣꕥꑣꕥꑣꕥꑣꕥꑣꕥꑣꕥꑣꕥꑣꕥꕥꑣ꧂

The transformation in my old colleague was rapid. His entire body, which appeared to be composed of a bent skeleton wrapped loosely in white parchment, seemed to deflate. His shoulders came down, his head dropped forward. He took another long draw on the pipe and raised himself just high enough to look up into my eyes. What I beheld were two gazing balls, as glassy and opaque as any you'd find in a wealthy man's garden.

"I'm turning Ahab and Daggoo over to you, Harrow," said Ishmael.

"What are you talking about?"

"They're yours. You'll do better by them than I will. You're a better man than I, George."

"Ish, you're talking utter nonsense."

"No, they're yours. I spent too long with them. Since they survived, they should have a chance at a different future."

The sight of him made me nervous. I lit a cigar to combat the sinister stink of the tar. "Ishmael," I said, "are you saying Ahab and Madi are *characters* you're giving to me?"

He nodded.

"That's lunatic. You're lost in some other place now, aren't you?"

Again, he nodded, then closed his eyes and leaned back in the chair. He set the pipe down on the side table. I found his situation wretched—a reminder of how quick the trip to Purgatory—and wanted to get him out of my house. I wished Misha were awake as I could summon more coffee . . . I poured myself a gin instead.

I began to fear that I was about to make a rash decision. I fought it, but it was strong. Reaching out to the table, I picked up the scrap of paper Ishmael had given me, supposedly the address where Ahab was being held captive. Before I could unfold it, though, I heard a knocking at the front door.

Turning around quickly, I saw the first light of dawn outside the window. I knew it must be Mavis. I put the paper in my vest pocket and took the article in its envelope out of my jacket pocket. Sure enough, when I got to the front door, Garrick's Mercury was standing before it. I let her in and we went back to the kitchen to talk. She sat down at the table, and I handed her the envelope.

"For Garrick," I said. "I thought it was going to be my last piece about Ahab, but it seems we're back in the hunt."

"Word is your friends were abducted outside the Crystal Palace."

I nodded. "I think I know where Ahab is being held. If I decide to go for him, do you want to join me?"

"Me and you against the Jolly Host insane with the midnight oil? How much?"

"Name your price," I said. "We get Ahab and we get away."

She looked around for a moment as if the answer to my question were floating in the air. "Forty dollars," she said.

"Fine." I shook her hand.

"Ten up front."

I gave her ten.

"What about Madi?" asked Mavis.

"He seems to have disappeared. My friend thinks he might have been murdered straightaway by Malbaster."

"Very possible," she said. "But Madi is resourceful."

"For his sake, I hope so."

"When?" she asked.

"I have to consider the situation," I said. "I just tonight got a tip on Ahab's whereabouts. It'll no doubt be within the next day or two."

She tapped the envelope on the table and stood to leave.

"Wait," I said. "I've got the address right here. You might know it."

I dug the scrap from my pocket, unfolded it, and brought it up to read. "Indian Caves."

"Where's that?" she said, squinting.

I shook my head. "I should have known better. It was given to me by Ishmael. You remember the *Mirror's* old copy editor?"

"Of course, I remember him," she said.

"It seems, he, himself, is on the smoke." I left the kitchen intending to go rouse Ishmael and attempt to learn more about the Indian Caves. But the front door was ajar and my office was empty. It appeared that Ishmael had fled and left me with nothing more than a location straight out of a bad pirate novel.

I turned to face Mavis who had followed me from the kitchen. "Meet me back here just after dark in two nights, ready to go," I said. "I'll do my best in the next two days to find out where the captain is."

By the time Mavis left, the sun was well up. I was exhausted from lack of sleep but knew there could be no rest until I discovered the location of Ahab's prison. In a matter of eight hours I went from resigning the captain to his ill fate, writing him out of my life, to now trying to save him. It struck me then that this foray into madness would be my ruin. The unremitting fact was that I was going to have to write an article now in which Ahab rises from the dead like Lazarus. It was a corner I'd painted myself into out of my desire to be rid of him. The only way out of the dilemma was if I were to be killed by the Jolly Host. There wasn't much solace in that direction.

I cleaned up, shaved, and put on new clothes. Taking my satchel, which held both the fid and Misha's pepperbox, I struck out on my self-appointed mission. I told myself I was out to rescue a friend, Ahab. But deep down, I knew that what I desired more than anything else was to regain my place in the story. Earlier I described the captain as "a character rent free from his pages," and now that could easily have applied to me.

There was no precipitation yet, but I could smell snow in the air. The day was gray and ice had formed overnight in the puddles at the sides of the street. I should have been, without sleep, drooping along like Ishmael. Instead I ran on breakfast gin. As I dove into the new day, I knew somewhere along the line there'd be a reckoning and I'd no doubt pass out from fatigue. The question of where and when made each successive hour more fraught with trepidation. I had great doubts about my plan, but as I've done for years in my journalistic pursuits, I pushed on, ignoring the obvious inanity of their origins.

All I had to go on were the two words Ishmael had scrawled on that scrap of paper: *Indian Caves*. Did they refer, perhaps, to a drinking establishment? A tourist destination? A historic site? I decided to follow my first instinct. "The Indian Cave" wasn't such a bad name for an out-of-the-way groggery. I knew most such places on Manhattan but had never heard of one by that name. There was a way to find out, though. I went directly to the offices of the *Gorgon's Mirror*. In the farthest back room, beyond the one where Ahab had slept on the fainting couch, there existed an unusual resource.

Luckily, when I arrived, Garrick was out, and the place was nearly empty save for the illustrator, Jack Coffee, bent over his elevated drawing board.

"Hello, Jack," I said.

He looked up and shook his head. "I'm drawing poor Ahab withered by the effects of the yellow smoke. Sorry to see he's through after this one."

I didn't stop to view the results but kept walking straight to the back. "You might see him again," I called over my shoulder.

"Harrow, you're shameless," I heard him say as I passed into the room that held the presses. The printers were there, setting type for the upcoming run. Beyond that room was the one with the fainting couch, and I saluted that rescue craft as I headed toward yet another room. I opened a final door and entered into a large, dimly lit space. Wooden apothecary cabinets, with their hundreds of drawers, lined the walls from floor to ceiling.

"Mrs. Pease?" I called into the gloom.

I scanned the room but could see only so far into the shadows. Presently I heard the sound of soft footsteps, and I turned in time to see an old slender woman shuffle out of the dark, carrying a lit candle in a shallow holder. She glowed as she came toward me, wearing a purple day dress with a starched white collar. Her snowy hair was cut short as a boy's and a pince-nez dangled from a chain around her neck. "What brings you, Harrow?"

"A question concerning groggeries. I'm seeking expert advice."

"I should think *you'd* be an expert."

Looking around, I asked, "Why doesn't Garrick get some light for you in here? How do you see anything?"

"I've gotten used to it," she said.

I squinted and looked closer at her face. The color of her irises had blanched for want of light. "You need to get some fresh air, Mrs. Pease."

"I arrive in the morning and leave at night. It won't be long now. Garrick said that when I go, he'll install another cabinet in here for me, and I'll become part of the archive."

I laughed. "This seems a good prospect to you?"

"Of course," she said. "Now, what do you want?"

"Ever heard of a groggery or perhaps something less legitimate than that called the 'Indian Caves'?"

She was still for a moment and then shook her head. "There's 'The Indian's Wife' over on Albany Street and 'The Green Indian' some blocks north of that on Vesey. There was once a place called 'The King's Indian,' on the southern end of the old collect pond, but that was back in the day. Story goes it was visited one night by an infestation of blue moths so thick that in order to clear them out, the owner set fire to his own establishment and it burned to the ground."

"No 'Indian Caves'?" I asked, getting a little impatient with the history lesson and trying not to show it.

"Let me check the system," she said.

She turned and walked away, taking the candle with her, and the darkness came up around me. I followed her across the room to a rolling ladder, which she climbed most nimbly, all the while holding her candle. She pulled something from one of the shelves before descending.

The archive was Garrick's dream come to life—shelves and drawers and cabinets containing various and sundry articles and clippings from myriad local newspapers and magazines—all catalogued, filed, and cross-referenced according to a system devised by Mrs. Pease. How the materials were chosen—and the criteria by which they were arranged—was a mystery. I briefly wondered what would happen if Mrs. Pease was no more, but I pushed the thought from my mind.

After descending from above, she handed me the candle and ordered me to follow close behind her. She led me toward the back of the room. Three times she stopped and dug through a few file drawers before moving on. I started to wonder if she knew what she was looking for or how to find it.

"Why all the stops?" I asked.

"Everything is cross-referenced so you can eventually get to anywhere from anywhere within the system."

I tried to picture what she was talking about but drew a blank. "I'm not getting any younger, Mrs. P."

"I just passed a note concerning the listing of your articles in the archive," she said as we pushed on through the dark from one wall of filing cabinets to the other.

"How are my pieces listed?"

"Under 'Feverish Wanking.'" She laughed.

"Less feverish, the older I get."

"Ahh. This is what I was looking for," Mrs. Pease said with a note of satisfaction. She pulled out a waist-high drawer and fished around inside with both hands. An exceedingly large book was her catch. "Back to the desk," she said. We turned around and I served as candleholder all the way back to her office area. Once there, she set the book down and opened it. She lit the gas lamp sitting on her desk, and we both leaned in to peruse the giant pages of colorful maps.

"These are Mitchell maps of Manhattan," she said.

She turned a few pages until she settled on a page that contained an image of the northern half of the island. "You see, here?" she said and pointed to a spot at the extreme northwest corner, bordered by the Hudson River.

"I've never been there," I said.

"Me, neither," said Mrs. Pease. She tapped the page at that spot with her forefinger as she spoke. "This is where the Dutch supposedly bought Manhattan from the Carnasee tribe for sixty guilders."

"I've heard the story."

"No doubt it's nonsense. There's an enormous tulip tree right here," she said, pointing with her pinky to be more exact. It's over 250 feet tall. If you can find that and walk due west toward the Hudson through the surrounding woods, you'll come across a considerable outcropping of schist rock. In those natural walls there are caves once inhabited by Indians on fishing expeditions to the area. Since the time of the Dutch they've been known as the *Indian Caves*."

My first reaction was disappointment, realizing how far I'd have to travel to find Ahab, all based on Ishmael's suspect word. I closed my eyes and tried to picture where the rocky shore met the Hudson. I couldn't see it. When I opened my eyes, Mrs. Pease was gone. I heard the sound of a file drawer sliding open somewhere in the distance and knew she had retreated deep into the system. I called, "Try to get some sun."

Her voice came back: "It's going to snow soon."

I let myself out.

18

On the street, the temperature had dropped. Walking aimlessly along, I tried to picture Mavis and I launching an assault on Malbaster and the Host at some cave in the woods in the northern wilds of Manhattan. Our odds of success struck me as less than promising. I was going to need at least a few more conscripts to the cause but couldn't think of anyone. I mulled the idea of asking Garrick to hire some thugs for me, but when I'd spoken to him about the end of the Ahab run, he hadn't seemed unduly upset that I was moving on from that theme. The chances that he would make the hinges squeal on his money chest and hand over cash for mercenaries was slim.

I thought of Misha, but she was getting along in years and had two bad knees. The only other possibility was my brother-in-law, Tommy, who might be willing to muster some police support. I headed south along the docks of the seaport where he usually could be found, either rousting vagrants or drinking free ale in one of the oyster joints. I finally caught up with him at a little place called the Rooster's Tooth across from the Coffee House slip.

He was sitting with the owner of the place, drinking a tankard, as usual. When I appeared before him, he sent the owner away and said to me, "George, you look like you've got something to say that I'm not going to like."

I sat down opposite him. I wasn't really sure how to begin. After all, he'd already warned me to steer clear of Malbaster and the Host.

"Well?" he said.

"Do you remember that fellow who was with me a week or so ago?"

"The one who had resolved to kill all the criminals in New York in order to save his boy?"

"Yes, that one. Ahab."

"What happened, George?" he asked wearily.

"He was snatched by Malbaster, and I have it from a reliable source the poor fellow is having his consciousness eradicated by the yellow smoke."

"Why are you telling me this?"

"I intend to rescue him."

Tommy took a swig of his ale and stared at me for a few beats. "What did I tell you?" he said.

"I couldn't stop Ahab from searching for his son. The man's obsessed."

"George Harrow, you can't bullshit a bullshitter. You couldn't stop yourself from writing articles about him for the *Mirror*. Did you forget that I'm your biggest fan? Even your own sister doesn't read your work as reliably as I do. You just ignored me. The way you saw it, you were in charge and nothing could go wrong."

"Tommy, I swear . . ."

"I warned you."

"It's a man's *life*. Don't the police want to catch Malbaster?"

"Where is he holed up?"

"Some place called the Indian Caves."

Tommy laughed. "Is this real or another one of your cockeyed stories?"

"It's true."

"You wouldn't know anything about a disturbance at a certain French restaurant in the Crystal Palace, would you?" he asked.

"Huh?"

"Word is Malbaster was on the scene. There was gunplay, a window was broken, and a colored fellow was tossing knives around."

"Sounds exciting," I said.

"I can't help you, George. I'll buy you a gin or two, but I can't muster forces for an assault on dreamland."

I gave up on Tommy. We had a few drinks and talked about Ivy and the kids and Mayor Westervelt's attempts to rehabilitate the police force. We parted amicably, and as we started off in opposite directions—I toward home and Tommy down toward the Battery—the last thing I heard him say was, "The fucking Indian Caves," followed by laughter.

I decided to go home and catch a few hours of sleep. Along the way an errant thought slipped into my mind: Arabella Dromen. Initially, I'd not considered her as an ally in the Indian Caves adventure, but only as a charming beauty my mind no longer had the wherewithal to resist. I watched her image float by behind my eyes, saw her smile, and noticed her hair was now undone and hanging loose. It flowed down over her shoulders and framed her alluring face.

I stopped in my tracks when I realized I might be able to convince her to come to the Indian Caves with Mavis and me to rescue Ahab. *I'll promise her a shot at Malbaster,* I told myself. With that thought in mind, I passed right by James Street and headed north. The image of Arabella Dromen revived me. In no time, I was standing on the sidewalk in front of her house.

I tapped the knocker on the front door and Otis answered. I thought he was going to chase me away, but instead he ushered me inside and led me along a dim hallway to a closed door. He stopped and gave two knuckle raps.

"Yes?" Her voice sounded through the wood.

"Harrow here to see you."

"Send him in," she called.

The butler opened the door and I passed into a room that was painted blue. Gas lamps cast wavering shadows across the walls. Arabella was sitting at a table, pen in hand, furiously writing. She wore a white muslin gown. I immediately noticed the smoldering pipe resting on a brass plate, smelled the opium swirling in the air. She motioned me toward a chair with her free hand, but her pen hand never stopped moving. The words rolled out upon the paper.

After filling two more pages, she laid the pen down and looked up. "Mr. Harrow," she said and smiled.

"Miss Dromen."

"Did you have something you wanted to tell me?" she asked.

It dawned upon me that I was staring at her. "Yes. I've come to inquire if you'd like to help me save my friend, Ahab, from a fate worse than death."

I told her about Malbaster and what I believed he was doing to the captain. I thought perhaps I was making progress when at one point she said, "Poor man." Then she lifted the pipe from the brass plate and pulled a small lamp with an open flame, no globe to contain it, across the desk to her. She held the metal bowl of the pipe over the fire and when the drug was smoking hot passed it to me. I took it, put it to my lips, and drew in that which I was just railing against in my description of Malbaster's undoing of Ahab.

I handed her back the pipe after three hearty puffs—I wanted her to think I was trying. Once in her possession she began the process again by filling and lighting it. "Is this what you want me to do?" she said. "Come with you tomorrow night to the Indian Caves? Attack Malbaster's operation and rescue Mr. Ahab? And if Malbaster is present, I get to kill him?" She took a voluminous draw on the dream stick.

Her straightforward summation of the affair struck me as funny, and I laughed. She tried to retain an expression of seriousness, but soon streamers of yellow smoke leaked out the sides of her mouth, and then burst forth in a torrent and swamped the room. All of a sudden I found my mouth dry and my eyelids heavy. I felt calm and giddy and dreamy all at once. Looking around, I noticed that the flickering of the gas lamps made the blue walls appear to move like undulating waves.

"What are you writing?" I asked.

"A story," she said. "A novel that I create extemporaneously. My hand moves faster than my mind. It's a tale told by the universe. I'm merely the conduit."

"Automatic writing?" I asked.

"Something like that. Dispatches from a transcendental state."

"For this you need the smoke?"

"It helps me connect with the everything."

"This is the work you spoke of last time I was here? *One Hundred Nights of Nothing?*"

She nodded. "I need to finish the manuscript or my publisher will be quite cross. I've tried to explain that one cannot just *summon* creativity at will, but . . ." And here she trailed off as her gaze shifted back to the papers on her desk.

"I'm in the booksellers all the time, looking for ideas. Why is it I've never seen your name on a book?" I asked.

"I use a man's name. Mr. Perseus Smith. Look for it. I'm in all the shops in town."

"Why a man's name?"

"Because I want to be paid."

"Can you tell me what it's about?"

"What else? The most important subject in the world. The life of a woman."

"Which woman?"

"Her name is Seraphita. She set out with her husband and child in a boat along with others, fleeing persecution. They sailed the great ocean, heading from north to south. After visiting a jungle country near the equator, a plague broke out aboard the ship and everyone on the vessel died but her. The boat was hailed by a whaling ship, but when the captain discovered that her ship had been infested with the plague, he would not take her aboard. Instead he had his men tie a long rope to a lifeboat and tow her, afraid for the health and safety of his crew.

"Seraphita wept at night for the loss of her husband and child, and the captain begged her to silence her grief as it was making his crew uneasy. But she could not contain her sorrow. In time, the ship's surgeon fed her bad meat and foul water in an attempt to quietly finish her off. Before that could happen, though, the captain cut the tow line and left her to the mercy of the currents. The poor creature was nearly dead from the poisonous food and dying of thirst. As luck would have it, the boat washed up on the shore of a strange island, uninhabited by men but full of wondrous and beautiful creatures. She lived out her life, and over time, transformed into a manticore."

Hearing again the story Madi had recently told me about a younger Ahab made me dizzy with shock.

"Do you know what a manticore is?" she asked.

I couldn't answer at first.

"It's a creature of many creatures," she said. "The face of Seraphita, the body of a predator cat, and the deadly tail of a scorpion."

"What if I told you I'd been chased by one?" I said.

"In your dreams?"

"In an old warehouse. The book, are you going to publish it?"

"It's my ambition," she said.

I wanted to respond to her but became instantly weary beyond reason. I no longer had energy to speak. My breaths came slow and rhythmically, my thoughts flowed like a stream, a passing of images becoming other images. Only my eyes remained open, and I was dreaming while still awake. Every few seconds Arabella came back into view and I caught a glimpse of her writing away like mad.

I was gone somewhere adrift in a tempest of thoughts and visions set to the sound of wind chimes tinkling, though there was no draft in the room nor any chimes as far as I could ascertain. The next thing I knew I was in Garrick's office, but sitting in his seat was Ishmael. "Look, Harrow," he said with the same kind of basso profundo voice as Garrick, "there is in fact a secret magical connection between the book and the voyage. You need to take control of the narrative." With that he puffed on a huge cigar and the smoke instantly filled the office. I choked, trying to catch my breath. There was suddenly a cup of water at my lips and the cool relief revived me somewhat. The smoke of Garrick's office cleared and I was back in the blue room, Arabella standing next to me, administering sips of water.

When I'd stopped coughing and gasping, she went back to her chair and left the water in front of me. "You've been away for over an hour, Harrow. Did you have a pleasant journey?"

I shook my head to clear it. "More than an hour?" I said. "It seemed mere minutes."

"Time, a maniac scattering dust," she said.

"That story you told me about the woman, Seraphita, is nearly the same story Madi told me about Ahab. Only in his version, Ahab was the captain in question."

"Every so often there are episodes where a confluence of fictions come together to shape reality," she said. "It's a time when, if understood in all its ramifications, the pen actually is mightier than the sword. From the moment I met you and Madi, I could feel that our stories had been mixing from long before that. Notice, my manticore has been appropriated by Malbaster. He must also be a fictioneer. What's the story he's telling?"

"Paranoia, fear." I said.

"I am a devotee of the works of Emerson and believe he's professing that the mind is a reality engine—it creates reality or at least in some part it helps to create reality. Malbaster draws his power from the fear he instills. He may not tell his story with ink and a pen, but in blood, and his book is terror. What's more, he's a consummate liar. In telling *you* the early story of Ahab, Madi somehow told me the early story of Ahab, and the woman in the boat infiltrated my vision. We're sharing in each other's plots."

I nodded, still in a daze. At first, I had no idea what she was talking about, but slowly it dawned on me that even I was in the insane position of having to agree with her. It was the only thing that even came close to explaining the corollaries between certain stories. How else to explain the predictive nature of my article that recounted, almost to a T, Ahab's fate. In reaction, I felt profound wonder and not a little fear.

"This phenomenon, the confluence of fictions, does it come and go, like the weather?" I asked.

"More like a fever," she said, and she returned to her work.

19

The day perished with a whimper into night and Mavis emerged from an alley a few buildings away from my house. At the same instant, Miss Dromen's private coach, piloted by Otis, drew to a halt out front. I was still slightly dazed from my experience with the dream stick, but at least now sober enough to reckon that Arabella's theory of the confluence of fictions was insane. I slipped into the cab and was unnerved to find Arabella dressed in men's trousers, a dark green cape, and a derby, and holding a short-barreled shotgun. I inquired if it was loaded and she laughed.

"It was my father's. He kept it aboard ship—an English coach gun."

Mavis, in black coat, black trousers, black hat, and a charcoal beard and mustache, entered the cab a moment after me. She sat next to Arabella. And then we were off. "The Indian Caves," I said aloud and shook my head in disbelief. The thought of it made me shudder.

"It'll be a few hours," said Arabella.

"You know how to get there?" I asked.

"Otis does. After you left yesterday, I sent him out to inquire about directions."

"And he found someone to tell him?"

"Otis is effective," she said. "He stopped in at Fraunce's Tavern and asked the bartender if he knew anyone with a good knowledge of Manhattan geography. A woman—older, alone, nursing a glass of claret—piped up and asked him what he was looking for. He told her, and she said 'Quite a coincidence.' But when she revealed the location she spoke with such certainty, he couldn't doubt her."

"He sounds useful," I said, and for some reason recalled Mrs. Pease's statement concerning the system, "You can get from anywhere to any-where."

"He'll be an asset in a fight. You'll see," she said.

I was sorry she'd mentioned the word *fight*. It was a part of the adventure we were embarking on that I least wanted to reckon. Turning away from her, I watched the night fly past. Otis was letting the horses go. The longer I watched, the more it seemed the coach was flying above the road. The wonder of that made me blink, and it became clear that the sensation of flight was merely an echo of the opium.

A moment later, the coach was back on the road, and I felt every bump. The springs squealed and I heard Otis, above, mumbling to himself. Arabella had said he was "effective." I wondered what that meant. I had noticed that her man was attired in full formal butler regalia for our outing, which seemed strange.

An hour on, Mavis nudged me awake with the toe of her boot. I came to and looked around the darkened cab. Arabella was slumped against the wall sleeping, her arms wrapped around the coach gun. Mavis moved forward in her seat and whispered to me, "Garrick said to tell you, 'No more with Ahab. That last piece was a fart in church.'"

"That doesn't sound good," I said.

"He said, and this is word for word, 'No one wants to read about the purgatorial sufferings of Captain Dimwit. Harrow's getting sentimental over this whole project. Tell him he'd better shake himself out of it."

"Did you warn him there might be one more Ahab piece?" I asked.

"I hinted at it."

"What was his reaction?"

"He said, 'Tell Harrow I don't give a donkey shit about Ahab anymore and neither does anyone else. Everyone's sick of it.'"

"A ringing endorsement," I said.

"I think he'd take one more if you insist," said Mavis. I was glad to hear that, knowing how astute she was when it came to cyphering Garrick's nature.

"Let's hope there's one more," I said.

After that I fell asleep for quite a while and woke suddenly when the coach came to a halt. The door opened and a frigid breeze blew through the cab. Otis was standing just outside.

"Let's go, Harrow," he said and helped me out of the conveyance. I had with me my satchel, minus the writing gear but plus Misha's pistol and the blasted fid. It was pitch-black wherever it was we'd landed. I could hear bare branches clicking together overhead. We were off the road, in the woods. I looked up and found that my eyes had adjusted to the dark. I saw the stars in the distance and heard Arabella and Mavis disembark. Otis strapped feed bags on the horses to keep them quiet while we were off raiding the caves.

"This way," he said and he led us through a thicket of trees to a clearing in which stood the giant tulip tree Mrs. Pease had mentioned. He lit a lantern there and held it up for us to see the towering wonder. Its trunk was enormous and it reached far higher than I could fathom. I watched Otis consult a compass and in the next second he led us away due west. I asked him if the lantern was a good idea. I was afraid we might be spotted.

"There's thick woods we have to traverse to get to the caves," he said. "I was told that without a lantern, we'd instantly be lost and in grave danger of falling from the outcroppings."

When he led us down a game trail that wound like a snake amid a labyrinth of low bushes and pine forest, I instantly saw the necessity for the light. It didn't make me stop worrying about being seen. For us to be successful in rescuing Ahab, we needed the element of surprise. I worried that we didn't represent anyone's idea of a formidable militia. My only defense was to ignore reality, which was something I had some practice in. Mavis, Arabella, and I followed in a cluster around Otis, all fitting snugly in the orange globe of lantern light.

We came into a clearing and as we stepped free of the tree line, it was obvious the terrain had changed. A few feet in front of us the ground went from dirt to hard rock. Otis put his hand up as a signal to us to be still. I froze and looked at him, trying to read from his expression what had spooked him. And then, like that, there was the tail of an arrow jutting out of his forehead. He gasped once and fell straight back at my feet. The lantern hit the ground, and from the corner of my eye, I could see a shadow approaching.

I turned and barely caught a glimpse of Mavis slipping into the woods. Arabella leveled her gun and put her finger on the trigger. She glanced at me and I could read in her expression that she knew it would be foolish to fire the weapon and call a swarm of the Host down upon us. She dropped the gun and we ran blindly into the dark, pursued by the assassin who'd murdered Otis.

Arabella, her cape flying behind her, ran swiftly, and I could hardly keep up with her. We were heading across an open expanse for the cover of the forest beyond. I was no more than fifteen feet behind her, when, in the middle of that enormous meadow, I tripped on a small outcropping of rock and went down hard, face-first. The fall knocked the wind out of me and jostled my brain. It took me too long to get up. I heard the footsteps approaching, and Arabella called back to me, "Harrow, he's coming."

I sat up and fumbled in my satchel to find my gun. My grasp closed twice on the fid before I finally got ahold of the pepperbox. At that point, I could hear the heavy breathing of the archer. He was steps behind me. I pulled the gun out of the bag and aimed into the dark. I squeezed the trigger, braced for an explosion, and nothing happened, nothing but a click. By then, I could smell his fetid breath, and the hair on my arms and neck stood up straight.

He loomed above me, a bow slung over his shoulder and his right hand holding a meat cleaver. Shaking, I spun the barrel of the pepper-box and fired. Again nothing. He raised the knife above his head, and I cowered on the ground, convinced I'd filed my last column. When no blow came, I dared to look up. In a pool of lantern light, I saw the archer facedown on the ground, the handle of a thin knife protruding from the base of his skull. Mavis set the lantern on the ground and reached out to help me up. Arabella joined us.

"What happened to your pistol?" said Mavis.

"Shit," I said and threw the piece into the woods.

"I wanted to run away," said Arabella, "but I was transfixed by what was about to happen."

"You mean me being hacked to death?"

"That is ghoulish, isn't it? But yes, that," she said.

Mavis put her shoe on the archer's head to steady it and pulled her knife from his neck. While she wiped it clean on a handkerchief, I asked her which way she thought we should go.

She put the knife and the handkerchief away and said, "Follow me." She picked up the lantern, and Arabella and I fell in behind her. As we moved in silence through the forest, I wondered if Mavis understood that when I asked her which way to go, I meant the most direct path back to the coach. Instead, she led us along a trail that worked its way down a steep incline, boulders strewn on either side. As we followed the lantern, Mavis warned us to watch our footing.

At the bottom of the hill we came to a cave. We stood before the opening like it was Garrick's maw of Leviathan. Mavis lifted the lantern and there was the sound of something within beating against the stone floor. Finally, it appeared out of the deeper dark—a chestnut horse, and riding it, was Madi. He dismounted and came forward to greet us. The horse followed close behind him.

I was, for some reason, overjoyed that he was alive.

"Harrow," he said. "Glad you survived the night at the Crystal Palace."

"Me?" I said. "How about you? How did you get away?"

"I told you he was resourceful," said Mavis.

"Did you know he was here?" I asked her.

"Not until a few minutes ago when I fled into the woods to escape the sights of the archer. I was making my way through the trees and the next I knew he was standing there in front of me with a torch."

"I saw you get kidnapped by the Host and Malbaster," I said to Madi.

He paid no attention to me but was kissing the back of Arabella's hand in greeting. His lips lingered on her third knuckle. He eventually backed away, but by then I was much less happy to see him. As for Arabella, her cape was draped around her like a shroud, and she had tears in her eyes, no doubt over the loss of Otis.

"I was taken," he said. "But when we got close to this area, I managed to leap through the window of the coach. I hit the ground and rolled and was up and gone into a thicket of trees before the driver could stop. I heard Malbaster croaking in his Pale King Toad voice, 'I want that nigger's head on a stake,' which hastened my getaway. I made my way south to Seneca Village, bought this horse, put together some provisions, borrowed a pistol and two throwing knives, and struck out immediately for this area. I knew they must be held up somewhere around here."

"Are you planning to rescue Ahab?" I asked.

"Harrow, I told you. I'm not out to rescue Ahab. My goal is to *kill* Malbaster—slit his throat. Ahab can go down with his own dilapidated scow of a life. To be honest, I'm surprised to see you here. Is that what you've come for, to rescue Ahab?"

"Not just Ahab, but you as well, Madi," said Mavis.

"You were a perfectly reasonable cynic when first we met, Harrow."

"That's what my boss said."

"Harrow's no cynic," said Arabella. "He's a man of enlightenment."

Madi laughed outright, and I couldn't help but both blush and smile.

"Have you seen Malbaster here, near the caves, in the past few days?" I asked.

"No, but I was hiding in a blind the other day and overheard two members of the Host talking. I'm almost positive I heard them say that the Pale King Toad would be here tonight to check on the progress with Ahab."

"They're turning him into another Bartleby," I said.

"All I want to see is Malbaster's neck," said Madi.

"What if we work together?" said Mavis. "We all take on both tasks—rescuing Ahab *and* killing Malbaster."

I nodded. "I'm in."

"So now Madi gets to kill the bloated toad? That was a pledge you made to me, Harrow," said Arabella, wiping the tears from her eyes.

"We'll kill him together," said Madi.

"That sounds promising," she said and smiled.

"And you'll assist us with Ahab?" I asked.

"I'll make an effort," said Madi. "But what I've learned about Ahab is that people die and the best of intentions evaporate when he's around."

He led the horse back into the cave and when he emerged, carrying a lit torch, he said, "Follow me. Low and quiet."

We did. I brought up the rear, content with that spot, since being in the lead seemed to invite arrows. I was concerned that the archer Mavis had killed was not a youngster from the Jolly Host but a large burly man. I wondered if we were going up against Malbaster's elite forces—his personal henchmen. I reached in my satchel and grabbed the fid. I was never so happy to have it, no matter how primitive it was. At that moment, it was worth a hundred pepperboxes.

Madi led us down along the Hudson. I could see the lights of a ship passing on its way to the city. It was a frigid night and the wind off the water cut right through us. The torch was less effective than the lantern had been in the pitch dark. I'd already tripped three times, and Mavis had caught Arabella a time or two as we made our way, unable to effectively navigate the uneven ground. We wound up in a thicket of trees that went some way to blocking the wind. As soon as we were all within the safety of the trunks, Madi put the torch out against the ground.

"That's it," he said. "We go forward from here in the dark. We're going to need the surprise."

"Are these Jolly Host or are they men we're up against?" I asked.

"Both," he said. "They're all unhinged with opium and laudanum."

"That'll make them easy to pick off," said Mavis.

"Where's the cave with poor Ahab?" said Arabella.

"Straight ahead. From what I could make out, it's one of the bigger, deeper caves. Malbaster has some dangerous-looking oafs directly guarding the captain.

"When we get to the entrance of the cave, I'll go to the left, and Mavis, you go to the right. We're the only ones with pistols. Harrow, you back Mavis up and Arabella, you come with me."

Arabella nodded. Without a further word, we headed due east on a rough path. It wasn't long before we saw lanterns blazing in the cave mouth. With every step I took, the more jittery I got. My only hope was that if we managed to free Ahab, his mind would still be intact.

20

What we were waiting for I had no idea. We stood in the dark, perilously close to the lip of the cave and peered in. I was only yards away from a stocky fellow with a sailor's pigtail, holding what looked like Ahab's own boarding ax. Behind him, sitting on a small boulder, was none other than the emaciated Usual Peters, a pistol in one hand and a bottle of Papine laudanum in the other. On Madi and Arabella's side of the cave was a younger man brandishing what I could have sworn was the spiked club that Fergus had used at Dutch Hill.

We could not see beyond the front vault of the cave, and from somewhere deep inside, a haze of opium smoke drifted out. The scent was intriguing and it made me slightly woozy. All of a sudden I noticed that it was snowing. I saw two flakes fall on the back of Mavis's coat. An instant later, she turned to me and grabbed me by the collar. "Ready?" she whispered. "I'm not waiting anymore."

She made her move, leaping into the mouth of the cave. She squatted and rolled and stabbed the pigtailed fellow in his groin with her knife, giving it a savage twist as she pulled it out by the hilt. Usual Peters staggered out of his chair to assist his compatriot, and she threw another knife that hit him directly in the Adam's apple. My God, the look of surprise on his face as he fell forward. I leaped in and smashed the first man across the top of the head with the blasted fid to put him out of my misery. He dropped like a sack of turnips.

By the time I turned around, Madi had made his move and his victim lay on the cave floor with one knife imbedded in his heart and another in his left eye. Arabella scrabbled in behind him and pulled a pistol out of the dead man's pocket. She stowed that and took up Fergus's club.

We moved quickly, Mavis retrieving her knives as Madi and Arabella pressed themselves against the wall at the back of the rock vault, and we entered a natural corridor that I hoped would lead to the captain.

Mavis and I made our way into the back of the cave. The corridor was dark, and at its distant end, there was a lit chamber curtained by a yellow haze. Fifty yards ahead of us, Madi and Arabella were huddled silhouettes against the distant glow, their bodies pressed close against the rock walls.

Mavis, on the other hand, strolled down the middle of the corridor, her hands in her pockets and a cigarette between her lips. She was as centered as a Brahmin about every task she took on. She had dispatched the three thugs that night with the same calm resolve with which she delivered Christmas hams to Garrick's business associates. I never knew her to initiate violence, but once engaged by it, there was no warning shot. She killed with precision and speed. I could not help but wonder at all I was getting for twenty dollars.

Mavis stopped and nudged my shoulder. She pointed ahead, and I looked up to see Madi's and Arabella's shadowed forms pass into the lit chamber. There were gunshots and screams. Mavis reached for her pistol and charged ahead. I clenched my fid and sped recklessly after her. Mavis was a few yards ahead of me when she entered the chamber. I lost sight of her as two more gunshots rang out.

I charged, weapon held high, into a place of utter stillness. Corpses littered the floor. Through the opium haze, I saw Ahab by the light of a flickering torch, shirtless, bearded, bedraggled, tied to a large, high-backed chair with armrests like a cheap wooden throne. His chin rested upon his chest and his breathing was labored. His eyes were open, staring at the rock floor of the cave. Mavis went to him and took her blade to the ropes.

I turned to the left and saw Arabella sitting slumped down against the wall. The club she carried was across her knees and the spike end was coated with gore. She was breathing heavily, not, she explained, from exertion, but in an effort to suck the errant smoke out of the air. I left her to it and looked for Madi. I found him at the opening of the chamber. He stood with his boot on the back of one of the fallen. Leaning over, he grabbed a shock of black hair and lifted so I could see the face of his victim. It was Gabriel. I nodded. "Alive or dead?" I asked.

"He'll live," said Madi.

We bound Gabriel's hands with the rope that had been used to restrain his father and shoved a handkerchief in his mouth to gag him. Madi started to walk the boy into the corridor, back toward the cave mouth. I quickly stripped one of Malbaster's dead followers of his long, filthy coat and gave it to the captain to cover himself. We then followed with Ahab in tow, weaving and stumbling into the dark passage. As we proceeded, the captain got his feet under him and was soon shuffling along at a respectable pace. All I wanted to do was escape from them all with my life.

Madi and Arabella waited for us in the entrance to the cave. "Hurry up," he whispered as Mavis, Ahab, and I came into view. I found Ahab's boarding ax on the cave floor and handed it to him. As our party left the cave, we heard the sound of an approaching stampede—the Jolly Host was on the hunt. I felt a jolt of fear run up my spine. I grabbed the captain by the beard and stared into his glassy eyes. "Run," I hissed. We ran. As we crossed the clearing, going hell-bent for leather toward the cover of the trees, the Jolly Host arrived. I heard their shouts go up and knew they'd spotted us.

We plunged into the dark of the woods, toward the thicket where we'd planned the assault. We went through there without slowing. As we ran, I became aware of two things: One was that Ahab, wasted and forlorn, was no more than a few yards behind me. The other was that it was snowing. This wasn't the flake here and there I'd noted earlier on Mavis's coat, but a full-fledged snowfall. I ran headlong into it, my fear blazing.

I could hear the Host as clearly as if they stood next to me. When I turned, I saw their torches sweeping through the woods behind us. We made it to Madi's cave, and he waved us ahead toward the trail lined with boulders that led uphill. Arabella and the prisoner, Gabriel, stayed behind with him. Ahab's bad leg slowed him on the hill, and I feared we'd be overtaken by our pursuers. He looked at us and yelled, "Go on. They'll get us all if you wait for me."

Despite my fear, I wasn't about to let go of him. I legged it back down the hill and grabbed him by the arm. Mavis did the same, and as the two of us sped the captain to the crest, the Jolly Host beginning the ascent behind us, she said, "Twenty dollars more."

"Fifteen," I said as we stopped at the top of the hill to catch an instant's breath.

"Agreed," she said. We resumed our hold on the captain and moved across the meadow. I heard a loud noise behind us, coming closer. Just as it was upon us, I realized it was Madi's horse. Arabella was in the saddle and Ahab's boy was strapped like a bedroll across its haunches. They flew by us, and the freshly fallen snow swirled behind them.

"As long as we can reach the tree line," said Mavis, "we can lose them in the woods."

The snow was coming down even harder now, limiting vision, and making the ground slippery. Ahab was huffing and puffing like a steam engine about to explode, yet we held on tight and kept him upright. As soon as we passed into the greater darkness of the wood, Mavis directed us toward a small thicket of trees that stood close amid the larger forest.

"Get down," she said. "We've only a second."

I dropped to the ground and pulled Ahab down with me. We all huddled with the tops of our heads touching, hoping to hide our faces from the light of the torches. Luckily, the snowstorm had only increased in its ferocity.

"Shhh," said Madi, and only then did I realize he was somehow among us.

The woods filled with movement all around. Flickering torches erratically revealed what the shadows hid. We lay in tense silence; I was nearly sick with fear. The sound of the boys' voices waxed and waned. I expected any second to be shot in the ass or stabbed in the back of the neck with an ice pick. But either they were too high on the smoke or we were too well concealed for them to notice us through the driving snow. In minutes they were gone, heading down toward the river, laughing and grunting and calling to one another like a pack of wild dogs.

Mavis whispered, "I remember the way to the coach," and we were off, running yet again. Now Madi held Ahab by the left arm as I had him by the right. Like the Host, we also were a single creature—yet we were awkward, slow, and dim. I'm sure the snow had helped us to escape certain death, but now the white fall was coalescing in dunes upon the ground. The gale picked up the fine frozen dust off the tops of these white hills and slapped us in the face with it.

Madi yelled over the wind, "Watch her footprints."

It was getting increasingly difficult to see Mavis through the storm. At moments, she was invisible. I turned my gaze to the ground and squinted, following one print after another. With neither a lantern nor a torch, we made our way back over treacherous ground toward the enormous tulip tree and the coach. Madi told us that Arabella was taking Gabriel to her home and that we were to meet her there if we got away. At this news, Ahab straightened, and I thought I saw a spark rekindle in his sad, old eyes. The only one of us near capable of piloting the conveyance was Mavis.

"An extra five if you get us back to Miss Dromen's alive," I said as we relieved the horses of their feed bags.

"Ten," she said as she handed her bag to me and climbed up into the driver's seat. She blew into her cupped hands and lifted the reins. I got into the cab, which was already crowded with Ahab and Madi. No sooner was I huddled in the corner than the coach jolted forward and sped away through the trees. We were going treacherously fast, and the wheels in the snow slid side to side behind the horses. I was going to stick my head out the cab door and yell up to her to slow the pace, but as I reached for the handle, I glanced out the window and saw the light of torches emerging from the woods.

I closed my eyes and turned my face to the wall like a child as we were buffeted by the wind and the rutted path. Eventually, I felt the coach decrease its speed, and I opened my eyes. Looking out, the torches of the Host were nowhere to be seen. I looked to my companions, neither of whom seemed in the least perturbed at our narrow escape from death. Ahab was just starting to doze off, and Madi was staring out the window, deep in thought. Before Ahab fell into the arms of Morpheus, I had a few questions I wanted answered.

"Captain, did you see Malbaster while you were a prisoner at the caves?"

Ahab came suddenly back to full consciousness. "Aye. He oversaw their treatment of me. Gave them orders on how to use the poppy to smoke my mind to ash. He came and went between the city and the cave. It's one of his hideouts."

"Did you make contact with your son?" asked Madi.

"I was able to tell the boy I was his father. He laughed at me at first. But I could tell him details about his mother only he and I would know. Her favorite flower, the black-eyed Susan; how her father died, at sea aboard the ill-fated *Cormorant*, a ship that was discovered with all hands missing, not a hint of a struggle, not a drop of blood left behind. I think my revelations terrified him. He'd pledged his allegiance to Malbaster."

"Did it give him pause to doubt the Pale King Toad?" I asked.

"I'm not sure, but at one point I thought he whispered something to me about *escape*. It may have been wishful thinking on my part, though. I was somewhere up beyond the crow's nest when I thought I heard it."

"And what of Malbaster?" said Madi.

The captain looked weary unto death. "Malbaster's head is like a prop. It's too large to be believed. And the placement of his face within that pale rock seems all crowded into the very center. The rest of his large form, at times, wavers tenuously between being and not. If I hadn't felt the back of his hand strike me across the cheek thirty-seven times, I'd have said he was a puppet or a person in disguise. He has a very refined manner, polite in speech."

"The curtesy of cruelty," said Madi.

"Aye. The thing that made me lose pieces of my mind wasn't the smoke, it was the lectures, his insane rationale for intimidating and murdering people. An inane corkscrew philosophy that pierced the heart of a world without humanity. At first it was frightening and then it was deadening. What a harangue. Spit flying, finger in the air. And in the end, it all could be traced back to the Puritans and the Great Awakening. Daft, I tell ya. Moby Dick was never so fierce."

We rode on for a quarter of an hour in silence before I asked him, "Was there magic?"

But both he and Madi were asleep.

21

Arabella beat us back to her place and had the boy tied into a bed by the time we arrived. She was out on the sidewalk, waiting to direct Mavis to bring the coach down the alley next to the house. I woke my traveling companions, and we disembarked beneath an old oak tree that blocked the moonlight. The snow had stopped falling, and the white ground was bright and slippery.

I was impressed with Miss Dromen. I'd assumed her an aesthete—the blue room, the opium. Not necessarily a phony, but something within hailing distance: a *transcendentalist*. But when she flew past in the dark, through the snow, with the boy strapped on the back of Madi's horse, my perception of her was altered forever. I'd been so wrong.

Madi and I helped Ahab into the parlor and set him down on a yellow satin couch. He was asleep or passed out before his head touched the armrest. Arabella looked down at his disheveled form wrapped in that greasy borrowed coat, and said, "He smells like the ocean's own turd." There was no alarm in her voice. It was a calm statement of fact. Madi laughed, and Arabella asked if we'd like a touch of libation. I was hoping for more than a touch.

I looked around the room: Arabella, Madi, Mavis, and I quaffed our tumblers of whiskey, Mavis alternating her swigs with deep pulls on a cigarette. The captain, out cold on the couch, did not imbibe. Arabella asked, "How long do you think it will be before they find us?"

I shook my head and Madi shrugged.

"A week if you're lucky," said Mavis.

"We'll have a few days to get Gabriel clear of the opium's hold, and then we'll have to be able to move him," said Arabella. "We need to be ready to leave in an instant."

Not a thought I wanted to dwell upon at the moment.

Madi said, "This isn't getting me any closer to finding Malbaster."

"Why chase him?" said Arabella. "He's coming to us."

"With the captain back in form, we'll be more of a force to be reckoned with," I said.

"When he's not playing nursemaid to his errant son," said Madi. "The boy's an albatross around his neck and now we have him around ours."

There was no disputing what he'd said. Arabella and I nodded. Mavis closed her eyes and folded her arms across her chest.

"I enjoy your company, Miss Dromen, but I'll be moving on tomorrow," said Madi.

"Wait," she said. "please hear me out. We're more effective when we work together. Our strength is in our number and in our ingenuity, which is unencumbered by smoke. We are set against an infernal machine powered by magic and hate, and at its center is Malbaster. It's not going to stop until we eliminate him. We've accomplished the first part of our mission, we've rescued Ahab and extricated his son. Now we must kill the Pale King Toad and thus destroy his evil engine."

"But I can't sit and wait for him to find us here," said Madi. "He may merely send the Host to overrun the place some night with orders to tear us apart."

"We need to draw him out, and if possible, draw him away from here. Do you gentlemen remember what I told you about Astor's store of opium somewhere on the Hudson side of Manhattan? I suggest that you two find it."

"Say we find it," I said. "Then what?"

"Then set fire to it and wait in ambush till Malbaster makes an appearance," she said.

Madi nodded. "That's as sound an idea as I've heard or had myself."

"How do we go about discovering the hoard?" I asked.

"I know it's on the West Side, somewhere near or along the river. You need to go there and wait surreptitiously for the Jolly Host to show itself—some act of malfeasance, bigotry, vandalism that appears in the local newspaper or that you catch wind of in a conversation. Then follow them. Eventually they'll be drawn to the source of their addiction. I doubt Malbaster puts himself in danger by frequenting the storehouse of tar. But he'll come out if his control is threatened." Arabella sat back in her chair and shut her eyes.

In moments, she was asleep and breathing steadily, her lovely chest rising and falling in a slow rhythm. So taken was I by the sight of Arabella at rest, I hadn't noticed that Mavis had gotten up and crossed the room. She tapped me on the shoulder, which broke my trance. "Harrow," she said. "I'll meet you here tomorrow night. I'll want my money and by then you'll need to have an article finished for Garrick."

"Certainly. How much do I owe you?" I asked, not looking away from the sleeping beauty.

"Seventy dollars."

"Good Lord, you don't come cheap," I said.

"You never think about that when I'm saving your life, do you?"

I laughed as did she. "Very well, seventy it is. I'll get Garrick to reimburse me somehow, I swear."

When she'd left the room, Madi said, "She's fierce."

"I don't think there's anyone in this life whose word I trust more. I do business with her regularly, but she always keeps her distance."

"No doubt she fears your penchant for the irrational," he said.

"Me? George Harrow, irrational? I'm the worst kind of realist."

"I mean your articles."

"Oh, well, yes. Madi, you'll be staying here till morning, will you not?"

"Yes," he said. Now his eyes were closed and he'd clasped his hands behind his head and leaned back in the deep velour chair.

"Good. I've got to return to my place and check to see that Misha is all right and to grab my writing equipment. I'm taking your horse. I'll be back by late morning."

"Very well," he said, but never truly woke.

I felt as though I were in a personal grudge match with gravity as I tried to pull myself out of the seat. The night's hugger-mugger had wasted me. I did sleep some part of each journey in the coach, which was all that made it possible for me to tear myself from the comfort of Arabella Dromen's parlor.

Out on the street, my satchel over my shoulder and collar pulled up high, the snow was nearly to my thighs. There wasn't a soul in sight. I guessed it to be perhaps 3 or 4 A.M. The icy chill of the night burned my nose and throat with each inhalation. From the front porch, I groped my way down the steps and headed for that side of the house where the coach was stored. I guessed I'd find a stable there, and eventually I did. Madi's horse wasn't budging after the flat-out run from the utmost north of Manhattan. I chose one of the heavier coach horses, a big white brute, and saddled him up by the light of a candle I found mounted on the wall near his stall.

The poor beast was as interested in a jaunt as his brethren, but I managed to coax him out onto the street, and we waddled along slow as molasses. I didn't require he trot. All I asked was that he keep me up out of the snow. I had learned how to ride when I was a boy on my uncle's farm in New Jersey, but it had been quite a while and so the attenuated pace was perfect for me. I'd seen enough excitement that night to last me till Judgment Day.

My only worry was being spotted by some member of the Jolly Host. Nothing moved in the streets and it was far too early for pedestrians. Even the riffraff stayed hidden inside wherever they could find shelter from the weather. I stuck to the sidewalk, but once we hit Chatham Street I took the mount into the middle of the road for easier passage. As we went along, the cold wind slapped me about, and I was good and awake after a few minutes. I began to consider what I might write for Garrick once I reached home.

As vehemently as the boss had said, "No more Ahab," I wondered how anyone could forgo a tale of skullduggery in and about the Indian Caves. I'd have bet fellow citizens would love to hear of that remote spot on the great Manhattoes, and there would be action galore. Granted, Ahab would be mucking around in the middle of the tale, bringing his unique brand of mawkishness, but at least he wasn't tied to a chair. I decided I would take the chance and slip Garrick one more final adventure with the lunatic Nantucketer.

It took me twenty minutes to reach my house. I tied up the horse in the backyard toolshed and let myself into the kitchen by the back door. The place was eerily still. I felt something was wrong, and when I passed from the kitchen into the hallway leading to my study, I encountered a frigid current of air coming from the front door, which I could now see was open. Reaching into my satchel for the fid, I clutched it tightly. As I passed the entrance to my office, the open front door, still three yards off, slammed shut of its own volition. I was startled into stillness. From within the room to my right came a vibrating voice— "Harrow, come and sit."

The thought of who might be there in the dark left me slack. Still, I obeyed and entered the room. There, in my desk chair, sat a man's body topped by a pale planet of a head. On his small scrunched face was an insipid smile, and his eyes squinted as if he was straining to see me. I thought of running, but Malbaster's magic drained me of energy. Or was that my own fear?

He was dressed in pin-striped trousers and a morning coat. His hand leaned on the silver dog head of a black walking stick. With the stick, he pointed to the chair across the room where Ishmael had sat during our last meeting. Although the dark engulfed us, Malbaster's head gave off an aura of luminescence by which I could see his tiny eyes shifting their gaze. A subtle bubbling noise came from deep within him, and we sat and listened to that subterranean turmoil for whole minutes.

Suddenly smoke issued from the Pale King Toad's mouth and nostrils, thin streams squeezed out from the corners of his eyes, billowed from his ears, and the glowing clouds filled the room. I was dazed by the time he next addressed me.

"George Harrow, you're a magician with words. I read your articles assiduously. Very entertaining." His voice was somehow resonant, as if he were calling to me from an empty, echoing cavern. "You scatter gapeseed like the Lord does blessings."

I wanted him to leave. As bleary and confused as I was, I kept my resolve to say nothing. "I'm afraid you and I have competing realities," he said. "And you and your coven of tramps—a madwoman, a murderous girl, a buffoonish sea captain, and—tsk, tsk, Harrow—a Negro. You've drastically lowered my estimation of you. You and these ruffians. I'm going to be forced to take measures." He stopped speaking and seemed to be waiting for me to respond.

I stayed quiet.

"You have stolen one of my young men. The fellow Gabriel. That requires retribution. Of course, eventually I'm going to kill you all. But for now, we'll start with this." He snapped his fingers.

I looked up, waiting to see what might happen next, when I heard in the distance the squeal of Misha's door hinges. A smile grew on his face as I heard her footsteps in the hallway. She was treading slowly. My mind was groping for a plan of action, something to say that might give us even a fleeting window of escape.

That's when I heard a growl come from the dark corner next to Malbaster.

"Oh, yes. I forgot to introduce you to my pet," he said.

Something moved in the shadows. The blue eyes and a multitude of teeth caught the fluorescence of his bulbous head and gleamed. "We've met," said a smooth, female voice. "I nearly made this wretch my dinner some nights ago at the old cotton warehouse. His treacherous little brat shot at me."

I never intended to speak, but I found myself asking, "A manticore—how is it possible?" Both Malbaster and the creature laughed.

"A manticore that speaks, no less," he said. "Fabulous. There's nothing that the combined will of the people can't conjure. Love generates great energy with which to form the world. But Fear and Ignorance aren't bad themselves, producing their own grim yet powerful magic. The secret, Harrow, is e pluribus unum."

As the words fell from his lips, Misha entered the room in her nightgown, her graying hair let down to the middle of her back. Her eyes were open and yet her gaze fixed on no one thing, as if she were sleepwalking. I tried to get up and go to her, but it was as if I were glued to the chair. "Run, Misha," I yelled, my words sounding like the buzz of a mosquito.

"I think your plotline, so to speak, is a little crowded, Harrow. I'm going to extricate you from such difficulty and remove this pointless character from your world."

"What do you mean, remove her?"

"Erase her as you might a faulty word when composing in pencil."

"What do you mean?"

The manticore slunk forward, ringlets bobbing like springs, padded paws silent on the office floor. She drew within two feet of Misha, and then the tail whipped out of the shadow behind the creature and stuck its poisonous stinger directly into the center of Misha's forehead. The tail pulled back, leaving a neat round hole leaking blood. I gasped.

"What I mean is what I said. I'm having her erased," said Malbaster. With that, the manticore opened wide its mouth and took a huge bite out of Misha's left buttock. She stood there wrapped in a trance, enduring it all. Still trapped in my chair, all I could do was watch in horror as my housekeeper, my friend, was vanished bite by bite. There was no blood or bone or viscera. Instead, there was nothing; each subsequent bite was like the pass of an eraser over words, wiping away that which was Misha.

The final portion was her face. The manticore used its teeth to lift the scrap from the floor and drop it in Malbaster's hands. "I'll have a bite," he said and took away a good portion of Misha's forehead. I groaned, unable to accept what I was seeing. When there wasn't a crumb of her left, Malbaster banged his walking stick against the floor twice, pointed to me, and commanded, "Sleep."

22

I woke in my chair, my cheek resting upon my writing desk. Nearby was an empty bottle of gin. One of my cigars had at some point rolled out of my hand and left a burn mark in the desk's wood surface. My head was heavy, my eyes bleary. I pushed myself upright, and as I rose, I noticed that my notebook was open and I'd obviously been working.

I picked up what was left of the cigar, lit it, and read through what I'd managed to scrawl in my weariness. It was not the adventure of the Indian Caves as I had planned. I vaguely remembered having the revelation, awash in gin, that perhaps a meeting with Malbaster at this juncture of my Ahab series might breathe new life into it and pave the way for not one but multiple new articles about the captain. Somehow my drink-addled mind had reasoned that the consumption of Misha by the manticore would excite the most primal reactions in people and draw them more deeply into the story.

At that moment, my housekeeper entered the room and inquired about her gun. I nearly cried in relief, realizing my article had been pure confabulation, and quickly closed the notebook. I knew that at some point I would have to suffer Misha's discovery of her unusual demise. But it would be days until the article was published. I came right out and told her I was nearly killed relying on the blasted pepperbox.

"But where is it?"

"In the bushes, somewhere at the northern edge of Manhattan."

"You just threw it away?"

"It was useless. A gun is supposed to shoot bullets," I said.

"It's been scary around here at night," she told me. "A voice out in the garden reciting poetry."

Her words made me shudder. I thought of how my article about Ahab's captivity was prophetic. If the manticore was nearby, it was too close. I asked Misha to take a few weeks and go to visit her niece on Long Island. "I'll give you money for the trip," I told her. "Take three weeks."

"What? Are you getting rid of me?" she said, her face becoming a grimace.

"Just vacation. Your position is safe. Trust me."

"I don't understand."

"It's too dangerous here for you. They know where I live. They'll come for you eventually. Only three weeks. I aim to solve the entire problem by then."

"We're counting on *you* to solve the problem?" she said, suppressing a laugh. "Might as well take a month while I'm at it."

"I'll send for you when I need you. Leave me the address. Get packed; I'll escort you to the ferry."

"And what'll become of you if I go?" she said.

"Chances are, nothing good, but if something were to happen to you, I'd never forgive myself."

"Oh, piffle, George Harrow. I'm not going anywhere. Besides, my niece on Long Island hates me and thinks I'm a meddlesome old bitch."

"I'd never suspected her of being that sharp," I said. Misha smacked the back of my head. "Okay, okay, stay, but you'll be here alone quite a bit and I, obviously, can't protect you. There are mythical creatures stalking the streets."

"I'll go right now," she said, laughing, "and sharpen the butcher knife."

Recalling Mavis in action at the Indian Caves, I wondered if I should get my housekeeper some knife-wielding lessons. In any event, I cut the mad article of my interview with Malbaster out of my notebook and secured it in an envelope with the *Gorgon* wax seal. After stowing that in my inside jacket pocket, I set to recording the adventure of the Indian Caves. Two new articles at once for Garrick.

Late that morning, I left with my satchel full of my writer's gear—pen, ink, paper, pencils, notebook, eraser, penknife, wax, matches, and the *Gorgon's Mirror* seal. Also in that bag was my last hundred dollars. I'd left twenty with Misha and I owed, out of what I carried, seventy to Mavis. I saddled the white horse and took a roundabout way to Arabella's, checking to make sure I wasn't being followed.

The streets were lightly traveled due to the snow and the wicked wind. A few people still scurried to work and on errands. Tramps huddled together for warmth like dogs under porches and in alleyways. Here and there was an itinerant fire in a barrel or gutter, spewing foul black smoke into the blue day and offering a bit of warmth to those without a home.

I didn't trust anyone. I particularly didn't trust anyone under twenty dressed in a shabby fashion. They may just have been youngsters on the street traveling to jobs at the seaport, but as far as I was concerned they were all the Jolly Host. I was becoming as suspicious and fearful as the Order of the Star-Spangled Banner.

I recalled the words Malbaster had uttered to me the night before in the Land of Nod. "The secret, Harrow, is *e pluribus unum.*" I didn't understand what that meant when I wrote it but recalled it came with such force. Back in school, I had been a scholar of spitballs, not Latin. Still, I knew it was our nation's motto—*Out of many, one.* Was Malbaster the *one* out of *many*? In the piece I'd written for Garrick, the Pale King Toad had told me he could smell the rotting oyster stink of fear and that it made him nostalgic.

I returned the coach horse to the stable beside Arabella's house. After peering up and down the street from behind a pair of juniper trees, I climbed the front porch steps. The door was unlocked. I retrieved the fid from my satchel and quietly let myself in. The vague scent of the poppy was in the air and all was terribly still. I entered the parlor to find Madi sitting on the yellow satin couch. He opened his eyes, smiled, and put his finger to his lips. Curled up asleep next to him, resting her head on his thigh, was Arabella.

He slowly, carefully, slipped out from beneath her and managed to wedge a throw pillow under her head. He stood and I followed him out of the parlor and into the hallway.

"What in God's name was going on back there?" I asked in an affronted whisper.

He stopped and turned to face me. I caught him smiling and didn't like it one bit. "You mean with Miss Dromen?"

"You know I mean with Miss Dromen," I said, losing patience.

"At around three in the morning, Ahab left to deal with the boy who was screaming to be released. All manner of threats and curses echoed through the house. When the captain got up, I sat down and closed my eyes. A while later, Arabella emerged from her writing room dazed on the smoke and sat next to me. We talked for an hour or so. She expressed her grief for the loss of her man, Otis, who'd been with her since before her father had passed. Eventually she must have fallen asleep and tipped over onto my leg."

"Somewhat unseemly. Wouldn't you say?"

"I wouldn't."

I was about to give him a piece of my mind when he turned to the left and pushed open another door. Inside, I saw Ahab, sitting shirtless and upright in a chair next to a four-poster bed. Gabriel lay there, ropes knotted around his ankles and wrists, his head on a cream-colored pillow the size of a cloud. His eyes were closed and he appeared to be fast asleep. The captain heard us enter and indicated two chairs. We sat, I at the foot of the bed, Madi across the bed from Ahab.

The captain looked as if he'd covered all watches for a week. His face was drawn and his hair had gone grayer than when I'd last seen him.

His eyes were dull and dark circled. Now that the boy was in reach, he dared not sleep for fear of losing him again.

"Madi says he's had some complaints," I whispered to Ahab, nodding down at Gabriel.

"Aye. A great caterwauling. He's professed his allegiance to Malbaster. Said the boulder-headed bastard would kill us all. There was much struggling against his bonds. I must hand it to Miss Dromen, she knows how to tie a knot like a sailor."

"Her father was a ship's captain," said Madi.

"I knew there was something worthwhile about the woman," said the captain.

"From what I understand, there will be more anguish to come for the lad," I said.

"Coming off the smoke will likely start this evening. Then he'll suffer sweats and pains and nausea and shivering and delusions," said Ahab. "I've seen it before."

"What does he say about your being his father?" asked Madi.

"Says he wishes I'd been swallowed by the white whale."

"He'll come around," I said.

Ahab shook his head. "No, no. I let the boy vent his rage, for it's I who've done him wrong. I could sit here forever in the quiet of this room and watch him sleep, knowing he is safe."

I looked over at Madi and saw him turn away. The captain was such a pitiful specimen, you couldn't help but commiserate with him. Even I felt the pricking of tears. To cover my emotion, I stood and announced that Madi and I were heading out to try to locate the warehouse holding John Jacob Astor's considerable stash.

"As soon as he's up and about and I've managed to corral his affections, we'll be on the spot to assist you, Harrow. I want to thank you and Madi for saving my boy."

"I'll take a dead Malbaster in lieu of thanks," said the harpooneer.

"Aye," said Ahab.

"We'll be back this evening," I said. "Should you need to flee, take the coach and try to make it to the New Rose Inn. To get there, follow the East River north. Tell Sally Cocharan I'm pleading with her to take you and the boy and Arabella in."

The captain quietly nodded.

After leaving the bedroom, Madi and I passed through the parlor. Arabella was just waking up, stretching her arms and yawning. When she saw us, she asked if we were off to the West Side. I told her we were and said the same to her as I did to Ahab about where to go if the Jolly Host should show themselves.

"I know the New Rose Inn," she said.

"I know you dropped the coach gun when we fled the Host, but have you got any other weapon?" I asked.

"There's a double-barreled percussion pistol in my writing room."

"Load it and keep it near you at all times," I said.

She nodded. "Oh, Madi, forgive me for falling asleep in the middle of our conversation. I was exhausted."

Madi waved away her concern and said, "Quite all right, but, you know, Harrow here is upset because when you fell asleep you leaned over and rested your head on my thigh. I'm afraid he feels your honor has been impugned."

"Yes, my honor," she said.

"I believe he's wary that I might have tarnished you."

"I just wanted to be sure everything was on the up-and-up," I said and could feel myself sinking deeper into the mire.

Arabella looked at Madi, raised her eyebrows, and said, "You know, of all people, Harrow's thoroughly on the up-and-up." Their laughter was damnably raucous. I left the room before it consumed me. Why did I couch my suspicions of Madi in the guise of superiority, when it was just straight-on jealousy? I'd thought it would give me license to be dishonest with myself but instead it made me a fool.

I slipped out the front door, dashed across the lawn to the juniper trees, and hid there waiting for him. I lit a cigar and asked myself what the hell I was doing. I was about to head off with the harpooneer to the West Side to follow the doings of the Jolly Host in order to discover a trove of opium, which we would burn, luring Malbaster out into the open, so that we might slay him. I knew I should flee this insanity, go back home, stay there, write my articles, drink gin, and trade insults with Misha. I wanted to fall asleep at my writing desk, concocting things that weren't real.

When Madi met me a few minutes later, we decided to go down to Chambers Street, so I could stop in at the offices of the *Cockaigne Times* and look up my old friend and competitor, Rufus Sharde. He was a man in the know and could more than likely point us in the direction of the Host.

The snow had melted somewhat in the morning's bright glare but by early afternoon the wind grew fiercer and turned it to ice. Our combined footfalls sounded like a regiment marching on eggshells. In addition, there were slippery patches in the road and on the sidewalk. We both came very close to falling more than once.

By the time we passed City Hall, I was frozen and fed up with the adventure before it had begun. In the park, a trio of turkey vultures perched in a dead elm. We passed beneath them and they followed us, circling above in the cold blue sky, their shadows ominous across the snow.

"I can't feel my hands, Harrow," Madi said and blew into them.

"My ears have fallen off," I said.

The birds followed us a few more blocks to the offices of the *Cockaigne Times* at the corner of Church and Chambers. I knocked upon the door and the copy boy answered. A voice behind him called, "Who is it?"

The boy responded, "Harrow."

"Let him in," came the reply.

"He got a colored man with him."

"Let them in, I told you," came the voice and then its owner appeared and swung wide the door to allow us entry into the fireplace warmth. It was such a relief to be out of the wind, I nearly cried. Sharde led us through the busy production room of the *Times* where off in the corner, the presses ran pages. We passed by a cluster of women who sat at a large table folding those pages together. They were all talking at once about various topics but their hands worked in concert like machines.

Once we reached Rufus's office, he said, "The first order of business is cigars and whiskey." I took a seat and tried to hug the chill out of myself. He gave each of us a drink and a smoke and then retreated to the chair on the other side of his desk. "Harrow, you looked like Jack Frost's father when you first came in from the cold. There were icicles in your hair and you were white as a wedding dress."

"I felt like his grandfather," I said.

"Is this your man?" Rufus asked and nodded toward Madi.

"This is my colleague, Madi."

"I know him from reading your recent articles about the sea captain. That series is brilliant, George. Brilliant."

"That's why we're here," I said. "We're trying to finish the story, but we need some information."

"On a day like this? You're out investigating, clear across town? Harrow, what's wrong with you?"

"We need to track something down."

"Track something down, are you serious? Aren't you spinning the Ahab story out of thin air?"

"Everything I've written has been more or less true," I said.

"I love the manticore," said Rufus and laughed. "A swift stroke of genius, but please, that's not even less true."

"It exists."

"Harrow, stay home and let your imagination do the work. I used to think there was actual wonder in the world, and when I started out, I went into the streets armed with my pen to find it. But the years have driven me inside for my articles. Dramas from my dark heart. There's nothing out there but grimy disappointment."

"I'd known that for years," I told Sharde. "Until Ahab swept by at high tide and shanghaied me into his service, I'd have agreed with you. But of late, the world's wonders intrude."

23

Sharde loved to lecture me, even though my articles were more popular than his and the *Gorgon's Mirror* outsold the *Cockaigne Times* nearly two to one. I couldn't completely ignore him, though. When I'd just started out in the penny press humbug business, working for the *Weekly Speculator,* Rufus had already been at it for a decade. He took me under his wing at the time and showed me the art and craft of confabulation. Without him, I'd never have risen to the position I now hold at the top of the mound of purveyors of print hokum.

The old journeyman hadn't aged well. His once-thick black hair had mostly flown away and what was left at the sides had gone steel gray. Also flown were several of his teeth. He appeared to have recently lost quite a bit of weight, and not in a healthful manner. *Frail* was how I'd now describe him. If it weren't for the fact that he was still a flamboyant dresser, what with his embroidered jacket, snakeskin boots, and dark Waddell hat with a bright red cardinal feather stuck in the band, he'd have passed for old broken-down flotsam of the streets. He stared at me through cigar smoke and smoothed his drooping mustache.

"The Jolly Host," I said to him.

"Ahhh," he said.

"We need to find them," said Madi.

"You've got to give me more than that, Harrow. I'm not coughing up information for you for nothing. Are you going to cut me in on your project?"

"Rufus, that might not be a good idea."

"You'd deny your old mentor a tidbit of a story?"

"You could very well wind up dead," said Madi.

"Mr. Madi, as Harrow's colleague, I'm not sure how much experience you have at the pursuit of wonder tales, but George can tell you I've been around the block more than once. There's little I haven't been through."

I looked to Madi and said, "Should I tell him?"

The harpooneer nodded.

"We're looking for a warehouse, either owned or once owned by John Jacob Astor, over on the West Side here. We've been told it contains an enormous quantity of opium. It's now controlled by the Jolly Host. We mean to destroy it by fire."

Sharde stubbed out his cigar and sat forward. "I know of the Jolly Host and their toad king, Malbaster. We've run into them a number of times and, I might add, run in the opposite direction as swiftly as possible."

"Where?" asked Madi.

"The Host, as I understand them," said Sharde, "are a gang with a purpose. And that purpose is not merely to enhance their income through robbery. From what I can gather, they're about driving the likes of yourself, Mr. Madi, out of Manhattan."

"The likes of myself? You mean fine, upstanding citizens?"

Sharde laughed. "Precisely. So, you won't find them down along West or Washington Streets in proximity to the Hudson. That's a good deal of old Protestant money along there. Either good residences or well-respected businesses. In the blocks farther back from the water, those businesses along Washington keep their goods in warehouses somewhat less lovely than their homes. A warehouse, a warehouse," he said and tapped his fingers on the desktop, thinking.

"We thought if we could just identify the Jolly Host and then follow them," I added.

"Better yet," said Sharde as if suddenly hit by a brainstorm, "Astor, himself, owned property due north of here, a twenty-minute walk, in the area around Varick and Vandam Streets. That might be where you need to look. There are warehouses he stored pelts in when he was in the fur-trading business."

"That could be very valuable, Rufus," I said. "Now, what was the last you heard about the Host?"

"Well, I don't know if you heard of this all the way across town, but not long ago, there was an incident at a place called Carpen's Cave. It was a theater where they'd put on productions of famous dramas, Shakespeare, Marlowe, et cetera. Supposedly the productions were very well done indeed."

"I've heard of it," said Madi.

"Ah, yes. Well, one evening before the show was supposed to go on, seemingly out of the blue, a crowd formed outside the theater. What the grievance was never made its way into the news. In minutes, a full-fledged riot was under way. The place was ransacked and burned. The proprietor, Mr. Carpen, was hanged from an oak outside the place and his wife and one of the other players were beaten to death. The crowd dispersed like a fart in a windstorm, and that, sir, was that."

"I take it these were not theater critics who led the assault," I said.

"Carpen was a black man," said Madi. "The entire business, players and set designers and musicians, all colored."

"That's right," said Sharde. "Charges were never filed. No arrests were made."

"And what was their crime?" I asked.

"From what I heard," he said, "Billy Niblo, owner of Niblo's Garden—you know the place, where Barnum first played—was broadcasting that Carpen's operation was underselling him and poaching his rightful customers."

"That was all Malbaster had to hear," I said.

"Their crime was they were successful," said Madi.

"Let it be a lesson to you," Rufus said, glancing at the harpooneer.

I could see Madi's muscles tense, and he leaned forward as if to spring from his seat.

"Easy, my friend," said Sharde. "I've nothing against you joining us in the pursuit of fallacious stories. My God, there's enough bullshit in the world to keep us all busy till the ends of our days. I welcome those of your persuasion. I merely offer a convivial warning to move cautiously through the white world. No matter the law on the books, danger still lurks."

Madi shook his head. "Sharde, seriously, you're a bigger fool than I first surmised. Do you really think I need you to tell me that? I'm here seeking a resolution to the murders of two innocent children. One of them black. I know full well the treachery of the white world."

I laughed to break the tension. "He's got quite a point, Rufus."

In that moment, I saw Sharde's age catch up to him. This idea he was just presented with, namely that a colored man does not need to be told what the dangers of being a colored man are left him verily stunned. Yes, the Jolly Host was perilous, but this attitude I now watched Rufus fumbling with might ultimately be more perilous for the plight of blacks in the city.

"Forgive me," he stammered. "You are correct, Mr. Madi."

"I'd not have gotten by without your corroboration," said the harpooneer.

Sharde seemed somewhat put out for the remainder of the time we spent with him. He wasn't upset at Madi. In fact, following the previous exchange, he seemed to warm to him. I think it was the fact that he realized the world in which he had been an integral part was quickly being left in the dust. Poor old scribbler. He no longer had his finger on the pulse of society. No longer was he a favorite paramour of the city. The daydreams he composed were slow and gray, and out of touch with the changing times.

I took the codger's condition to heart, seeing myself in his decline in not too many years. Before we left, I gave him a hearty hug and found him near weightless, like a bird—all feathers and air and hollow bones. He escorted us to the door and, as he had done for so many years, bestowed some advice upon me at our parting. "Stay true to your imagination, Harrow," he said as I stepped back out into the frozen world, and these words lodged in my mind and struck me as something important to consider. "Be safe, my friend," he said to Madi, and the harpooneer shook his hand and thanked him for the fire and the drink.

We headed north as Sharde had suggested toward Varick and Vandam. As we crunched along through the snow on the sidewalk, I said, "Rufus isn't such a bad soul."

"To you, Harrow," he said. "But think how I felt when he told that story of the theater being destroyed and the owner hanged. I'm sure he never lifted a finger to achieve justice for those people, nor did any of the other 'not such bad souls' in Manhattan."

"Do you think when all this is over, granted we're not killed, that someday we'll be friends?"

"Well, you're not such a bad soul, Harrow," he said and we laughed.

"Fuck you," I said.

One thing we'd not considered was how we were supposed to determine which buildings were warehouses and what each warehouse contained once we'd reached our destination. We weren't there at the corner of Varick and Vandam for more than five minutes before Madi noticed a tarnished plaque on the two-story brick building in front of us. A penny-green patina covered the no-longer-bright copper sign, which read: *J. J. Astor.*

Madi looked at me, and I shook my head. "What are the chances this is the very building we seek? I would never even put something like this in one of my articles."

"Too coincidental?" asked Madi.

"Too expedient *and* too coincidental."

"But could it happen in real life?"

I weighed the possibilities and came to the conclusion fairly quickly that perhaps it could. "Maybe," I said.

The block was empty, not a soul in sight. Next door on the right there was an empty lot of about two acres, and, on the left was another redbrick building, although in much worse repair. Madi and I peered in the glass sidelights on either side of the door we faced. There was nothing moving inside. I scanned the windows of the two buildings across the street, both two-story places like the one behind us. Their empty windows were like Malbaster's dead black eyes. We tramped through the snow, waist-deep in places, skirting the vacant lot for nearly a hundred yards till we reached the back of the building.

There, we found a large wooden door, rudely built of thick planks. Wider and taller than the front door. I supposed it was used as a means to get large items in and out of the building. It differed in another way from the front door, too: it was obviously unlocked and slightly ajar. Madi walked up to the door and pushed it fully open. I feared the complaint of rusted hinges might be heard all the way to Broadway.

"This is too much," I said. "If there ends up being tons of opium in this building, I don't know what I'll do. The entire scenario is unbelievable."

"It strikes me as unusual," said Madi.

I came to stand next to him at the open door, a rectangle of darkness. "Matches?" he asked.

I reached into my satchel and removed the matches and the small candle I carried to affix the wax seal of the *Gorgon*. I lit it, enlisting Madi to help me block the wind. We stepped through the open doorway, and I was immediately struck by the scent of old wood and mildew.

Stepping into the darkness, it took a moment for my eyes to adjust to the candlelight. Slowly, our surroundings were revealed. Old furniture, stacked in no particular order, one piece upon another, to the ceiling: a chair atop a table atop a couch. There was a narrow canyon that cut through the middle of the wooden chaos. Every few steps, we stopped and surveyed what lay on either side of us.

We found a staircase leading to the second floor and ascended. Upstairs wasn't quite as dark, thanks to the pale winter light coming in through the windows. There were boxes of old books as well as a wide selection of taxidermized creatures gone to rot, the fur shedding upon the floor, the yellowed stuffing showing through open wounds, glass eyes askew. The most impressive piece, which was in better shape than most, was a moose that towered over the peaceable kingdom of deteriorating beasts.

We soon ascertained that this warehouse wasn't the one we sought, and we left the way we'd entered. We crossed the street to inspect the two warehouses there. Upon finding the Astor plaque on those two buildings, we contrived a way to gain entrance that involved the breaking of glass and spent hours inspecting their contents. For our trouble, although we found not one ball of opium tar, we discovered barrels of spoiled grain and wine; boxes of nails and coils of rope; the pelts of at least two hundred foxes, martins, and otters; the teeth of wolves; and bear claws from woodland behemoths.

The fabled warehouse of smoke may have been just that, a story told by an old sea captain to his daughter. But one thing was for certain: Astor had enough detritus in the three buildings we went through to sink a dozen clipper ships. And when all was said and done, the old Croesus couldn't take it with him. It was impossible to fathom having that much wealth. It would leave me with no reason to write or daydream stories, and what kind of life would that be?

It was dark when we exited the last of the warehouses. Our first foray to the West Side had been less than fruitful, and I was slightly put out that I'd diminished my cinnabar candle by more than half in our search. Out on the sidewalk the winter remained relentless. Although the snow had by then stopped falling, what was on the ground was harder and slicker. It struck me that I'd never seen an area of the city proper more desolate and lonely than the area around us.

"Do we head back to Arabella's or stay around here and see if we can locate the Host?" asked Madi.

"I have to meet Mavis," I told him. "We'll get an earlier start tomorrow."

He seemed reluctant to give up the search just then, but I convinced him to accompany me by reminding him of the distance we had to cover. We traveled a block south to Spring Street and took that east. We passed into a slightly busier section of town—a few people on the street, passing hansom cabs and coaches now and then, lighted windows, and the smells of dinnertime mixed with the scent of chimney smoke. Both Madi and I were tired and silent as we trudged along.

We'd made it to Spring and Mercer, about a block from Broadway, when there came the sound of charging horses and squealing wheels. I looked over my shoulder and saw a coach-and-four turn onto Spring Street behind us and come flying in our direction. It moved fast in the evening gloom, weakly illuminated by the two gas lamps, one on either corner of the street. I leaped backward and pulled Madi with me up against the wall.

The conveyance, with its monstrous black horses, bore down on us and the left two wheels skipped up onto the sidewalk. We flattened ourselves against the brick building, and the coach sped past us, missing us only by inches. As the coach passed, I caught sight of a white blur. Something was tossed out at us from the open window of the cab. It hit the wall between our heads and fell to the sidewalk.

In the next instant, the coach turned north on Broadway. At our feet was a duffel bag. Madi grabbed it by the drawstring.

"Is there something in it?" I asked.

"Yes," he said. "Let's get up to the next streetlamp and we'll see what it is."

A few yards from Broadway, beneath a flickering gas lamp, Madi turned the bag over and shook its contents onto the ground. Something rolled out and plopped into the snow. At first I took it for a melon or a cabbage.

"What in God's name?" I said, moving out of the way of the lamp-light.

Madi toed the thing with his boot, turning it over. A human head, severed at the neck, stared back at us, a gnarled piece of spine and tissue and blood trailing from the point of brutal decapitation.

"Harrow," said the harpooneer. "I believe it's Sharde."

I looked down and nearly vomited. Instead I groaned and doubled over with fear. Then, in the distance, we heard the shouts of the Jolly Host. Madi grabbed me by the arm and we dashed across the street and disappeared down an alley.

24

I couldn't shake the sight of Rufus's head. His eyes seemed to stare into mine, and he wore an expression as if he were about to say, *Harrow,* and give me one of his unwanted nuggets of wisdom. How had Malbaster known where we'd been earlier that afternoon—and had they followed us after our visit to Rufus's office? I was numb. Only my legs worked. Madi dragged me away.

We ran from one alley to another, heading south, back toward Chambers Street, managing to keep a hundred yards ahead of the Host. We heard their echoing cries behind us, their clambering through the canyons of brick walls and the overturning of trash bins, the scattering of hogs. They moved like a wave. As we broke out onto Franklin Street, I slipped on the snow and went sprawling into the road just as a coach-and-two was passing, heading for Broadway. The driver pulled hard on the reins, and the horses reared to avoid trampling me. Madi grabbed me by the back of the coat, and in one fell swoop, brought me around to the side of the cab, opened the door, and tossed me into the back of the conveyance.

"South on Broadway," he yelled to the driver, who didn't see, as the harpooneer got into the cab, that the swiftest of the Jolly Host was upon us. Before slamming the door, Madi kicked the assailant in the throat. The coach started up and we were away not a moment too soon. It took me nearly all the way to Chatham Street before I could catch my breath. My first words were a thank you to my companion. His response was, "Harrow, I hope you have money to pay for this ride." I assured him I did. When we reached Chatham, I ordered the driver to head north on that street for Bayard and Arabella's house.

"Well," said Madi, "we were looking for the Jolly Host. There's no argument that we definitely found them."

"Or they found us. How did they know we'd been to see Sharde? Was that Malbaster in the coach that passed us? The one who tossed the head?"

"We'll know for sure where we stand when we reach Miss Dromen's place. If it's still in one piece and the others are alive, it'll be clear that Malbaster and his gang don't know everything yet."

"Somehow they tracked us to the *Cockaigne Times*, though."

"Or it could be that an employee of the paper saw us there and reported our whereabouts to the Host," said Madi.

"Possible," I said, and I dreaded what we would discover at our destination.

Even with the snowdrifts in the street hampering our progress, we made it to Arabella's quickly. I diminished my last twenty dollars by forty cents, and we thanked the driver for a job well done. Alighting from the coach, we didn't bother with hiding behind the juniper trees before scurrying to the front door. The situation was too critical. We bolted for the porch, and I was happy to discover that at least this time the door was locked.

I tapped on it as lightly as possible, not wanting to alert the neighbors. We waited for a few moments, but there was no answer. Madi brushed me aside and pounded on the door.

"Shhh," I admonished.

"It's more dangerous to loiter on the porch in plain sight than to make a little noise," he said.

I took solace in the cover of night. Another minute passed and I was envisioning finding them all with their throats slit, or worse, their heads cut off like poor Rufus, when the door swept back and there stood Arabella wearing her white muslin writing garb, holding a pen in her left hand and exuding the aroma of the poppy. In her right hand was a pistol. Her eyelids were only half open and when she saw us she broke into a wide smile.

"Who goes there?" she said and stepped aside for us to enter. She led us down into the parlor. Mavis was already there, sitting on the yellow couch, her hands clasped across her stomach and her hat tilted back.

"There's stew in the kitchen," said Arabella. Madi went to help himself and she followed him.

I reached into my jacket pocket and retrieved the two envelopes, one with my Malbaster dream and the other the tale of the Indian Caves. When I handed them to Mavis, I said, "I need the old man to follow me on the order of these two."

"He's been somewhat steamed lately," she said. "He was complaining that you're never at your desk. He hasn't seen you in an age. What's this article you refer to about?"

"My meeting with Malbaster."

"You met him?"

"No, but the subject seemed like something I could make hay with."

Mavis raised her eyebrows. I knew that wasn't a good sign, but shrugged it off. Garrick could give me a tongue-lashing when it was most convenient for him. I didn't care. At that point, I'd have just been happy to make it through our ordeal alive. I reached into my trouser pocket and pulled out the sweaty dollars I owed Mavis. I counted out the bills as I handed them to her.

"Good?" I asked.

She nodded.

"Are you staying here?" I asked.

"Are you joking?"

"You think we're in danger staying here?"

She smiled. "I like to keep moving."

"It's going to be tough for us to get out of here with Ahab's son if something happens."

"You need to plan to always be planning," she said.

I laughed.

"The boy has the jibbering sweats."

"He's unwell?"

"Puking his guts up into a bucket," said Mavis. The thought of it made me woozy.

"Do me a favor, when you're in my neighborhood, look in on Misha. Let me know if anything seems amiss."

She nodded.

"Keep a tally and I'll even up with you when the entire gambit is over. We just have to pray that Garrick doesn't fire me."

"I don't pray," she said.

I promised her I'd have another article for her in three days. She left and I locked the door behind her.

Madi and I sat in the kitchen, eating stew. I wanted to say to him that I couldn't clear the image of Sharde's decapitated head out of my own, and somehow, I knew he wanted to tell me the same, but neither of us mentioned it. Instead he told me he thought we'd made some good progress on the West Side.

"What are you talking about? That was a disaster," I said.

"Irony, Harrow. You don't recognize your own tools?"

"I don't know what you're talking about," I said. "Everything I write is emotionally true. And here's a truth for you. It's imminent that we're going to be overrun here by the Jolly Host. They'll swarm upon the walls, break through the windows, and slither down the chimney."

"We have to get out of here," he said.

"That's what Mavis said. Keep moving."

We made a bond that while one of us slept, the other would remain awake to be vigilant against the Host. The thought of being attacked made the spacious home feel claustrophobic. Since returning there, the urge to run throbbed like a drumbeat just beneath the thin layer of my rationale. When Madi left the kitchen to lie down for his hours, I headed to Arabella's writing room. I hesitated for a moment and then knocked on the door.

"Harrow, you may enter," she called.

I wondered how she knew it was me. I opened the door into the blue room and I couldn't make out a thing through the yellowish-white fog. I took a deep breath, closed the door behind me, and dove in. I swept my arms through the swirling smoke and headed toward where I knew she'd be—at the low table, sitting cross-legged on a large cushion.

Eventually, there was a brief break in the cloud cover, and I found Arabella hard at work, the pen looping and scratching out her vision that, according to her, arrived so rapidly that to think would slow her down and she'd lose the story.

I took the same seat as I had last I was there, in the chair across from her. "I want to speak to you, Arabella."

"Speak," she said. Her eyes did not meet mine, but stayed trained on the paper, assiduously tracking the relentless progress of words.

"I'm worried you might not be ready for what's coming," I said.

"What's that?" Still her hand moved.

"The Jolly Host. It may only be days, hours, minutes, before they'll be sweeping through this place, beating, skewering, and shooting us."

"I'm ready."

"How can you be ready? When you greeted us tonight, you seemed more than half asleep on opium. Do you think it's truly a good idea to be smoking it in this house, what with Ahab's son trying to wrestle free of the drug's grasp?"

"It can't be avoided," she said.

"Why? Are you also addicted?"

"No. I can't get addicted. My body reacts to it in a different way than most people's."

"Isn't that what all the addicts say?"

"It's true, Harrow. I'm not making it up."

"What's the difference?" I asked and already I began to feel a slight effervescence at the edge of my consciousness. My mouth went instantly dry.

Keep in mind, she continued writing throughout this entire exchange. "I can resist its negative aspects and use it to nourish and open the seed casing of my mind," she said.

I had to try not to laugh. "Is that really important now, considering all that's happening?"

She stopped and laid the pen down on top of her pages. I could make out through the fog that the ink she used was violet. She stretched and yawned and in that moment was perhaps the most beautiful as ever I'd seen her. "Look, Harrow. I know what I'm doing. Do you really want to know what that is or would you rather simply trust me?"

"I'd feel better if I knew," I said. With those words, the blue walls began to undulate and it seemed we were all at sea. The stars were slowly showing themselves and somehow she was now snuggled next to me as the tiny craft we were in was lifted and lowered by the gentle surf.

"If you must know, I'm trying to reassert myself over the character of the manticore. We need the creature on our side. I'm laying a trail of blood and drawing her back into my fiction."

"And for this you need the smoke?"

"It helps me achieve the state I need to cast my story spell."

"How did Malbaster wrest it from you to begin with?" In my mind's eye, I saw the island Arabella had told me about where her heroine, Seraphita, was washed ashore and transformed into the manticore.

"It must have been through the boy, Gabriel. Time has no direction on the astral plane. Malbaster's effect on the boy has an effect upon his father, who is tied together with me in our current venture. The Pale King Toad explored the cosmos of this, our story. Saw my creation and snatched it with impunity."

"Very well," I said, my legs trembling as I stood. I was slightly dizzy from the smoke of her exhalations, and I knew if I didn't escape at that moment, her explanations would tie my thoughts in knots. It was better I left while I still realized she had lost her grip on reality.

"Do you see what I mean, Harrow?" she said, lifting the pen and beginning to write again.

"Interesting," I said. When I got out in the hallway, I leaned against the wall for a minute, taking deep breaths. I had promised Madi I'd stay awake for four hours while he slept. After five minutes with Arabella, I was ready to lie down and succumb to the sleep of unreason. My nightmares made more sense than her theories, and at the very least I could hide from our troubles. Mavis's words came back to me, and I repeated in a whisper, "Keep moving." I pushed off the wall and went in search of Ahab to get a report on the boy.

I knocked on the half-open door of the room in which Gabriel was our prisoner/patient. Ahab answered in a weary voice, "Come in." I entered and took a seat by the end of the bed. The captain was wringing out a wet rag. He placed it flat upon his son's forehead. The boy looked terrible—an ashen complexion, heavy-lidded eyes half open above puffy dark circles. I noticed a bucket of vomit and a nasty aroma, an amalgamation of puke and sweat and fear. Every now and then Gabriel gave a violent shudder.

"I'm no doctor, but he doesn't look tip-top," I said.

"Harrow, always a master of understatement," said Ahab. He was finally free of the coat we'd taken off the dead man at the Indian Caves and now wore a billowy white shirt patterned with violets.

"Have you slept, Ahab?"

"I doze off and on. Trying to keep the boy comfortable. The worst part has been wrestling him out to the outhouse. My God, what a task. He can barely stand.

"We're in the heart of the squall now," he said. "Another day of this hellish withdrawal and we should begin our ascent out of the darkness.

I swear, Harrow, it's like he's possessed by an evil spirit. After he comes around, the hard part will be to keep him off the poison. I'll stay by his side as long as it takes."

I didn't mean to say it, but I felt it. "You're a good man, Ahab."

"No, mate. I'm a bad man trying to do good."

"As you wish," I said. "By the by, your fashion sense is stunning. That shirt is something."

"Arabella made it for me from a dress left behind here by a very large housekeeper she once had. Took the scissors to it and a needle and thread and turned a circus tent into a nicely fitting top for me. She also combed my hair."

"Your beard's coming back," I said.

"So it is. She asked if I wanted a shave as well, but I'd already put the poor woman out with all our mess."

"To tell the truth, Captain, I think, minus the fact that her man, Otis, took that arrow to the noggin, she's enjoying this venture more than just about anyone else. More than me, I can assure you."

"I don't know if I'm enjoying this. But I'm thankful for the chance to be with my son." Ahab turned his gaze to the dozing boy. "I spoke to him about his mother both while he was awake and asleep, and I told him about my life at sea. When he's awake, he no longer fights me, but simply stares, watching my mouth moving and listening to the words pouring forth. As of yet, he's spoken no civil word to me. But he hasn't called me a *ghost* in at least half a day."

25

I had hours to wait before Madi would relieve my watch, so I sat with the captain. We didn't converse but listened instead to the boy's breathing overlaid by the sound of the winter wind howling outside the windows. Somewhere in those longest minutes of the night, Gabriel suddenly awoke with a fit of coughing. The noise roused me from my stupor. I'd not gone to sleep, but I might as well have. I'd lost track of how long I sat there, a citizen of the vegetable kingdom. My brief encounter with the opium engendered in me a weariness that sleep couldn't touch.

The boy seemed to be upset about something. It was painful to see Ahab attempt to administer to his son. This tough, gruff old sea captain was at a loss when it came to tending a sick child. Eventually Gabriel quieted and sank back into slumber.

The sounds of breathing and the wind returned. Ahab leaned close to the now sleeping Gabriel. His lips were moving, and I heard a low murmuring, but it was difficult to make out what he was saying. I watched as Ahab wrapped his son in words, the way a doctor would treat a wound with bandages, and my mind wove a story from those faint sounds.

Ahab filled the boy's head with images of the great green ocean in both fair and foul weather. There was much talk about the sun, and an entire story wherein the starry constellations walked and breathed at night above the ocean. The captain was haggard, and yet he droned on with determination, casting his spell. He leaned his elbows against the edge of the bed with his hands clasped and his forehead resting upon them.

I'm almost certain he spoke about the most beautiful spot on Earth—a sea cave, its stalagmites and stalactites studded with chunks of crystal that lit like stars when the morning sun slipped into the opening at low tide. There were pink starfish in the knee-high surf and green seal-like creatures that swam around and through a visitor's legs. Ancients had left an altar there hundreds if not thousands of years earlier and the legend had it that if you were to leave an offering of fish or flowers, your life would be blessed with serenity. This place was on a small atoll a hundred and fifty miles due east of New Caledonia and the same distance southwest of Fiji.

Apparently, he was taken there by a group of Brits canvassing the islands of the Pacific, looking for exotic plants in order to gather seeds and specimens for Kew Gardens, the Royal Botanical Society. They'd allowed Ahab to join their expedition as long as he was willing to pitch in with the work on board ship, and if he was patient with their studies and their searching, they promised to drop him as far east as the Pitcairn Islands, where eventually an American ship would stop on its way back to Boston. For one with few funds and no position to bargain, the captain took them up on their offer.

The story snaked its way back into that beautiful cave and from somewhere in Ahab's mumbling I became aware that when the grotto lit with the morning sun, a voice would rise out of the ancient altar and the spirit of a creature on two legs and sporting long flowing hair, the strands of which were imbued with volition like the limbs of an octopus, would be seen to walk away upon the water. I saw all this as he carried on with his incantatory telling. There were swirling colors and a rising tide that might trap them in the cave. And I feared being trapped in the cave myself. I dove into the water to swim for it and soon found I could breathe even though submerged. The water slowly became the night and stars and I was floating, turning slowly head over heels, and . . .

"It was here that I learned the secret to life," Ahab said to his son.

I woke suddenly and before opening my eyes, I thought of Madi and how I'd let him down. At that instant, someone smacked me across the face with the back of his hand. The blow stunned me and chased my consciousness to the brink of darkness. Still, I hung on and opened my eyes and caught sight of Bartleby leaning over me, a glimmering string of drool descending from the corner of his lips toward my open mouth. He had a knife in his hand.

He raised the weapon, and in the moment that followed I saw how he'd been patched since our last encounter with him. The gash Madi had left in his throat had been rudely sewn shut, and ropy scar tissue, whiter than his already deathly pallor, marked where cuts and scrapes had healed without medical attention. He stank like an old foot. What was he? I saw the knife descending and brought my knee up as hard as I could, smashing him in the balls. The knife altered its course and went wide, sticking into the back of the chair.

I shoved him with all my might and he reeled backward across the room. I noticed Ahab was no longer in his chair and Gabriel was gone from the bed. I was stunned by the thought that my weakness might have cost us all our lives. Bartleby gathered his haphazard deathless energy and came at me again. I heard windows breaking in the distance and fire crackling, and I smelled smoke, this time not the poppy. I stood, trembling, and prepared to meet him in battle.

That's when I heard Arabella's voice behind me. "Duck, Harrow," she yelled. I had been staring at the emaciated bone-shop horror that was my assailant, frozen in fear and had only just lowered my head when I heard the gun go off. With the first shot, Arabella blew off a chunk of Bartleby's forehead and forced him backward. I bolted from the chair and moved toward her. She told me to duck again as she aimed her double-barrel pistol. As crumbling brain matter fell out of the ragged wound, Bartleby stumbled toward us like a feeble old man looking for the bathroom in the middle of the night.

She put the second bullet square in the middle of his face and that knocked him over. I felt her hand on my shoulder, and she pulled me with her through the house. We made it to her writing room and she shut the door behind us and locked it. I noticed that the low table she worked upon was kicked over and revealed an open trapdoor. "Hurry, Harrow, they're waiting for us," she whispered.

"What about Madi?" I asked. "Did you get him?"

"Of course," she said. "Did you think me some dithering opium addict fallen asleep on the job?" She was loading two more percussion caps into the pistol. "Now move or they'll be upon us."

I started down the set of steps leading through the rectangle of darkness in the floor. Arabella followed closely, after shutting the trapdoor behind her. When we reached the bottom of the steps, she said, "Straight ahead. It leads to the stable." I put on speed and eventually tripped forward onto a set of steps ascending out of the darkness, putting us in the stable with the coach-and-four. Madi stood at the top of the stairs holding a lantern.

"You're in the coach, Harrow, with Miss Dromen and the boy," he said.

Arabella asked him, "Did you bring George's satchel and my notebooks?"

"They're in the coach," he said.

"Do you know where we're going?" she asked.

He nodded and went to his horse, which was saddled and waiting for him. Then I noticed that Ahab was on the driver's bench of the coach, and an intuitive sense of uncertainty flashed across my mind. Madi's match went out. Arabella and I scrambled into the coach and pulled the door shut. A match flared to life in her fingers, and I saw Gabriel huddled in the corner shivering.

"Now," she yelled and I heard the great doors of the stable sweep open. We began to move. As we turned left on Bayard, I heard the hoofbeats of Madi's mount head off to the right. The next I knew, we were jostling and bouncing through the night at top speed. It was hard to hear with the racket of the coach traveling over rough road, but I was too nervous to stay quiet.

"Where are we going?" I asked.

"I have a place on St. John's Park," said Arabella.

"Madi and I were in that area today."

"It was a very posh neighborhood at one time, but its charms are quickly diminishing. Still, I thought we could confound the Jolly Host for at least a few weeks if we holed up there."

Gabriel hid his face in the corner and it sounded as if he was weeping. I looked at him and then to Arabella. She pointed at the boy and with her other hand pinched her nose to indicate that he stank. I was trying to ignore the fact that he'd most certainly shit his trousers.

"I'm working on gaining control of the manticore," she said. "Once I have her back in my possession, we can strike."

"How exactly do you get her into your *possession*?" I asked.

"I write to see where her story is going, to find a place where I can meet her and regain control. What I'm looking for in the storyline is a cross-roads, a juncture where the boundaries of our personal tales intersect with the tales of others. I must be on the lookout for it every time I put pen to paper. And when it presents itself, I must act swiftly and decisively. If I can do that, we'll have the manticore grind Malbaster to salt for us."

Gabriel's aroma comingled with Arabella's fanciful nonsense made me slightly ill. I closed my eyes and leaned into my own corner of the coach. Through slightly parted lids, I saw Arabella, her face partially lit by moonlight, staring out the window at the passing night. In all she was a remarkable woman. Not but twenty minutes earlier, she'd saved my life from that persistent revenant, Bartleby. On the one hand, I had the overwhelming suspicion that she was, in her way, as crazy as Ahab, what with her theories of intersecting fictions and the like. My God, I'd never heard such twaddle, and yet I'd have to say, I trusted her implicitly. Even when three sheets to the wind on the opium, she had a clearer head than I.

Ahab eventually slowed the horses to a reasonably brisk walk. If one wants to remain anonymous, blasting around Manhattan in a coach-and-four isn't the way to do it. I was delighted we'd slowed. I don't think Ahab had slept in days and I didn't fancy winding up in a ditch. I lost track of where exactly we were. My presumption was that we'd gone north and then west, perhaps on Walker Street. I looked over to ask Arabella, but it appeared she was wrapped in deep contemplation. She had lit a small lantern within the coach and its dim light cast her face in a soft glow, making it seem more beautiful than ever.

Gabriel sat up straight. He looked at me as if I'd summoned him to consciousness. His face was flushed and his hair wild. He was a handsome young man, or at least would be with some convalescence. I didn't see any trace of Ahab in his looks, which was all for the better I suppose.

"Relax, my boy," I said. "We'll be there soon enough."

I recognized for the first time that he was wearing the old overcoat we'd lifted off the dead man at the Indian Caves. His expression didn't grow less frantic with my advice. Instead of leaning back into the corner, he lunged past both me and Arabella and hit the handle on the door. It flew open, the wind burst in, and he leaped out into the dark. I heard him hit the road with a grunt. After I yelled for Ahab to stop, I could hear Gabriel's footsteps headed back downtown.

By this point, Arabella was alert. She looked around, noticing the boy gone and the door ajar. She grabbed her pistol off the seat and jumped out the open door after Gabriel. I supposed I bore some responsibility, and although the last thing I wanted was to be gallivanting around in freezing temperatures at four in the morning, I also leaped out and followed Arabella. In a moment, Ahab was beside me, begging to know what had happened.

"It's your blasted son," I called to him over the wind. "He's escaped. Go back and get the coach and try to follow us."

He stayed beside me. "Harrow, if he manages to get back to Malbaster, I'll lose him forever."

"Go," I yelled at him and was surprised that he responded to my command.

Since meeting the captain and being drawn into his quest, I'd done more running than is seemly for a man half my age. Still, I poured on what speed I could, hoping to catch up to Arabella.

It was dark and cold and I couldn't tell if snow was falling or if the wind was merely whipping up what had already fallen. I stayed in the middle of the road as the traffic of carts and cabs had tamped down the drifts and made the going easier than on the sidewalk. Every block or so, I'd come to a gas lamp and standing beneath it I'd turn in each direction to see if I might catch a glimpse of Arabella. By my estimation, we were somewhere close to Broadway when I finally caught up to her.

"Have you seen him?" I asked.

"I lose sight of him and then I catch a glimpse."

"Is he insane?"

She shook her head. "At times, he seems to have a destination in mind, but he switches course, probably to put us off his trail."

"Where do you think he's going?"

"Well, what does he want right now more than anything?"

"The smoke."

"He could be heading for Astor's stash."

Two blocks over, we saw him pass like a phantom beneath a gas lamp, and we were off.

Arabella and I tracked Gabriel for more than an hour, until it was nearly dawn. I thought for sure he would ultimately elude us, but she proved to be an effective hunter. Her quick thinking allowed us to somehow get ahead of him and trap him in an alleyway near the corner of Chapel and Thomas Streets. I was loath to enter the dark maw of the passageway to extricate him. Arabella had her pistol, but it wouldn't have done to shoot the lad. The best I could think now was to call into the shadows within which he hid and try to convince him that it was a good idea to come with us. My attempts were met with silence.

We noticed that the sun was on the rise, and the last thing we wanted to do was be seen making a scene in broad daylight. News on the street in Manhattan travels faster than a spark on a fuse. We needed in the worst way not to be brought to the attention of the Jolly Host. I was so sick of them and wanted more than anything to get to Arabella's place by St. John's Park and sleep without worry for a few hours.

"We've got to get away from here," said Arabella. "I'm going to go and get him." She held the gun up in front of her and moved slowly into the alley.

"Do you think that's a good idea?" I asked, certainly not following her. She shook her head at me in seeming annoyance.

As she moved into the alleyway, the sun came over the buildings across the street and followed her to vanish the night. Gabriel was nowhere to be seen. The alley's only occupant was Arabella. She walked to the middle of the passageway and turned in a circle. "Where?" she said to me.

Within the next heartbeat, he'd appeared, as if from thin air, grabbed her by the throat, and seized her gun. It happened so suddenly, I literally jumped in the air, both feet leaving the ground. It came to me instantly what a stew of fine-feathered shit I was in. My two options were to flee, my old standby, or to challenge Gabriel and rescue the moment. Let it not be said that Harrow shirked his heroic duty. I inched toward the situation like a bowl of jelly, frantically searching for the words with which to intercede.

"Now, now," was the best I could do. I saw Gabriel's finger tighten on the trigger. The barrel was resting against Arabella's cheek. I felt that if I said one more word, he'd fire and tear her face off. I even tried to hide the fact that I was breathing. For a solid minute, we stood frozen, staring at each other. The boy's look was one of anguish, and the eyes were piercing, seeing through me to somewhere far away. She, on the other hand, shot a look at me that as much as said, *Do something.*

I hung there between their gazes until I heard wheels and hooves on the cobblestones at the top of the alley behind me. I turned to see Ahab on the coach. When he spoke, it was in a voice from the deep ocean. "Gabriel," he said. "Come now. Come to your father."

To my amazement, the young man dropped the gun and released Arabella. He walked forward with his head down. I stepped aside to give him a wide berth and watched as he continued to the coach and hoisted himself up on the driver's seat next to Ahab, who put his arm around the lad's shoulders. I looked at Arabella and she at me with wonder. The captain had talked his way into Gabriel's head, which didn't seem completely for the best. Still, he had the boy and we were all safe, on our way to St. John's Park.

26

The second Dromen property was even more spacious and beautifully appointed than the first. Arabella said it had been her father's place. When we trundled Gabriel through the front door, Madi was waiting for us, dressed in a jade green silk robe and slippers. He smiled when I commented on his costume, and he told me he'd found it in an upstairs bedroom closet.

I wandered down a hallway, found the first open room with a bed, and lay down. I didn't care if the Jolly Host was coming down the chimney or if Bartleby was hiding in the closet, I needed sweet sleep. While out cold I had a series of dreams, none but one that I could recall.

I cleared my eyes before the window and stared out at the lowering sky. It was time to find Madi and to go in search of the opium warehouse. Back in the parlor, I encountered Ahab and his son. Gabriel had cleaned up and put on new clothes. He still looked beset by withdrawal from the drug, but he was no longer twisting and snarling like an animal in a trap. Even Ahab had tended to his appearance. He had groomed his beard and exchanged his violet-patterned shirt for a formal white one. Miss Dromen's dead father was a font of fashion. Eventually I, too, would no doubt look through his wardrobe for a change of clothes.

Ahab turned upon my entering the room and when he saw me, he said to his son, "This, my boy, is Harrow. He's been assisting me in my search for you. I want you to apologize to him for leading him and Miss Dromen on their early-morning hunt."

Gabriel, his complexion grayer than the overcast sky, nodded in my direction and asked for my forgiveness.

"Quite all right, son," I said, ever magnanimous. There was no sense in relating how I'd wanted to punch his face while trudging through the snow at four A.M.

I found Madi in the kitchen, brewing a pot of coffee. As I poured myself a cup, I said to the harpooneer, "The captain's son looks like he's coming around."

"But can we trust him?" asked Madi.

"You should have been there," I said and related how Ahab had given one calm, simple command and the boy had acquiesced.

"While you were asleep, Harrow, we asked him if he knew where the store of opium is. He said he knew that one existed but he'd never been to it. Malbaster kept its secret whereabouts shared with very few. 'I tried to follow them to it once,' Gabriel told us, 'but I got caught and the Pale King Toad had them give me a beating.'"

After a brief meal, Madi, Arabella, and I set out with eyes and ears open for news of the Jolly Host. She took Madi's horse and went north on Washington up past Canal Street. I went back to Chambers Street, thinking it would probably be safer for me to poke around there than Madi. Madi went as far south as Liberty and canvassed the area from the Hudson back to Broadway for signs of promising warehouses or criminal activity.

This we did for three days running and each of us saw undeniable signs that the Host were at work on the West Side. On her second day, Arabella broke up an assault on a young Irish woman who was innocently carrying laundry to wealthy clients. Three scruffy, empty-eyed members of the Host had the young woman on the ground and were tearing at her garments, when Miss Dromen rode up behind them and shot one in the ass with her pistol. The other two came for her and she shot one in the kneecap and beat the hell out of the other with the butt of the gun. When all was said and done and the assailants were gone, she helped the poor girl to her feet, smoothed her dress, and assisted her in gathering the laundry tumbled from her cart.

She told us about it that evening, saying, "It was the best thing I've done in an age. Once we're finished with Malbaster, I might become a vigilante who rides throughout Manhattan shooting the peckers off scallywags who dare to test a woman's honor."

Madi had stories to match Arabella's of the abuse he witnessed perpetrated by the Host against his people or the Catholics. It was roving packs of three or four grubby young men, set on making trouble for all those scorned by the Order of the Star-Spangled Banner. I saw the same. And with my connections in the penny press, I got reports of other, more clandestine crimes—bodies hung by the neck in an old burnt-out warehouse near the Hudson; a place of worship for the poor, ransacked and set afire; and a lot of thievery, of individuals and also of small businesses run by blacks and Germans. Malbaster's minions kept up a constant barrage of fear in those communities. At the least, they injured people and when they knew they could get away with it, they committed murder.

Gabriel told us that the participation of some of the boys made no sense, as they were from the very communities targeted by Malbaster. So many unthinkable acts—children beating a parent to death with an iron pipe; setting fire to the only ramshackle school available to them; threatening violence against their neighbors—all of that could be satisfactorily explained by the opium, if you knew the opium. However, Malbaster did not allow the papist or the colored members of the Host to get too powerful. Once they'd done his bidding for a few years, he would cast them off and in turn they would be harassed, beaten, robbed, and killed. Only white male Protestants got a lifelong membership.

On our second night of searching for signs of the Host, we met back at Arabella's home. Sitting in the kitchen at the table, drinking a midnight cup of coffee, Madi made an observation that got me thinking. He said, "I've memorized, as you have, the sites of a number of incidents involving Malbaster's army, but I wish I could somehow fly above the streets and watch the whole thing unfold, get the big picture and chart the comings and goings of the Host as if they were a colony of ants. It would be easier to see where the action is concentrated and maybe even to discover the opium stash by seeing the areas of concentrated activity."

On the third day of the search, I decided to break from the cold and retired to a pleasant neighborhood groggery. Finding a comfortable chair in a quiet corner, I ordered a whiskey with hot water and honey. Taking my notebook, ink, pen, pounce pot, and eraser from my satchel, I set out to chronicle a dream of the manticore I'd had a few nights previously. With any luck I could spin my nocturnal phantasm into a piece that Garrick would print.

That dream was murky, and although there was a thing or two I could recall, try as I might I could not come up with enough material for a full article. I sipped the toddy and rubbed my eyes, and when it seemed not a single idea would arise, the door to the establishment opened and in walked a woman outfitted in riding gear and carrying a short shotgun over her right shoulder like a soldier on parade. She headed directly for me. When she reached up and doffed her sizable hat, I realized it was Arabella.

The last thing I needed at the moment was company, seeing as I had to turn out an article before the sun went down. Still, she looked lovely as ever and was, for me, always a welcome sight.

"Are you busy, Harrow?" she asked.

Her smile was so disarming, I shook my head even as I whispered, "Deadline. How'd you find me?"

"Easy. I asked if anyone had seen a handsome fellow with a satchel round his neck. The policeman on the corner pointed me to this establishment."

"Why were you looking for me?"

"I'm bored sneaking into and trudging through old warehouses. There must be a better way to find Malbaster. I can't say what would be better but this seems excruciatingly slow."

"And yet," I said, "Malbaster seems everywhere and nowhere."

"That, Harrow, is not far from the reported actuality. My father always spoke of him as if he was a living, breathing, man, but there is much mythology about the Pale King Toad."

I pulled my notebook and the portable inkwell closer. I uncorked the bottle and dipped the steel nib of my pen into the blood of my profession. "Now, about this mythology," I said.

Arabella proceeded to tell me all she knew. As she spoke I brought my considerable talents of embellishment to bear and gave her testimony form and direction.

It was said that Malbaster was not born from the womb of a woman, but instead coalesced like an angry storm cloud during a riot in the Five Points brought on by nationalist factions attacking a dance where Irish and colored mixed. To the best of anyone's recollection, the great white planet of a head was nowhere to be seen when the trouble started, but as things went from bad to worse——from bashed heads and busted kneecaps to shivved kidneys and discharged pistols——more participants seemed to recall his hulking presence. It was as if he was whirled together in the tumult of the mob's hatred and fueled by the fear of those who were persecuted. He quickly consolidated and expanded with each anguished cry.

From the bloody remains of the dance hall melee, toting a billy club in one hand and a ten-inch blade in the other, he floated away from the chaos and disappeared down an alleyway when the police showed. It was said that the cops gave chase, but, upon investigation, that alley, which had no outlet, proved to be empty.

Thence forward, those with a nationalist bent began to notice Malbaster at gatherings of the Order of the Star-Spangled Banner and various Know-Nothing events——wherever persecution was in the offing. It was not that he was seen arriving and leaving, but more that he simply appeared among the throng of true believers when the vitriol grew most fervent and disappeared when the hate was a cooling ember.

His bulbous head was roundly admired, as it was perceived a symbol of intelligence. "Think of the load of brains what is contained therein," claimed those whose proof of acumen and judgment was itself in short supply. For those wretches of the unwanted classes who came in contact with the phenomenon of Malbaster, that inflated head bespoke so much foul air, as if a pin might be employed to prove there was nothing beneath the surface.

At times, he was asked to speak, and it was evident he was no orator. His vocabulary was limited, but he spoke in such vague generalizations that the throngs of his compatriots found in his words enough room to nurture their own grievances and fears. His message was one of selfishness. "Life and resources and wealth are limited. They should be only for those of us who resemble those of us. All others should be driven out and/or dispatched of." A simple enough ideology for the masses.

Then, some years ago, Malbaster began to attract a following of young men and boys, some of whom had parents among the persecuted. It was his demand of strict allegiance, his dim encompassing philosophy, his childlike messages of "Me First," and a quest for the reclamation of white Protestant superiority that had never gone missing. There was also something else, some unknown factor, that had them following him like rats behind the piper of Hamelin. Soon enough it was discovered not so much to be sorcery but instead, plain and simple, the spell of the yellow smoke.

He engendered his followers with his spirit and as time went on, and their numbers grew, they engendered him with theirs. That negative energy reportedly gave him power beyond normal ken. Some called it magic, others thought it worked more like animal magnetism or the techniques of Franz Mesmer. In combination with the tar, he was capable of producing hallucinatory effects that frightened or delighted his followers into his mind-set.

It was in 1847 that Astor first discovered someone had been stealing from the secret store of opium that he had amassed during his years in that trade. It had once been his intention to loose the drug upon New York society, creating a catalyst for greater trade from which he could reap a windfall. As he got older though, Astor's disposition changed and his desire for yet more wealth gave way to a predilection for cultural and political causes.

When he died, it was reported that Astor was worth twenty million dollars, but in reality it was half that amount. The newspapers reported that he died of "natural causes." At eighty-four, his body simply failed him. One of his most trusted valets, a young man by the name of Otis Truc, testified to any who would listen that his employer, on the day before he planned to hire private investigators to track down who had been stealing from him and to order the destruction of his opium stores, was visited by a pale, large-headed man. Following that private meeting, Astor was beset by harrowing hallucinations, visions of finger-length demons tormenting him. Eventually, he fell into a coma and never recovered.

It was the young lads who followed Malbaster, the horde he'd named "the Jolly Host," for reasons none can guess, who first referred to him as the Pale King Toad. They claimed that he had a damp, dank aroma, the smell of mildew and moss. He spoke not from his chest and lungs but from the waggling waddle beneath his chin, and the sound reminded one of a frog's call in early spring. In addition, his flesh, if you were unlucky enough to come in contact with it, was clammy and cold. His gaze was unblinking and sly as a snake's and, when he witnessed the anguish of those he put to torture, he was as unmoved as a toad.

No one knows how vast Malbaster's operation is. There's a certainty that it extends beyond the boundaries of Manhattan. There are accounts of him having appeared at lynchings as far south as Georgia and at anti-emancipation rallies as far west as Kansas. Funny thing is that despite all the blood that's been shed and the cruelty dispensed, he and his followers claim to be in the employ not of nationalist extremists but of God himself. They see their work as a glorious moral crusade against the shiftless, the backsliding, the inferior who have infiltrated the shores of the New Eden and like Satan, who leaped over the wall of the Garden, are here to undermine the foundation of all that is good and wholesome.

Malbaster cannot be killed. To shoot him, to stab him, is to attack a pervasive idea. He cannot be imprisoned, for what wall or iron bars can contain a notion? He strikes outward from his ephemeral center and inflicts physical harm on those struggling to make a place in a new world. He is Leviathan, a white behemoth, a superstitious dread, crackling with the million individual sparks of petty intolerance, humming with a chorus of idiot bigotry.

When Arabella finished with her mythology of Malbaster, I asked her, "Was the Otis Truc you mentioned your valet, Otis?"

She had to catch her breath as the recitation of her truths seemed to upset her greatly. She was flushed in the face and subtly trembling. "Yes," she said, moving her hand across her left eye as if perhaps brushing away a tear. In one sure draught, she finished off her toddy and called to the barkeep for another.

For my part, I took my penknife out of my satchel and proceeded to cut the article from the notebook. I found her summation of Malbaster stirring but altogether outlandish. There was something of religious oratory to it, and it carried much of the same exaggeration. Still, I needed an article, and here was one. Malbaster, an evil for the ages. I saw him as more a petty criminal with a murderous streak, who used said intolerance as a means of financial gain. That said, my readers desired the fantastic in some form or another, and with this piece I offered a bogeyman that would be the more effective because they just might dimly recognize something of themselves in the monster.

27

On the way back to her home on St. John's Park, I strode along-side Arabella who rode atop Madi's horse. The dark came early as the month was drawing closer to Christmas. The snow had partially melted and the going wasn't as rough as it had been earlier. We passed a child selling gourds and small pumpkins looking the worse for wear as they no doubt had been picked months earlier. Still, Arabella bought an armful from him, and I got the honor of carrying the load. Once we were a block away from the house, she told me to throw them in a waste bin.

I asked about her progress with the manticore.

She shook her head and told me, "It's an arduous process, Harrow. I've reached the point in my story where I can make the creature recite her poetry for me, but I wouldn't trust her with your life."

"That's not a comfort," I said. "Does Malbaster suspect that you're trying to reclaim her?"

"He must know something's afoot. I'm sure I've affected the creature to the point where she's not answering his call with lightning speed any longer."

"Have you a sense of how much more it will take for you to be successful?" I asked.

"Not yet. I need to write through it more. If we could distract Malbaster with our attack on his opium, I think I could steal her."

"You know, I believe I can locate the warehouse where Astor stored the tar."

"How's that, Harrow? Prayer?" She laughed.

Her response cut me to the quick. If anything, I wanted her to consider me at least reliable. "See if I don't come up with the answer tomorrow. You'll accompany me. If I'm right, you'll owe me an apology."

"Very well."

As we approached Arabella's place, I heard a voice call my name from the park across the street. I was rattled, for being recognized anywhere other than in the neighborhood of my home or work was alarming. I looked up and saw a figure walking unhurriedly toward us. Arabella, still upon the horse, had pulled her pistol.

"Don't shoot, Harrow, or your article will never reach the *Mirror* on time." With that, I recognized the voice and the figure. Arabella begged the messenger's pardon for having drawn on her. Mavis shrugged.

We entered the house through the back door and were not inside longer than a heartbeat before it became clear that a crisis was unfolding. We heard Ahab's voice, bellowing, "Open up, boy, or you'll ruin everything." Arabella, Mavis, and I followed the cries to the room in this house that Arabella used for her writing. Ahab was pounding on the door and Madi stood behind him, looking aggravated.

"What's the uproar?" I asked as we all crowded into the hallway.

"Last night," said Madi, "Gabriel noted the scent of the smoke emanating from this room. He's locked himself inside."

"All will be lost," cried Ahab melodramatically as if he were no longer a real person but had stepped freshly from Ishmael's book.

"Let's be calm," I said.

"Miss Dromen, I beg permission to break the door down," said the captain.

At this, Mavis stepped between him and the door. She took an exceedingly thin blade from somewhere in the waist of her trousers, stuck the point of it in the keyhole, turned her wrist, and the door swung open. She marched in straightaway. The rest of us gathered at the entrance as she strode toward Gabriel. It was clear he was trying to light the pipe.

"Give it to me," said Mavis.

He rose from the chair at the desk and backed away.

She advanced and reached for the pipe.

He put his elbow out to block her.

And that was it for Mavis, who was willing to entertain foolishness for about a solid moment. With one snake-strike right cross, her fist connected with Gabriel's chin. I saw his eyes roll up, and, as he fell to the floor, she reached out and snatched the pipe from him. Ahab rushed in, the sound of his ivory leg tattooing the wooden floor, and took her in his arms.

"My dear, you're an angel!" he proclaimed.

The captain gathered up his boy and threw him over one shoulder like he was hauling a sack of potatoes.

Later, after Gabriel had come around, Ahab didn't harangue his son about the incident. He seemed to understand that the boy was wrestling his own angel or demon and that it did no good to browbeat him any further. Instead of punishing the lad, he made him help in the kitchen where he concocted for us a sailor's stew of onions and carrots and mutton that turned out close to edible.

After dinner, I sat with Mavis in the parlor and asked for news. After assuring me that all was well with Misha, she said, "Garrick, though, says you've gone round the bend in your articles, and he keeps threatening the empty air that your termination is in the offing, but I've heard from Jack Coffee that your Ahab pieces are actually selling like hotcakes. I think the boss just wants to see you. When you're gone too long, he fears you'll be snatched away by a competitor. Someone told him you were recently at the *Cockaigne Times*."

"He's got nothing to worry about," I told her and then laid out the tale of what had transpired as a result of our meeting with Rufus Sharde.

"Malbaster means business," she said, having winced only slightly when I described my old mentor's head rolling around on the street. I suppose that for Mavis, a wince was as good as a gasp.

I fetched my satchel and took out the new article on Malbaster's mythology, an envelope, and my seal. As I was dripping hot wax upon the envelope leaf, I said to Mavis, "You've got one hell of a punch."

"You mean Gabriel?" she said.

"Have you punched anybody since?"

She shook her head and looked away shyly. "He's sweet," she said.

I almost dripped hot wax on my hand, but tried to stay calm. "Sweet?" I said, keeping a straight face.

An instant later I felt the barrel of her pistol poke my ribs and saw a fleeting smile cross her lips. I noticed that even after I'd given her the sealed envelope, she lingered awhile in the parlor, sitting on the yellow satin couch with Gabriel, who'd come in from the kitchen. They spoke in near whispers, conspiratorially, the way young people do when vultures like the rest of us are lurking.

The next morning, we were up early, and Arabella and Madi and I took the coach, Arabella driving, to the offices of the *Gorgon's Mirror*. The previous evening I'd made the outlandish promise to them that on the morrow I'd reveal the location of Malbaster's stockpile of opium. They were, of course, skeptical, and who could blame them, but it was too difficult for me to explain. The remaining snow had turned to slush in the bright morning sun, which brought the temperature at least five degrees above freezing for the first time in two weeks. The city was a muddy, melting mess.

Unfortunately, Garrick was in his office when I tried to sneak by and slip my compatriots in with me. I heard him bellow "Harrow!" as we were making for the back rooms, and I froze in my tracks. And so it was that we were drawn into his smoke-filled lair and I was made to explain everything. I stammered as I introduced him to my coconspirators. The old man sat there, staring disapprovingly, but managed a genial-enough nod for both Arabella and Madi.

"Now, Harrow," he said, "what in God's name are you up to? Mavis dropped off your article late last night, and I read it this morning, and I fear you're off your chump. Manticores and fellows with balloon heads, opium, scheming nativists. Where is all this leading? The public loves a good confabulation, but have you not gone too far?"

Madi and Arabella were afforded chairs but I had to stand before my employer like a child brought up to the front of the class to recite before a strict teacher. "Well, sir, what I've written so far is all true."

Garrick laughed. "It can't be. It shan't be. I'm paying you to bamboozle the public, not me. This can't be anything but hot air rising between your ears. And another thing, where's that Ahab fellow? You've exchanged him for this lovely young lady and a black man?"

"You've read the articles, sir," I said. "My friends will attest that what I've written is mostly true."

"The manticore certainly exists," said Arabella, "in a manner of mythic fictional confluence."

Garrick gave me a puzzled look.

"Miss Dromen's a transcendentalist," I offered, and he nodded as if that explained everything.

Garrick looked at Madi, and the harpooneer said, "I'd not claim the same level of truth that Harrow does for his writings, but there is enough of it in them to the point where you should believe him."

"Harrow, I've told you I'm done with this. I've given you firm orders to move on. Mavis swears she's passed on my directives."

"Mr. Garrick, I . . ."

"But I must admit, the damn *Mirror* is selling better than ever, and I can't refute the fact that it's because of this cockeyed story you've been penning piecemeal, like a mosaic, a tile of the goings-on here, a tile there, leaving it to the reader to discern and comprehend the whole."

"Then what's the problem, sir?"

The old man shook his head. "It's very different."

"Yes, sir."

"A foolish consistency is the hobgoblin of little minds," Arabella slipped in.

"How much more of it is there, would you say?" asked the boss.

"If our journey to see Mrs. Pease today goes well, not much longer at all."

"Mrs. Pease?" he asked. "I've not heard her name mentioned in these offices for quite some time. Is she still back there?"

"Every day, sir."

"I'll have to look to see what I'm paying her. What about Ahab?"

"He's with his son, whom we found and secured, as I related in the article, battling forces of evil at the Indian Caves."

Garrick threw his head back and laughed. "Harrow, Harrow, Harrow, you are an inveterate bullshit artist of the first water. I loved the Indian Caves installment. All right, onward then. Stir up some more whim-wham for our customers and finish this hugger-mugger."

"One thing, sir."

"What?" he said, tamping out his cigar.

"I'll need more ready cash to keep the carnival running."

"Oh, ready cash, as opposed to cash that is not so ready—what?—to be spent?"

Madi was giving me a look as if to say, *How can you put up with this pompous ass?* He just didn't understand Garrick, because, as I knew the old man would, he swiveled round in his chair and reached for his treasure chest. He inserted the key on his watch fob and opened the thing. The hinges squealed. He brought out six three-dollar bills. "Eighteen dollars, Harrow, and that's the end of it. I don't care if you're bringing down the bleeding devil himself."

As I stepped forward and took the money, Madi said, "That may be exactly what we're doing."

When our business was concluded, Garrick nodded to my companions and said, "A pleasure meeting you both." They rose and we headed for the door. At the last moment, as I passed the threshold into the editorial room, he called to me, "You must retain a zest for the battle."

"Yes, sir," I called over my shoulder.

I led my friends through the offices, and when I passed my desk, I reached out and ran my hand over the scored and ink-stained surface. I suppose that like Garrick, I too wanted to return to the world of daydreams that didn't bite back. I'd already tried to step out of this adventure once, though, and didn't like it at all. There was something powerful in being part of it.

As we made our way to the far back room and Mrs. Pease's system, I tried to explain to Madi and Arabella how it worked. Neither of them made any indication that they understood the drift of it, and when finally we arrived and stepped inside, Arabella said, "Why, George, you've brought us to a darkroom."

"Mrs. Pease," I called out. We stood for a few moments and Madi told me that all the excitement had finally gotten to me. "No, no," I said, "look," and pointed. From off in the dark distance, a small flickering light appeared as if the room were two city blocks deep. "Our answer approaches."

I introduced her to Madi and Arabella and she sat down at her desk. The pince-nez came off, and she rubbed her eyes. "I'm just back from a tour of the system."

"What did you learn?" I asked.

"Too much."

We stood around the desk in the candlelight and no one knew where to begin. Finally, Madi asked, "Do you know the Jolly Host?"

"I can't remember anything I've read about them, but I know they're in the system," said Mrs. Pease.

"They're a street gang of sorts," I told her. "I need any information about crimes they've committed west of Broadway, most important, where those crimes took place. I want to compile those locations and plot them on a map like the one you showed me when I was last here."

Only after saying it out loud did it strike me how inane my scheme was. Things just didn't add up. I was about to apologize for wasting all our time, when Mrs. Pease looked up, smiling. "I can do that," she said. She put her specs back on and lifted her candleholder.

Arabella slipped into the desk chair as Mrs. Pease slipped out. I lit a match and by its dim light found two more chairs. A quick search of the desk turned up two more candles, which I lit. And then the waiting began, the minutes growing heavy, inflated like Malbaster's head. From far off in the dim hallways of the system, I heard filing cabinet drawers opening and closing, and then the faint sounds of a baby crying. I cocked my ear and leaned forward, and from a different direction there came a vague impression of howling. A moment later, I was unsure I'd heard anything other than the three of us breathing.

28

We sat in silence for so long, I nearly fell asleep. After a period, perhaps twenty-five minutes, perhaps an hour—it was hard to tell how long, sitting there in the dark—Madi finally spoke and broke the spell.

"So this place is wall-to-wall file drawers, in which articles from all the papers in the city are catalogued?"

"That's right."

"Why is it so damned dark?" asked Arabella.

"That was my question," I said. "If you look closely at Mrs. Pease, you'll notice she's losing the color from her eyes like a fish living in an underground pool."

"Certainly strange," she said and shook her head.

"If she does as you've asked, she'll return with a map that notes all the places the Host have been reported disturbing the peace in recent years?" asked Madi.

"I got the idea from you," I said. "Do you remember mentioning that you wished you could be above the street and see it all laid out below you?"

"Ahhh."

"There's only one problem," I said.

"What's that?"

"The problem is," said Arabella, "you're assuming that wherever they store the opium will be at the *center* of their operations. There's a crass old saying about woodland creatures, Harrow—perhaps you don't know it—but it is, 'Wild animals don't shit where they eat.'"

"I take it that's a metaphor," I said. "Here's another one. The opium is the heart of Malbaster's operation, the center of his power."

"I like it," said Madi, "but Miss Dromen is right. Yours seems to be *Gorgon's Mirror*–type wishful thinking."

"We'll see," I said. "If it turns out to be as wide of the mark as you suggest, I'll somehow make it up to you both."

More time passed, and just when I thought we might have to send a search party after her, I noticed the faint glow of Mrs. Pease's candle approaching.

We watched the candle flame grow in brightness as it floated through the far-off dark. "Speaking of metaphor," said Arabella, "I imagine that this is what happens when we conjure a memory. Everybody has a Mrs. Pease behind their eyes."

"I think of this place as the memory of New York City," I said.

Mrs. Pease placed her candle on the desk. She laid a large sheet of paper in the pool of brightness. I saw it was a chart of Manhattan Island with streets and some buildings clearly marked as they were on the Mitchell map she'd shown me on my last visit. Arabella vacated the chair and let the librarian sit. We gathered round her as she fished a sharpened pencil from her desk drawer.

In less than two minutes, working, as far as I could tell, solely from memory, she circled about a dozen and a half places on the map, all west of Broadway, south of Franklin Street, and north of Albany.

Madi leaned over Mrs. Pease's left shoulder and said, "Where's the center of the activity?"

"Seems to be the very west end of Fulton Street, right down on the Hudson," said Arabella.

"Have you ever been there?" asked Madi.

"I must have passed it," she said, "but I don't recall."

"Same here," I said. "Mrs. Pease?"

"Oh, many years ago, I had a lover over that way. He was delightful.

Quite a romantic. We ended up marrying. That would be Mr. Pease, passed on now ten years."

"Do you recall the area?" I asked.

"No, and after all this time in the dark and living alone, I remember less the face of my husband, although sometimes I feel him trying to reach me from the other side through the system."

"Lovely, I suppose," said Arabella.

Mrs. Pease's reverie waxed bizarre and the further she went with it, the more I doubted my assumptions about the location being represented now by what was on the map. So we took it, thanked her profusely, and made a rapid departure. As we passed through the offices, Garrick spotted me and waved for me to reenter his lair. I waved back and kept walking, too excited to tarry. I wanted to see what was there on Fulton Street.

Back at the coach, Arabella called down from the driver's seat, "To the Hudson."

I nodded and Madi and I got in the cab.

Minutes later, we were there on the corner of Fulton and West Streets. We left the coach in an empty lot and walked toward the water, finally stopping beneath the eaves of an empty boathouse. We unfolded the map and held it between us, studying it. None of the buildings that lined the street were big enough to hold what I'd envisioned as a mountain of opium. The surrounding structures were well-to-do residences with hedges and lawns. I couldn't imagine any one of them harboring a nefarious cargo.

"What's that?" asked Madi, pointing out toward the river.

Across West Street and down at the end of a long pier was an abandoned oyster barge. It was basically an enormous floating warehouse that could easily accommodate thousands of boxes of tar. The exterior was chipped blue-and-white paint stained with rust, a few of the windows in the pilot's cabin were smashed, and its wood was barnacled and splintered, but it was most definitely seaworthy.

"Perfect disguise," said Madi.

It seemed unlikely, and Arabella didn't think much of the idea. I wanted to get away from my embarrassment of having dragged them over to the Hudson on a wild-goose chase. And then Madi said, "Look, there's a boat . . ."

We could just make out a small boat carrying two men, one rowing. We kept our eyes on it for quite some time as it pulled up to the barge and, within a matter of minutes, began a return trip. When they reached the shore, they were carrying wooden chests. We could also see at least one man who remained behind to guard the barge. He had a rifle and appeared to be alone. We stood there for an hour while two more dinghies visited the oyster barge, picked up wooden chests, and returned to shore. As we made our way back to the coach, we concurred that the oyster barge must be the hiding place of Astor's opium hoard.

Back in the coach, we began our return journey from the Hudson docks straight across Manhattan. I was anxious to check in on Misha before doing anything else. All Madi could do was talk about the coming confrontation when we would lay waste to the opium-filled barge and finally destroy Malbaster. "It won't be long now," he said, a half-crazed, murderous glint in his eye. "I'm ready." I looked away.

I was anything but ready. Honestly, if it weren't for the promise we'd made to help each other, I'd have given Madi the slip. We were going to war with Malbaster on an epic scale, compromising his livelihood and threatening his means of influence over the Host by setting fire to his opium. It was about to get very dangerous and very harrowing for old Harrow. When I'd started the whole danse macabre, my goal was solely to reunite Ahab and his son. That, I'd accomplished. To continue down this road, to risk my life to see the grotesque Malbaster slain, had lost its appeal. Still, I'm a man of my word. And beyond that the story had gotten its hooks in me; I was compelled to see how it would play out.

Arabella pulled the coach-and-four over to the curb in front of my home, and I got out. Not wanting to draw attention to our presence, I suggested she and Madi drive around the streets for a few minutes, and I'd be out presently. By the time I knocked at the front door, the coach had turned onto South Street and disappeared. There was no answer. I knocked again. Nothing. I turned the knob and the door opened.

"No, no, no," I whispered to myself as I made my way through the foyer to the hallway, my insides churning. How foolish I'd been to leave Misha on her own. What was I thinking? I should have put my foot down and made her go to Long Island. She would have resisted but I could have threatened to terminate her employment. I looked into the writing parlor, which was empty.

As I approached the entrance to the kitchen, I saw something that staggered me. There, sitting at the kitchen table, was Bartleby. The near-skeletal ghoul, face partially blasted off by Arabella's pistol shot, was dressed in a black short coat and was slowly bringing a steaming cup of something to his lips. I stood in the hallway stunned, horrified, fascinated. I was shaken from my paralysis by Misha's voice, which called out, "George Harrow, is that you?"

I stepped tentatively into the kitchen, and sitting across from Bartleby was Misha, also holding a steaming mug of something. "What's going on here?" I asked, my glance shifting back and forth from Bartleby to my housekeeper.

"Well, this old bag of bones came by to make a stab at me today. Look at the face on him, like he's caught between a shit and a sweat."

"He attacked you?"

"If you can call it that. He had a knife but all's he could manage was like a blind newborn pup searching for its mother's teat."

I grimaced at the metaphor.

"In any event," she said. "I heard a noise, turned around, and there the pathetic creature was—arm upraised, holding a knife. Took a swing—missed me completely, dropped the blade, and sort of fell into me. So I smacked him hard and shoved him into that chair. Then I gave him a talking to and reminded him of his manners and the basics of gentlemanly conduct." She sniffed as if in disapproval.

"Misha, he's a killer."

"He's a hellish *mess*. There's not much left of him. He's been sorely abused. Looks like someone used his hatchet face for target practice. Once I started telling him off, I didn't give him a chance to get a word in edgewise. I harangued him for an hour straight and then gave him a nice cup of hot coffee. The only peep out of him was a quiet, 'I'd prefer not to,' when I asked him if he liked being one of Malbaster's thugs."

"What are we going to do with him?" I asked her.

"We're not going to do anything with him." She leaned close to me as if sharing a secret and whispered in my ear, "He's spent. He's had the spirit beaten, stabbed, and shot out of him. All there's room left for in him now is a kindness and a hot coffee."

I shook my head to clear it. Misha had subdued the persistent revenant with a lecture on etiquette and an offer of hospitality. Why hadn't we thought of that? I considered Bartleby as he sat there, staring out of his one good eye left in that ruined face and drinking his coffee. For a moment, I saw him as Misha did: a poor, abused fellow, roped into nefarious service against his will. "Okay," I said, "get rid of him."

She stood up and walked around the table to stand next to him. When she lifted her hand to touch his ragged cheek, he flinched and cowered away as if she were about to strike him. "There, there, now," said Misha. "Here's what you need to do. Finish your drink straightaway. Then, I want you to walk down to the East River, jump in, and when you touch the bottom, walk to Japan."

The entire scene was so ridiculous. I couldn't help but give a snort of laughter, which drew a disapproving glare from Misha. She shooed me away with a wave of her hand. Meanwhile, Bartleby slowly lifted his cup and drained off what was left, losing much of it through the gash in his throat in the process.

His good eye was so devoid of glimmer or gleam that it was very much like a blue-and-white pebble set into an ivory skull. White hairs that had once sprouted on his chin and head had turned to salt and fallen away. Malbaster had made a mockery of poor Bartleby, robbed him of any self. Finally, he pushed back his chair and rose. I heard the hinges of his joints squealing. He made a feeble genuflection toward Misha and staggered out of the kitchen and down the hall. Of course, we followed.

Bartleby left by way of the front door, shambled down the walkway to the street, and headed for the East River. Without thinking, I followed, keeping five to ten paces behind him as he made his slow way toward the river. As we crossed South Street, I became aware of a carriage following our strange parade. Turning, I saw Arabella atop the coach-and-four, glaring at the pitiful husk of a man stumbling along.

At the river's edge, Bartleby walked along a pier that jutted out over the water. When he came to the end of the dock, he stood at the edge, the soles of his shoes half on and half off the wooden planks. For the first time since I'd laid eyes on him, he achieved a perfect stillness, as if he were grasping at a memory of a memory. Then he grunted and raised his hand in either self-astonishment or witless chance.

Arabella stepped up behind him and pulled the trigger. The blast tore off the short coat and ripped away whatever meat had been left on his back. The oddest thing was that there was no blood at all. For the briefest moment, I could see into him, and it was all bone, ribs like the shattered rafters of a fallen cathedral. Then he was gone, blown out over the water. I watched him fall, and then I watched the green river swallow him.

I turned and stared at Arabella. "Why?" I finally managed to ask.

"It was something I really wanted to do," she said and gave me that disarming smile.

"Out of revenge?" I asked.

"No. But when this story is finished, I want it to remain that way. Each, in turn, is due his offing."

Who knew what she meant by that? There was nothing more to say. We turned and left whatever remained of poor Bartleby, scuttling across the ocean floor toward Japan, and headed back to Arabella's place on the park to plan for the final siege of our war on Malbaster.

❦❦❦❦❦❦❦❦❦❦❦❦❦❦❦❦❦❦❦❦❦❦❦

29

It wasn't long before the conversation turned to fire. We were sitting in Arabella's parlor: Arabella, Madi, Ahab, Gabriel, Mavis, and me. All of us, except for Mavis, who quietly shook her head at the proclamations of so many armchair generals, expounded our plans to attack the oyster barge and flush Malbaster out into the open.

Ahab called for a headlong charge and said he could see himself swinging the boarding ax over his head. Arabella said, "We need bullwhips and poison gas." Madi called for a stealthy, late-night strike. Gabriel said, "I can't wait till they light that cargo on fire." Personally, I was making the case for drilling a hole in the bottom of the barge and sinking it all, lock, stock, and opium chests.

Eventually Mavis got up from where she sat on the floor next to Gabriel. She stood in the middle of the room, and said, "You people don't know what you're doing. Let me tell you what our plan is going to be." Since we'd all seen the accuracy with which she threw a knife, we shut up and listened.

She began by saying, "Why don't we use a bit of each of these plans? Put them together and make them work. I agree with Madi that we should approach our mission with the utmost care. In other words, we want to get on the barge, light the fire, and get off the barge. Our plan is simple: threaten the Pale Toad King's most precious asset and draw him out into the open where we might have a fighting chance against him."

Ahab spoke up. "All right. Who will volunteer to sneak on board and light the fires?"

"Forget volunteers," said Mavis. "Here's who's going. It'll be me, Arabella, and Harrow. Madi, Ahab, and Gabriel will wait in the shadows across the street from the pier for Malbaster to show. He'll be in a carriage or coach. You'll have to be prepared to ambush him. Then we kill him quick and get out of there." She turned to Gabriel. "How many of the Host will come running if they see the barge on fire?"

"Not many. A dozen perhaps. He didn't trust the location of the hoard to more than a few. Mainly his older, longtime henchmen," said the young man.

I thought about what Gabriel said earlier and said, "When that cargo starts to burn, the entire West Side is going to be inebriated."

"There's nothing to be done for that," said Mavis. "At least the opium will be destroyed when we're done."

I couldn't help but sneak a glance at Gabriel. His expression was wistful; no doubt he was picturing the sinking stash.

Mavis continued. "The timing is going to be everything. We want to start out late enough that we can move under cover of darkness, but not so late that the fire will burn itself out before an alarm is raised."

"Spermaceti oil," declared the captain. "That's the ticket. It'll burn long and clean and bright."

"Oil, yes," said Mavis. "And to add to it, 100-proof booze and turpentine, just to be sure. We soak as many crates as possible and then torch them."

"How are you getting aboard?" asked Madi.

"We'll borrow one of the skiffs left down by the piers and row out to the barge. There's only one guard as far as we can tell, so we'll climb aboard the stern, make our way into the storage area, do our work, and retreat. Back into the dinghy, then to shore to help you three with Malbaster."

"And what of Malbaster, once we have him?" I asked.

"After he's been taken, what happens to him is up to you lot. I've nothing to do with it," she said.

The following day, each of us took a portion of that money Garrick had fronted me and we fanned out across the city to gather supplies for the assault on the barge. Ahab and Gabriel went to South Street to buy oil; Madi bought turpentine; Mavis, the alcohol. For my part, I went in search of a firearm. The fid had served me surprisingly well, but we were now approaching the endgame and I needed something with a little more punch. I was able to secure a nice used pair of Colt Navy revolvers.

The very fact that I was participating in a plan that called for the manufacture of torches was enough to make me nervous. What once made sense now seemed so grandiose. Was there nothing simpler we could do than burn ten tons of opium on an oyster barge to get to Malbaster? Why did it have to be so dramatic? But this seemed to be the plan Fate had written for us. There was no getting out of it, the story was set.

Later, while Madi and Arabella sat in the kitchen inspecting the two pistols I'd bought that morning, I sat with Ahab and Gabriel in the parlor, smoking a cigar and poking around with questions to see if I could squeeze one more *Mirror* piece out of Ahab before the end of it all.

"What can you tell me about, Captain?" I said.

To my surprise, Ahab, who usually went quiet the moment he knew I was fishing for an article idea, unfolded his arms from across his chest and opened his hands outward as if he were presenting me with a gift. "Come with us, Harrow," he said. "We have something for you." He stood and put his finger to his lips in order to signal that we were to move quietly.

Gabriel lit a candle in its holder, and we left the parlor. Halfway down the hall, we came to a door, which Gabriel opened. Before us was a set of steps leading down into what I surmised was a cellar of some kind. We descended: Ahab leading, followed by me, with Gabriel bringing up the rear. When we reached the bottom, the young man held the candle higher, and the expanse of a full basement became clear. Ahab headed across the room to a workbench, and we followed.

He went to the back end of the bench and picked up something quite large. The candlelight revealed that he held a harpoon in his hand. He stood it on its butt end, and we all gazed at its double fluke pointing upward. "We bought the shaft to hold the head today when we were at the seaport," said the captain. "But this fluke has a story behind it."

I'd not really thought of Ishmael's book much since our adventure had begun, but as Ahab spoke, I seemed to recall that in the novel, Ahab had the blacksmith, Perth, fashion a harpoon for him that was pulled straight from the burning forge and plunged into a cooling bath composed of the blood of the ship's three harpooners—Queequeg, Tashtego, and Daggoo (Madi). I had a strange suspicion, and I blurted out as much without thinking.

Gabriel's eyes widened and Ahab made his forgetting-how-to-laugh face, which no longer terrified me. "You're correct, Harrow."

"How can that be?" I asked. "It was that very double fluke you hurled at Moby Dick in the heat of the fateful hunt."

"True," he said. "And yet I have it now. This is the story about how it came back to me. After my convalescence from the brutal damages visited upon me by the white whale, I fled the Gilbert Islands. For some reason, I thought of my boy and suddenly had a desire to find him that was as true and righteous as my desire to track Moby Dick had been dark and destructive." Here he paused and put his hand on Gabriel's shoulder. The boy smiled very faintly and looked at the floor.

"I've already recounted for you my experience in Australia where, awaiting a ship going east, I was put up with a ghost. Well before I even made it to that port, I'd already stopped at several others. My homeward journey rivaled that of Odysseus. One such stop was at an island that at the time was unnamed. There was a small British settlement there of about 150 people. The ship I'd paid to take me to Australia, a Dutch clipper, *Heilige van de Golven* (*Saint of the Waves*) put in there in wait for another ship bringing teak wood from Burma.

"The small village lay at the base of a towering dormant volcano. It had a general store called the Pink Frog, no doubt named for the brightly colored creepers that filled the night with song. It was amazing to me how much stuff was crammed into that store. The old widow who ran it, a Mrs. Trumball (Mr. Trumball had been lost at sea) could find anything in that chaos. She had everything a sailor might need. There were books in English, Dutch, and German; sewing goods; dried food; biscuits; tinned meats; knives; pistols old and new; taxidermied wildlife from surrounding islands.

"Mrs. Trumball was a tough, tightfisted proprietor. I'd once seen a sailor try to lift a thin cracker of hardtack. He quickly shoved it in his mouth when he thought she wasn't looking. Oh, but she was always looking. She grabbed him by the throat with one hand and shoved a knife in his ribs with the other, forcing him to spit out what he'd stolen.

"About a week before my ship was due to leave for Australia, I was in the crowded store, searching for something or other when I came across the two-fluke harpoon head wrought by Perth the blacksmith, forged in the blood of the harpooneers, and which I'd buried deep in the white flesh of Moby Dick.

"You might say, 'Ahab, how can you be sure it was the same?' But it's unlike any other—a wicked, snarling tool of death. In Ishmael's book I say that the nails that were melted down to recast the harpoon 'will weld together like glue from the melted bones of murderers.' I, of course, never said that. I was never as dramatic as the book alleges, although I was quite mad at the time and fully believed the ritual of the harpoon's creation would imbue it with greater killing power. I had flung that very harpoon at the creature, and in response, the white menace laughed and showed me how deep the world truly was.

"I knew the instant I saw it what it was. I asked Mrs. Trumball where it had come from. She told me she got it from two fishermen who'd brought it up in a net a few miles north of the island. I had to have it and bargained with her. The price she set for it was not unfair, but I had almost no money. I'd made it this far relying on the brotherhood of seafarers, fellow captains who agreed to transport me as a professional courtesy. But I still had a long way to go.

"Nonetheless, I struck a bargain with the widow and missed my ship for Australia. The next ship I could catch wouldn't be in for another six months. I sacrificed an entire half year just to hold the harpoon. It made no sense to me no matter how much I thought about it, but I did it all the same. I had the harpoon head in my possession and agreed to work for Mrs. Trumball to pay off my debt. She let me stay in a back room of the store, where she set up a cot amid buckets and brooms. But the work was not at all what I'd expected.

"I was to go deep into the island's interior, into the humid, shockingly green jungle, and collect feathers. She told me there was a bird in the jungle that was covered in a tricolored striped pattern. It was said that one of those colors was a color never seen by anyone before. Mrs. Trumball told me she prized those feathers of unknown color very highly. 'Bring me just three of those,' she said, 'and your bill will be paid.'

"So I went out into the jungle. It took a few days to become accustomed to walking there. At first the exposed roots, soft ground, and divots made it slow going with the whalebone leg, but I had a job to do. I put everything of myself into being a good feather hunter. Mrs. Trumball let me take her dog, Suigui, a black hound, a very reliable beast. Besides my companion, I had an old blunderbuss for protection and a bag round my neck to collect feathers in.

"Nearly every day I went into the jungle, Mrs. Trumball would say, 'You know, if you don't see any feathers on the ground, load up the old buss and knock a few of the rascals out of the trees. It won't matter, there's always more of them.' Instead, I played fair and only took the feathers that had fallen. It wouldn't have paid to have the birds against me.

"Six months later, when the ship for Australia arrived, I was waist-deep in the mangrove swamps. Although I'd long paid off my harpoon-head debt, my feather collecting had become something of an obsession. As I trekked through the jungle with Suigui, searching for feathers, I wrestled with why I felt the need to have the double fluke so desperately. Was it because I thought I might face Moby Dick again? Or was I grasping for a bygone time when my crew was alive and with me? Or was it because the flukes had been bathed in the three harpooneers' blood—did I need that connection?

"One afternoon, as I scoured the jungle floor for feathers, my eyes caught sight of a bird emerging from a hole in the ground. The bird was the size of a house cat, with a short neck and beady eyes on either side of an orange beak. Its feathers were striped in maroon, yellow, and . . . some other color that to this day I cannot describe. Up to this point, I'd never seen one of these birds, despite all the feathers I'd found. It stared at me, unblinking, its head cocked to one side. Suigui stood still beside me; I found I couldn't move. A feeling of panic enveloped me, as if I were momentarily glimpsing in those inky black eyes what awaited after death.

"And then, as if it had come to a decision, it squawked, spread its wings, and flew away, leaving three feathers drifting downward in its wake. I felt as if I'd woken from a dream and suddenly remembered that this island was but a temporary stopover on my journey. I'd tarried an entire year, chasing bird feathers, when my son needed me. I hobbled all the way back to the village as quickly as my ivory leg would carry me and just managed to catch the ship for Australia."

"You can give me no hint of the color?" I asked, thinking if I massaged this poppycock into an article, I'd need something more.

"I swear I can't, man. But I can tell you what the natives of the island said. Something Mrs. Trumball never warned me about. Only a handful of islanders had ever seen the bird. Of those who did, supposedly all died in battle, which for the natives was a happy conclusion to life. As for me, though, I've only just found my son. Dying at this juncture, battling Malbaster's grimy legion, is not a happy conclusion. So . . . what I'm trying to say, Harrow, is that the harpoon is a gift for you."

"Wait, Ahab, what does this mean?"

"Well, after all is said and done, you did help me find my boy. And so

I give you this lance. With this harpoon you have a chance to defeat the thing that is Malbaster."

"Where are you going to be?" I asked.

"Gabriel and I are leaving. We're taking a back way out. Call it cowardly, call it a father protecting his child. But we are going. I need more time with my son." He grabbed my collar as if to shake understanding into me.

"I grasp your point," I said to him. "But we have a deal with Madi."

"I truly don't want to renege, but I've not come this far to simply give up my life. I want at least a year or two with the lad."

Losing Ahab and Gabriel would put us at a definite disadvantage, but I tried to put myself in his place. "Do what you must, Captain," I said.

He handed me the harpoon and I took it. He then put his arm around his boy's shoulders and said, "Let's go."

To my surprise, Gabriel suddenly shrugged off his father's arm and turned on him. "I won't do this. We've made a commitment. You go on," he said to Ahab. "You're the one with the curse on his head. I'll meet up with you after the job is complete. Besides, I want Malbaster dead more than anyone."

For the first time since he entered the story, I thought of Gabriel as more than just a lumpen body draped across the back of Madi's horse, or the pale near-corpse lying in bed, the captain's words laving him like the waves of the sea. Now, suddenly, he was a person, and through the dim candlelight I saw the character in his face. Sad green eyes and a shock of dark hair hanging down over one eye, the vaguest mustache sprouting.

Ahab had tears in his eyes, and he must have remembered how to cry. "You're right," he said to Gabriel and put his arm back around the lad's shoulders. "I didn't come all this way to set a bad example for you. We must honor our commitment." We went back upstairs with the blood-forged harpoon and showed it to Madi and Arabella and, in turn, they showed us how to load the guns.

Later that night, as I sat writing in the kitchen, trying to put some meat on the bones of Ahab's bird feather story, I heard the front door creak open and close. The only other person awake was Arabella. She was in her writing room working on her insane bid to bring the manticore under her control and no doubt polishing up her favorite bullwhip. I got up and went to the front door and peeked out the sidelight window. It was lightly snowing, and among the shadows I could just make out the silhouettes of Gabriel and Mavis sharing a kiss.

30

ꞏꙅꙚꙚꙚꙚꙚꙚꙚꙚꙚꙚꙚꙚꙚꙚꙚꙚꙚꙚꙚꙚꙚꙚꙚꙚꙚꙚꙚꙚ

The following evening, after darkness fell, Mavis, Arabella, and I found ourselves in a rowboat on the Hudson River. I had a list of complaints about this situation; for starters, it was freezing, and we were lucky the river wasn't iced over. My second complaint was that I was the designated rower, and whenever I brought an oar up too quickly and water splashed or a paddle slapped the surface, eyes were rolled, and I was shhhhh'd. My third and perhaps biggest gripe was that of the two guns I'd bought the previous day with the money from Garrick, I got to carry neither and was stuck again with the fucking fid.

Mavis took one of the new guns and gave the other to Madi. I told her I thought Madi was determined to kill Malbaster by slitting his throat. She simply shrugged. "And what about the gun you already have?" I asked. She told me she'd given it to Gabriel since he was going to be part of the ambush and would need it more. She reminded me that if our plan was executed perfectly, we shouldn't need any guns whatsoever.

"Then why do you need the new one?" I asked.

"If we're being shot at, would *you* rather be shooting back or would you rather *me* be shooting back?"

I had to admit, in a gunfight, I was, as Garrick might have said, "useless as Millard Fillmore." We borrowed a dinghy north of Fulton, beneath the pier at the end of Barclay Street, and rowed amid the pilings of the dock at Vessey. We circumnavigated a ship to reach the oyster barge. The night was pitch-black and the moon lost behind thick cloud cover. In the bottom of the small boat there were four bottles of our fire starter concoction, three torches, and a shiny bullwhip. I carried my empty writing satchel around my neck, having left its contents at the house. Other than that, I had two boxes of wooden matches and, of course, the perfidious fid.

Mavis wore her fake charcoal beard. She'd told me she wore this disguise when engaging in dangerous activities so that in case she was seen, she might be mistaken for a small man. Arabella, on the other hand, wore a rather flamboyant ensemble: riding pants, a silk blouse, a velvet vest, and patchwork coat; atop her head was a derby with a tricolored feather in the band.

It was easy enough to get to the back of the barge. The vessel was enormous. The fifty or so timbers that formed the base were whole tree trunks. Luckily, a ladder hung off the stern to the waterline. Arabella wore her bullwhip around her neck like a pet snake as she ascended from the dinghy. I followed her, trying to hang on to my bottle of fire starter and a torch. Her pungent perfume, a combination of fruit and flowers that I found intoxicating, wafted tantalizingly in her wake.

Behind me, Mavis very untantalizingly poked my ass with her torch to prod me along. When we made it over the side onto the deck, we crouched, huddled together in the dark silence, alert for any sound that might indicate the presence of a night watchman. Once satisfied that we were alone, we began to move, with the pale moon providing the light.

It was slow going across the uneven deck, which was strewn with all manner of junk—coils of rope, empty baskets, winch parts, rakes, netting. But we reached the back wall of the onboard warehouse and stopped to get our bearings. Mavis told Arabella and me to stay hidden and quiet, that she was going to figure out the location to the entrance of the opium storehouse. An anxious few minutes passed and then I heard the squeal of hinges, followed almost immediately by three gunshots and a scream.

I don't know what I was thinking, but I stood up, intent on charging to Mavis's rescue. Just then a man came running around the back of the warehouse, holding a rifle. When he caught sight of me, he lifted the gun to his shoulder. Arabella sprang up out of the shadows and I heard that whip moving through the air. With a loud crack, the tip punched the gunman in the side of the face and sent him sprawling, the gun dropping from his hands.

Arabella approached the prostrate, unconscious man to see if he was still breathing. When she found that he was, she drew a knife from her belt and severed each of his Achilles tendons. Even in the dark, I could make out the unhesitating efficiency with which she completed her task. I suppressed a shudder as I followed her around a corner and toward the warehouse door.

The door was ajar and lamplight shone out. All was silent save for the whistling of the wind and the lapping of the pilings below. We crept along the outer wall and when Arabella kicked the door open and leaped through the entrance, she found three dead bodies and Mavis staring up at the stacks of wooden chests. I gazed up at the ranks of boxes that disappeared into the darkness. A mountain of opium.

Mavis broke the silence, gesturing to the three dead men and saying, "I didn't see any others, so this must be all who were left on guard."

"There's one on deck incapacitated," said Arabella.

"Well," said Mavis. "Just in case we missed someone, I'll keep an eye on the door while you two set the fires. She pointed toward a lantern and bottles of oil. Holding her gun in one hand, she picked up a torch with the other and said, "Got a light, Harrow?" I found a match and set fire to the thing, which she held high above her head as she trained her pistol on the warehouse door. "Get to it," she said.

Arabella and I worked as a team. I'd spill some oil all over a bunch of cases and then move down the row. She'd follow with her own torch, sending the stacks up in flames. I had to wonder at the stockpiling of the drug—the degree to which the wealthy acquired and stored things put to shame even my most imaginative stories. I thought about the Astor warehouse we'd investigated. So much stuff just sitting there. It was as if he were saving up things to start another world.

After ten minutes or so of spilling and sparking, I paused to survey our handiwork. We were deep into the towering conglomeration of chests, which were blazing all around us. We had been so intent on our task that we now ran the risk of going up in flames ourselves. I turned around to look for Arabella, who should have been right behind me.

The air was thick with smoke and a cloying, sweet aroma; my eyelids felt heavy and my mouth was as dry as cotton. I saw her through the flickering firelight, standing stock-still and breathing deeply. Half of me was inclined to join her, and the other half knew I was in trouble. I ran back to her. "Arabella, we'll be burned alive," I said. She dropped to her knees and reached into a large inside pocket of her coat and pulled out a notebook. A pencil appeared as if from nowhere. The next thing I knew, she was writing.

Our plan, our mixture, our fire was going too well. The heat was intensifying, flames creeping into the alleyways at the base of the wooden mountain. We didn't have long before it would be too late and we'd not escape. "Arabella," I said, "we've got to keep moving. The fire."

Her voice, as if in a dream, said, "This is important, Harrow. I'm nearly there." Her hand flew over the pages of the notebook, birthing scribble. I wondered if what I was looking at was really language. I tried to control my fear as the fire crackled around us. From within the rush of flame, I thought I heard a strange and sonorous voice, reciting poetry.

I spun around in confusion; the movement left me dizzy. Not too far off, the flames looked like petals of bright lilies undulating in a breeze. The smoke was yellow and thick like tea-stained cotton, enveloping the flowers. In the next instant, the blossoms exploded and it was all fire, and panic set in. I heard Mavis's voice echoing through the warehouse, calling for us. Yet Arabella scribbled on. To my left, suddenly, a fierce snarl and a line of iambic pentameter. I turned and there was the manticore, its scorpion tail hovering in the air above its head.

If I'd not been intoxicated by the smoke, I could have made a run for it. But my legs had turned to sand. She came toward me, her blond ringlets bobbing above her sleek shoulders. Her eyes were an unforgettable blue—the deepest, clearest, Caribbean water lit by a star from below. All that was left to me was to shiver.

She didn't stop to grind my head into a pencil point with her three rotating rows of teeth. Instead she passed me by and went directly to Arabella, who seemed not to notice that a monster leaned over her, drooling. I tried to scream, but my mouth was too dry. I watched in horror as the creature went to work on Arabella's lovely face. But, as in my dream, there was no blood. It was as if every bite was a pass of the eraser.

Bit by bit, Arabella disappeared. The thick yellow smoke swelled around them like an ocean wave and they vanished into it. At that moment, Mavis grabbed my arm and pulled me away. As we fled, I had a hallucination that we were running through a city on fire—I saw flames leaping from the windows, heard people screaming. When we emerged from the warehouse and into the cold night air, Mavis backhanded me across the face to wake me up. We made our way to the barge's stern where she had stowed three of the opium chests.

I don't mind telling you, the chests were heavy as hell as we carried them, slung across one shoulder down the ladder. Mavis made two trips to my one. I sat in the front of the boat and tried to reconcile my feelings for Arabella Dromen and the fact that I had witnessed her disappear one bite at a time. An unkind thought occurred to me: after all her opium-induced scribbling, she is erased. There was something classically ironic to that, but I cared for her too much.

This time, Mavis rowed, a roll-up stuck in the corner of her lips. Her charcoal beard had faded. I told her what had happened to Arabella. "Bloodless," I said, "like eating the wind." Mavis stopped rowing and pulled up the oars. She took the cigarette out of her mouth and blew smoke at me. The water lapped at the sides of the boat as we drifted in the current. "Harrow, you have to wake up. Too bad for Miss Dromen, but we have to deal with Malbaster when we get to shore."

She took up the oars again and started rowing. I huddled in the bow, still unable to get the picture of Arabella slowly disappearing out of my mind.

"Listen," Mavis said, softly. "It's not like I don't feel awful about what happened. But right now we don't have the luxury to dwell on it. Once we're safe ashore—once we sell these blasted chests of opium and split the money with whoever else of our party survives—that's when I'll think about it. Arabella is dead. I want to live."

My mind was still racing, but I knew she was right and kept my peace. She brought the boat in beneath the dock, and we quickly tied it up and removed the cargo. Once the wooden chests were stacked away in the bushes out of reach of the tide, we proceeded up the shallow incline to the road. We both turned at the same time and looked back at the oyster barge that was ablaze, the wild light reaching into the heavens.

We met the others on the corner across from the Fulton Street dock. Arabella's coach-and-four was there, positioned at the side of the road, with Madi holding the reins in the driver's seat, ready to block traffic on West Street. Standing on the sidewalk were Ahab and Gabriel. The captain had somewhere acquired a new top hat and peacoat—no doubt from the funds Garrick had donated to the end of this business. I couldn't begrudge it. Ahab looked revived, sharp, and proud to have his son standing next to him. He swung the boarding ax slowly, practicing, what I surmised, was his killing blow.

Gabriel, on the other hand, looked somewhat peaked. He stood near the horses, shivering, one hand shoved in the pocket of the filthy thug's coat, his other holding the pistol in a wobbling grip. It was Ahab who inquired about Arabella. I shook my head and waved away his question. Mavis interceded. "Gone," she said. "Harrow says she was eaten by the manticore."

All of them, including Mavis, wore a forlorn expression, and soon enough they looked away and shook their heads in silence. It wasn't long, though, before Madi interrupted the reverie, pointing out into the sky beyond the dock, where we saw clouds of opium smoke rushing at us from the burning oyster barge. The storm moved faster than a running dog and swamped us before we could react.

Within the realm of the smoke, the streetlamp was a godsend. Its glow, though dimmed by the clouds, was still strong enough to allow us to see one another. Together, we waited in the pale-yellow night, our gazes glazed. Reality, such as it was, was slightly frayed at the edges. Madi, sitting atop the coach, drank from a canteen and kept his head cocked as he listened for movement up the street. Gabriel leaned against the lamppost, yawned, and smiled. "That's the ticket," he said, between deep breaths. Mavis sat on the sidewalk with her back against the wall of the closest building, smoking a roll-up and staring out at the flames. Ahab stood ramrod straight, as if at attention, awaiting the order to attack.

God knows what each of them saw before his eyes. As for me, it was the bird of the unseen color from Ahab's tale. It flew in and out of the fog at the end of Fulton Street, a swooping shadow. How I knew it was the bird of the unseen color, I'm not sure, for I never really got a good look at it. I was trying to remind myself to wake up, when from somewhere beyond the clouds, there came the sound of hoofbeats on cobblestone.

"Here we go," said Madi and grabbed up the reins. Before the coach pulled away from the sidewalk, Ahab opened the cab door, reached in, and drew out his harpoon. "From hell's heart, I stab at thee," he said.

31

When the coach appeared out of the smog and encountered Madi and his team blocking their way, the driver pulled hard on the reins and the lead pair of black horses reared to a stop only inches away. It was clearly the same coach that had been used in Malbaster's getaway from the Crystal Palace and to kidnap Madi and Ahab.

"Move it along," said the driver.

Madi pulled out the new pistol and shot the man twice in the chest. The body tumbled out of the driver's seat and into the road. The coach's cab door opened and a trousered leg appeared. Before the fellow could get out, Ahab was upon him. He grabbed a shock of the man's dark hair, whipped his thin form around and buried the boarding ax blade dead center into what turned out to be Ishmael's forehead. Blood splattered and the author's distant voice uttered the phrase, "Good Lord." My old copy editor, obviously under the influence of the opium, didn't die at once, but staggered to and fro with a look of astonishment in his eyes, the surprise that comes with being slain by your own creation. When he did finally succumb to the wound and fell onto the street, dead, Ahab spat upon him and said, "Who's the author now? Make a ghost of me, will ya?"

The cab door swung shut and as a curtain was drawn over the window we couldn't see in. Blood pooled in the street and had sprayed across the side of the coach. The captain was breathing heavily. I could tell by his expression that he just wanted to get the job done and be finished with it, kill whoever else was in the coach. As he moved for the door, Mavis stepped in his path and told him to wait. "Stick your head in there and you're asking to be shot," she whispered to him.

Ahab relented and backed up a step. As he did, Gabriel came forward to join Mavis and his father. She and the lad pointed their guns at the door of the coach, and the captain lifted his harpoon prepared to strike. And from his seat on Arabella's rig, Madi aimed at the same target. I stood there with my fid in my hand, nervous, scared, and hallucinating a drizzle of small white flowers drifting down through the smoke.

Time passed and not the slightest noise or movement came from the cab. Mavis called up to Madi to make sure no one had gotten out the other side. "I'd have shot them already," was his answer.

"What about those blue moths coming out of the coach?" said Ahab.

"Moths?" I asked.

"A torrent of them. Does no one else see them?"

"I see the smoke keep changing into people, like a phantom Jolly Host," said Mavis.

"You're beautiful," Gabriel said to her.

Without turning she lackadaisically reached back and smacked him in the face. "Look alive," she said and he smiled.

At any second, I expected to see the coach turn into a pumpkin and the horses into mice. With that thought, the cab door opened, and a bright beacon of light streamed out into the night, reflecting off the swirling fog. The beam was brighter than any lantern could produce, and it stunned us. No one spoke. Even Ahab was subdued by it.

Then the springs on the coach squeaked and bounced a bit as a fig-ure exited through the door. The instant I saw the giant pale head con-trasted with the black suit, I knew we had Malbaster in our trap. What were the odds? He moved toward our group with an otherworldly smile on his face. The balloon head bobbed up and down as he halted and took a position ten yards away.

"Gentlemen," came the strange voice. Mavis stepped forward with the pistol pointed directly between his eyes. The Pale King Toad snapped his fingers twice and her gun became a bird, squawked, and flew out of her hand. Madi's pistol followed suit. "You all know my friend," said Malbaster and made a half turn toward the coach. From out of the bright beacon light emerged the manticore. She leaped to the ground, moving with a slow dreamlike grace, and took up a position next to her master. The blue eyes scanned over each of us.

"This mere girl took a shot at me once in the cotton warehouse," she said, nodding to Mavis. "I don't forget such treachery."

Mavis's ruined charcoal beard must have fooled Malbaster for a moment. "Ahhh," he said. "I smell it now, an Irish slut. In that case we'll kill her last."

Mavis drew the thin blade from the waist of her trousers, but before she could think to throw it, Malbaster had nodded at her, and instead, she plunged the blade into her own thigh and cried out.

"Shhh, dear," said Malbaster, "you'll summon the police."

I stumbled to her and helped her to the ground, pulled out the blade, which hadn't sunk that deep into the muscle, and stanched the bleeding with my handkerchief. As all this transpired, Gabriel had stepped forward with his gun, the only one remaining, and aimed it at the marshmallow globe.

"Gabriel, my boy, you've fallen in with a bad crowd. A Negro hardly worth a bullet, a slatternly Irish whore, a lunatic seafarer who claims to be your father, a pathetic scribbler of poorly written tripe, and where is the other crazy bitch?"

The manticore laughed aloud at his question. Understanding shone in Malbaster's expression. "A shame," he said. "I hope her mental confusion didn't give you too much indigestion."

Although his aim was wavering, Gabriel kept the gun trained on Malbaster.

"Now, my boy, seriously, don't you miss the life of the streets? I was about to make you prince of the Jolly Host, ruler of your own throng of ne'er-do-wells to command as you see fit. What in God's name do you want with this powerless scrum of lackeys? Come back to me. This opium that burns is only a quarter of all the stores I have secreted throughout the city. Your days and nights will never be without it."

I wanted to *move*. My anger at Malbaster had reached foolish proportions, and I was all set to take him on, but his magic had me trapped as if my feet were buried in the ground. It must have been the same for the others. I saw Ahab flailing his arms wildly trying to be rid of the spell and Madi, long knife in hand, attempting, with no luck, to pull himself to the edge of the driver's seat of the coach.

"What do you say, Gabriel?" asked Malbaster.

"I'm through with you," said the boy.

"Well, in that case, I'll just have to kill the girl right now, for I sense that it's she who draws you away from me."

"It's all of them. My family."

"We're your family. I'm your old dad, and the Host are your brothers. Who took you in?"

"And made me sick. Made me do sick things."

"Okay," said Malbaster. "I don't want to kill you and I'll even spare the bearded girl. But I'm afraid that the others must die. All you need do is shoot that jackass who claims to be your father."

It was easy to see that Gabriel was trying to resist his old master's commands. His body trembled and his arm shook wildly. Slowly, the lad turned around and aimed the gun at Ahab's head.

The captain watched, as did the rest of us. He said, "Don't worry, boy. Save yourself and Mavis. You must go on to live your life. I've done what I can. Forgive me my sins."

It was obvious from the expression of anguish on Gabriel's face and how he shook that great pressure was being put on him. I noticed that the manticore now rose from her haunches and stood ready to pounce. I feared I'd be the first to go. For all my own scribbling, Lord knows I deserved to be erased. Still Gabriel held out, although it was clear his finger was tightening on the trigger.

Out of the corner of my eye, I noticed a strange movement from the manticore, as if a sudden wave had flooded through her body from head to tail. I shifted my gaze to her, and to my awe, noticed her blond ringlets straighten and darken. Her cheeks, which accommodated those extra sets of teeth, smoothed and flattened, and if I wasn't mistaken, her paws were becoming hands before my eyes. I shook my head at the hallucination. Or was it? The scorpion stinger that had bobbed at the end of her tail in the air above her head was suddenly nowhere to be seen.

I grunted involuntarily when I realized what was happening. It was too amazing. Too much for even George Harrow to take in. Malbaster hadn't noticed, concentrating, as he was, on willing Gabriel to shoot his father. But I watched the entire transition as Arabella Dromen stepped out of the melting form of the manticore. The creature's sleek cat body transformed into the powerful physique of the friend I believed to have been erased. Mavis must have been watching too, because she grabbed my ankle and whispered up to me, "Throw her the fid."

I threw it in an arc as Arabella moved toward Malbaster. She caught it in one hand, and as his concentration was broken by her movement beside him, Arabella rammed its spiked end with all her strength into his stomach. She leaped away once the weapon was planted. The Pale King Toad made a prolonged toad noise, a deep croak like a machine running down, as yellow smoke poured out of the wound.

Gabriel, suddenly free of Malbaster's control, turned and fired a shot at him. The bullet went wide. It didn't matter, though, because Madi launched himself off the driver's seat of Arabella's coach and landed on the pale villain's back. He still had the long knife in his hand and, in one quick, savage motion, he dragged it across Malbaster's throat, leaving a gaping, smoking wound.

We all drew closer to the corpse of the Pale King Toad, who lay lifeless, like a heap of laundry in the middle of West Street.

"That's it?" said Mavis.

"Where's the blood?" asked Gabriel.

"Aye," said the captain.

Arabella pointed and said, "What's that?"

The smoke had stopped pouring from the gash in his throat, but now there was something pushing its way out from inside Malbaster, a puddle of white goo come to life. It wriggled and undulated its way out of him, and it was huge. At its tallest point the blob that slowly crawled forth from within him was twelve feet. We watched it being born. Once it was free, it headed for the river like a snail without a shell.

Ahab took off after the blob with a vengeance. I don't know how he moved so fast on that whalebone leg. By the time we crossed the street and climbed down the rise on the other side to the bank of the Hudson, the captain already had the dinghy untied and was twenty yards out into the water. He wore his top hat as he rowed methodically, following the white, half-submerged hump of the blob. The head of Ahab's harpoon could be seen jutting out over the prow.

"What are you doing?" I yelled to him.

"Finishing the job, Harrow," he called back. "Making the world safe for my son." I saw his silhouette wave before he disappeared into the smoke-filled night. And then, I could have sworn I heard laughter off in the darkness. That's how Ahab left my life, as suddenly as he'd entered it. I would never see him again.

The very next instant, I opened my eyes and I was in my parlor at home, sitting at my writing desk. I turned my chair around and saw Gabriel and Mavis across the room each curled into a corner of the couch. Madi slept in a straight-backed armchair, his chin resting on his chest. Arabella lay across the floor wrapped in a dark blue blanket patterned with golden stars. I sat in silent thought until daybreak when Misha appeared in the entrance to the parlor and announced that she'd made coffee and would make eggs for any who wanted them. I stumbled out of my chair, went to her, and gave her a kiss on the cheek.

I never did find out how I finally got home the night of our battle with Malbaster. I must have succumbed to the fear and smoke. I was told by Arabella that I should thank my brother-in-law, Tommy, without whose intervention things would have been far more complicated.

Madi told me later that by the time the police showed up, a moment after I'd passed out, the three bodies—coach driver's, Malbaster's, and Ishmael's—were all gone, vanished.

As it turned out, while the rest of us were chasing Ahab down to the river's edge, Mavis stayed behind and moved the three chests of opium into Arabella's coach. Each weighed fifty pounds, and when all was said and done, Arabella took only one of the chests as part of our deal. We sold the other two to a shifty denizen of the underworld and made quite a profit on it. The drug was rather rare at the time in New York. Later, in the '60s, opium use would peak in Chinatown and then the drug would be in the Manhattoes to stay. During those years I wondered if it had been shipped in or if someone had discovered the other three stores of Astor's hoard.

With the money we made, Madi and I set aside a portion to give to Fergus's wife and child to help them get along. Otis had no family. Mavis used hers to rent an apartment for her brothers and Gabriel and herself. Arabella used her cut to publish a novel under her own name, a feminist fairy tale concerning a manticore and inspired by the works of Margaret Fuller.

Before a month was up I had a visit from Madi. He told me that our adventure had made him think about his own mother and father back in Guinea, and that he'd decided to travel there with the rest of his opium money. "There, I'll make enough to return to America and buy land and acquire the right to vote. I'll search for whatever remains of my family. My religion, which the ocean washed out of me and the equatorial sun evaporated from my heart, calls to me at night from the distant end of my memory. I'll return, Harrow," he assured me. "I will be back."

I told him I believed he would and accompanied the harpooneer to South Street where he embarked as a seaman again on the clipper *Maximus* bound eventually for Dakar in Senegal. Just before he boarded, I told him Seneca Village was to be dismantled and the residents evicted. He looked past me for a moment, shook his head, and said, "I'm coming back, Harrow."

"Why would you want to?" I asked.

"To finish the job. Make the world safe. Malbaster hasn't gone anywhere. You can't slit his throat. His is the irrational viciousness of white suspicion. The Pale King Toad is still out there," he said before taking his leave up the gangplank.

As it turned out, Arabella was never romantically interested in either me or Madi, for when the Malbaster affair was a year behind us, she took up with a lovely young woman, Julianna, who was every bit as rough and ready and full of Emersonian phrases as Miss Dromen. Still, we had lunch a few times a year. I'd go over to the St. John's Park house and we'd sit in front of the big picture window at the front of the place, sipping tea and eating dainty sandwiches that seemed to be made of nothing but bread, lettuce, and air.

The conversation was always filling. I tried whenever I saw her to get her to talk about where she had been during the interval between when the manticore had devoured her in the warehouse and she had reappeared in place of the creature next to Malbaster. Only once, when Julianna had excused herself to go to the kitchen to get another pot of tea, did Arabella say, "I was in your hearts." I wasn't quite sure she was serious, for after she'd spoken the words she laughed aloud and I couldn't help but join her.

And what about old Harrow, you ask? I carried on, writing my articles for the *Gorgon's Mirror*. They remained popular for some time, although never so much as when I wrote of Ahab's quest. I stayed with Garrick nearly eight more years confabulating hokum at my steady pace and excellence until he passed away on a terrible winter evening. They found him frozen the next morning, clutching his chest, in the gutter outside the *Mirror*. At the funeral, I remember holding Mavis to me, a grown woman by then with children of her own. She sobbed upon my shoulder, having loved the old man more than anyone should have. Nearby, with his hand lightly upon her back, was the steadfast, sad-eyed Gabriel, who turned out a better man than his father might ever have dreamed.

Notes in 2s

2 Streets

While delving into the past in preparation for this novel, I came across an online copy of a Mitchell map (Mitchell being the name of the company that made it). It depicted the lower half of Manhattan ca. 1850. This was a real boon to me as I could trace my characters' adventures around much of the city. I found that having it always available on my computer while writing, being able to see the lay of the land and where streets intersected, made it a kind of talisman that allowed me to daydream more deeply into the fiction. One thing to keep in mind, though, is that some of the streets of 1850s Manhattan do not have the same names today. Take, for instance, Orange Street, which plays a part in this novel. If you were to ask someone today where Orange Street is, an in-the-know New Yorker would tell you, "Brooklyn Heights." Of course, they would be right. But in the 1850s, there was also an Orange Street that ran parallel to Mulberry Street, in Manhattan. Today it's called Baxter Street.

Check out the Mitchell map for 1850 Manhattan if you want to follow the action in my book. You can find it at: https://upload.wikimedia.org/wikipe dia/commons/4/4e/1850_Mitchell_Map_of_New_York_City_-_Geographi cus_-_NewYorkCity-mitchell-1850.jpg.

2 Places

For those readers who are hearing about Seneca Village and/or the Indian Caves for the first time, I want to let you know that both places are/were real.

Unfortunately, Seneca Village no longer exists. It was a settlement of free African American farmers who bought the land from a fellow named John Whitehead. In 1825, Whitehead began selling off parcels of his land, which was situated along what is now the western side of Central Park, and the village soon came into being. There are numerous theories about how it came by the name Seneca Village. I tend to think the moniker was related to the Roman philosopher, whose work was often favored by African American thinkers of a political bent. The village was successful, and it grew as the villagers welcomed Irish and German immigrants, who were spurned by much of New

York City establishment for being "papists." There are reports that Native Americans also found a home there. The same black midwife birthed both white and black children; villagers worshipped side by side in the village's three churches. It was a remarkable place, a true melting pot, and one I wish were better known.

Then, in 1855, plans were made to create Central Park on a large parcel of land that encompassed Seneca Village. Ultimately, the villagers were evicted in 1857 (some violently), leaving the way clear for a new playground for the city's elite—who would build homes in the area—and disbanding a site where blacks owned land (and thus had the right to vote) as well as a viable integrated community that flew in the face of the nativist and Know-Nothing factions. I was unable to find many books about the village, but there are some good online sites that will give you more information, if you are interested.

The Indian Caves seem like something I might have made up solely to provide a Romantic locale for one of the scenes in my novel. Doing something like that is certainly not beneath me, but in this case, I did not have to do any inventing; they exist. They can be found at the very northern part of Manhattan, in what is now known as Inwood Park. The presence of Native Americans in this area, namely the Lenape, reaches back to pre-Columbian times. The caves found here were used by the Indians as stopovers while on fishing expeditions to what are now called the Harlem and Hudson Rivers. It is said that there was a nearby tulip tree, which stood 165 feet high and had a 20-foot diameter, beneath which a Dutch representative, Peter Minuit, bought the island of Manhattan from the Canarsee tribe of the Lenape Nation for sixty guilders' worth of beads and trinkets (approximately twenty-four dollars). The story is obviously a confabulation worthy of the humbug of George Harrow. Still, the caves are real and worth a day trip to Inwood to check out. The tulip tree, unfortunately, was taken down at some time in the 1930s.

2 People

I try not to populate my "historical" novels with too many historical personages, as I find they often clutter up the works. In *Ahab's Return*, I kept it to two: Catherine Thompson and John Jacob Astor, diurnally opposite in disposition, race, and class. Neither is ever encountered in the flesh, so to speak; they are only perceived as powerful forces working their will from offstage.

I'd like to help revive the memory of Catherine Thompson. I discovered her while doing research on Seneca Village. Thompson, at age seventeen, started and ran a school for black children in the basement of the African

Union Methodist Church in Seneca Village. She is credited with educating scores of children and her school was integral in inspiring New York City to create some of the first official "colored" schools. I am a teacher and I find her an inspiration and a reminder that although every teacher has the potential to be a one-person school, few would have the courage. In *Ahab's Return*, Catherine plays a role as Madi's teacher, and she inspires him to seek justice for the murdered children of the village. After reading about this trailblazing educator and contemplating what little is known of her life, I concluded that her dedication to the children of Seneca Village would have had to encompass a desire for future political and legal parity for them and, in keeping with this, she could never have let the loss of those children stand.

John Jacob Astor, on the other hand, is well known in the annals of history— someone you may have read about in high school or college. Most who know about Astor know that his initial fortune was made in the fur trade, but not as many are aware that he later became involved in smuggling opium into China. He'd purchase tons of it in Turkey and then, using his merchant ships, move it to ports like Canton (Guangzhou). When China eventually cracked down on the practice, Astor reverted to unloading the drug only in Britain. He then used his opium money to invest in New York City real estate. Of course, the premise in *Ahab's Return* is that he stockpiled tons of the drug in secret locations within the city. That's more George Harrow speculation, but not completely beyond the realm of the possible. (Note: Based on my research, it seems that opium didn't take hold in Manhattan to any real extent until later, in the 1860s.)

2 Many Books

The following are some of the books I used for research while writing *Ahab's Return*, in case readers are interested in learning more about the world I've tried to depict in its pages. I've broken the list into two basic sections: *Ahab* (Melville's character and the whaling life) and *Manhattan* (the history of the city and its citizens). I've also read all of Melville's fiction from "Bartleby the Scrivener" to *The Confidence Man*, and even waded through *Mardi*, his dense, Busby Berkeley–esque musical of the South Seas. Of course, a good deal of my research was done on the web and in the databases of Ohio Wesleyan University, where I teach part time.

Ahab

↦ *Ahab* by Harold Bloom. One volume in Bloom's series of Major Literary Characters. If you've never seen any of these volumes, they're compendiums of essays about a given major literary figure. Joining Ahab in the series are Faust, Satan (*Paradise Lost*), Gatsby, Clarissa Dalloway, Emma Bovary, Hamlet, and so on. I think there are about thirty volumes in all. I didn't really borrow anything from this book, except for the realization of the multiplicity of ways in which Ahab may be perceived. It inspired me to be bold with my own view.

☞ *Ahab's Trade: The Saga of South Seas Whaling* by Granville Allen Mawer. Everything and anything you'd like to know about the history of the whale fishery in the South Seas.

☞ *In the Heart of the Sea: The Tragedy of the Whaleship Essex* by Nathaniel Philbrick. A wonderfully readable nonfiction account of the tragedy at sea that influenced Melville's writing of *Moby Dick*.

Manhattan

☞ *Five Points: The 19th-Century New York City Neighborhood That Invented Tap Dance, Stole Elections, and Became the World's Most Notorious Slum* by Tyler Anbinder. The definitive book on this treacherous lower Manhattan neighborhood. A book of great riches for the fiction writer, depicting the way of life for the lower and immigrant classes of early Manhattan.

☞ *Gotham: A History of New York City to 1898* by Edwin G. Burrows and Mike Wallace. A serviceable overview of the history of early New York.

☞ *City of Dreams: The 400-Year Epic History of Immigrant New York* by Tyler Anbinder. Another fine book by Anbinder, focusing on those who came to America to find a new life—their problems, challenges, contributions, and triumphs.

☞ *The New Metropolis: New York City, 1840–1857* by Edward K. Spann. A book I found at a garage sale that just happened to focus on exactly the time period I was writing about.

☞ *P. T. Barnum: America's Greatest Showman* by Philip B. Kunhardt Jr., Philip B. Kunhardt III, and Peter W. Kunhardt. An excellent, lavishly illustrated biography of Barnum. Barnum plays a part in the life of the city during the time of my story. His influence may be felt as well in the sensationalist penny press newspapers like Harrow's *Gorgon's Mirror*.

☞ *Black Gotham: A Family History of African Americans in Nineteenth-Century New York City* by Carla L. Peterson. A fascinating study of the African American experience in Manhattan through Peterson's own family history (from 1819 into the new century). This book explodes assumptions about the role of African Americans in New York.

↬ *Root and Branch: African Americans in New York and East Jersey, 1613–1863* by Graham Russell Gao Hodges. A remarkable book that offers a comprehensive history of African Americans in New York from the very first until 1863.

↬ *My Seneca Village* by Marilyn Nelson. I was unable to find stand-alone books about Seneca Village. For information on it, I relied heavily on the Internet. I did, though, find this one children's book of poems, which is worth the read for both adults and children (age five and up) seeking an entry into the phenomenon of the village. This book boasts both great research and terrific writing. Nelson is a nationally recognized poet and a former poet laureate of Connecticut.

Acknowledgments

No one embarks on a voyage like this without help. A debt of gratitude to my agent, Howard Morhaim, without whom I'd never have gotten out of port. Also to the book's editor, Jennifer Brehl, an ingenious editor, collaborator, and friend, who kept a steady hand on the wheel and navigated this craft through treacherous waters. A word of thanks to my son Derek for the cover's manticore and to Owen Corrigan for the cover's design. And of course, to the family, without whom the journey would be nothing.

About the author

About the book

Read on

Insights,
Interviews
& More . . .

Meet Jeffrey Ford

Jeffrey Ford

JEFFREY FORD is the author of *The Physiognomy, Memoranda, The Beyond, The Portrait of Mrs. Charbuque*, the Edgar Award–winning *The Girl in the Glass, The Shadow Year*, and *The Drowned Life*. He lives outside Columbus, Ohio, and teaches writing at Ohio Wesleyan University. ∿

Reading Group Discussion Questions

1. How do you feel about an author ransacking a classic for parts to create a new work of fiction?

2. If you had to choose one word to describe George Harrow, what would that word be?

3. The story of *Ahab's Return* is relayed by a prevaricator of speculative articles. What effect does that have on your perception of the tale?

4. What is the proper balance of "fake news," "innate truth in fiction," and "utter veracity" in life, politics, and art?

5. This novel has been described as a "fabulation." How is it different from a work of "fantasy"? Or, is there really no difference between the two? For those readers familiar with *Moby Dick,* is that novel a work of "fabulation" or "fantasy" or neither?

6. There is a theme of anti-immigration running throughout *Ahab's Return*. How do the sentiments of the Know-Nothing movement and the Order of the Star-Spangled Banner match up with similar anti-immigrant sentiments today? ▶

Reading Group Discussion Questions
(continued)

7. The success of Seneca Village in the 1850s seems to be a great story of tolerance and disparate people living together in harmony. Why do you think so few people have heard of it?

8. Which of the characters in the book would you trust with your life?

9. Discuss the nature of Malbaster. Is he a monster, a man, or some amalgamation of sinister ideas?

10. How do the fantastic elements— the manticore, Bartley, Mrs. Pease's "system"—work in the novel? How do they affect the story?

11. What is "the confluence of fictions" discussed by Harrow and Arabella Dromen?

12. Why does Madi leave at the end? Do you think he will eventually return to America? ∾

An Excerpt from Jeffrey Ford's *The Shadow Year*

On New York's Long Island, in the unpredictable decade of the 1960s, a young boy laments the approaching close of summer and the advent of sixth grade. But when a night prowler is reported stalking the neighborhood, he and his brother, Jim, appoint themselves ad hoc investigators, and set out to aid the police—while their little sister, Mary, smokes cigarettes, speaks in other voices, and moves around the inanimate clay residents of Botch Town, a detailed cardboard replica of their community they've constructed in their basement. Ensuing events add a shadowy cast to the boys' night games: disappearances, deaths, and spectral sightings capped off by the arrival of a sinister man in a long white car trawling the neighborhood after dark. Strangest of all is that every one of these troubling occurrences seems to correspond to the changes little Mary has made to the miniature town in the basement.

Not since Ray Bradbury's classic Dandelion Wine has a novel so richly evoked the dark magic of small-town boyhood. The Shadow Year is a masterful re-creation of a unique time and place, and a hypnotically compelling mystery. Now available in hardcover from William Morrow, an imprint of HarperCollins.

IT BEGAN IN THE LAST DAYS OF AUGUST when the leaves of the elm in the front yard had curled into crisp, brown ▶

tubes and fallen away to litter the lawn. I sat at the curb that afternoon, waiting for Mister Softee to round the bend at the top of Willow Avenue, listening carefully for that mournful knell, each measured *ding* both a promise of ice cream and a pinprick of remorse. Taking a castoff leaf into each hand, I made double fists. When I opened my fingers, brown crumbs fell and scattered on the road at my feet. Had I been waiting for the arrival of that strange changeling year, I might have understood the sifting debris to be symbolic of the end of something. Instead, I waited for the eyes.

That morning, I'd left under a blue sky, walked through the woods, and crossed the railroad tracks away from town, where the third rail hummed, lying in wait, like a snake, for an errant ankle. Then along the road by the factory, back behind the grocery, and up and down the streets, I searched for discarded glass bottles in every open garbage can, Dumpster, forgotten corner. I'd found three soda bottles and a half-gallon milk bottle. At the grocery store, I turned them in for the refund and walked away with a quarter.

All summer long, Mister Softee had this contest going. With each purchase of twenty-five cents or more, he gave you a card: on the front was a small portrait of the waffle-faced cream being pictured on the side of the truck. On the back was a piece of a puzzle that, when joined with

seven other cards, made the same exact
image of the beckoning soft one but
eight times bigger. I had the blue lapels
and red bow tie, the sugar-cone-flesh
lips parted in a pure white smile, the
exposed, towering brain of vanilla,
cream-kissed at the top into a pointed
swirl, but I didn't have the eyes.

A complete puzzle won you the
Special Softee, like Coney Island in a
plastic dish—four twirled Softee loads
of cream, chocolate sauce, butterscotch,
marshmallow goo, nuts, party-colored
sprinkles, raisins, M&M's, shredded
coconut, bananas, all topped with
a cherry. You couldn't purchase the
Special Softee, you had to win it, or so
said Mel, who, through the years, had
come to be known simply as Softee.

Occasionally Mel would try to be
pleasant, but I think the paper canoe
of a hat he wore every day soured him.
He also wore a blue bow tie, a white
shirt, and white pants. His face was
long and crooked, and, at times, when
the orders came too fast and the kids
didn't have the right change, the bottom
half of his face would slowly melt—
a sundae abandoned at the curb.
His long ears sprouted tufts of hair as
if his skull contained a hedge of it,
and the lenses of his glasses had
internal flaws like diamonds. In a
voice that came straight from his
freezer, he called my sister, Mary,
and all the other girls "Sweetheart."

Earlier in the season, one late ▶

afternoon, my brother, Jim, said to me, "You want to see where Softee lives?" We took our bikes. He led me way up Hammond Lane, past the shoe store and the junior high school, up beyond Our Lady of Lourdes. After a half hour of riding, he stopped in front of a small house. As I pulled up, he pointed to the place and said, "Look at that dump."

Softee's truck was parked on a barren plot at the side of the place. I remember ivy and a one-story house, no bigger than a good-sized garage. Shingles showed their zebra stripes through fading white. The porch had obviously sustained a meteor shower. There were no lights on inside, and I thought this strange because twilight was mixing in behind the trees.

"Is he sitting in there in the dark?" I asked my brother.

Jim shrugged as he got back on his bike. He rode in big circles around me twice and then shot off down the street, screaming over his shoulder as loud as he could, "Softee sucks!" The ride home was through true night, and he knew that without him I would get lost, so he pedaled as hard as he could.

We had forsaken the jingle bells of Bungalow Bar and Good Humor all summer in an attempt to win Softee's contest. By the end of July, though, each of the kids on the block had at least two near-complete puzzles, but no one had the eyes. I had heard from Tim Sullivan, who lived in the development on the other side of the school field, that the kids over there got fed up one day and rushed the truck, jumped up and swung from the bar that held the rearview mirror, invaded the driver's compartment, all the while yelling, "Give us the eyes. The fuckin' eyes." When Softee went up front to chase them, Tim's brother, Bill, leaped up on the sill of the window through which Softee served his customers, leaned into the inner sanctum, unlatched the freezer, and started tossing Italian ices out to the kids standing at the curb.

Softee lost his glasses in the fray, but the hat held on. He screamed, "You little bitches!" at them as they played him back and forth from the driver's area to the serving compartment. In the end, Mel got two big handfuls of cards and tossed them out on the street. "Like flies on dogshit," said Tim. By the time they'd realized there wasn't a pair of eyes in the bunch, Softee had turned the bell off and was coasting silently around the corner.

I had a theory, though, that day at summer's end when I sat at the curb, waiting. It was my hope that Softee had been holding out on us until the close of the season, and then, in the final days before school started and he quit his route till spring, some kid was going to have bestowed upon him a pair of eyes. I had faith like I never had at church that something special ▶

9

An Excerpt from Jeffrey Ford's
The Shadow Year (continued)

was going to happen that day to me.
It did, but it had nothing to do with ice
cream. I sat there at the curb, waiting,
until the sun started to go down and
my mother called me in for dinner.
Softee never came again, but as it
turned out, we all got the eyes. ◯

Have You Read?
More by Jeffrey Ford

THE DROWNED LIFE

There is a town that brews a strange intoxicant from a rare fruit called the deathberry—and once a year a handful of citizens are selected to drink it. . .

There is a life lived beneath the water—among rotted buildings and bloated corpses—by those so overburdened by the world's demands that they simply give up and go under. . .

In this mesmerizing blend of the familiar and the fantastic, multiple award–winning *New York Times* notable author Jeffrey Ford creates true wonders and infuses the mundane with magic. In tales marked by his distinctive, dark imagery and fluid, exhilarating prose, he conjures up an annual gale that transforms the real into the impossible, invents a strange scribble that secretly unites a significant portion of society, and spins the myriad dreams of a restless astronaut and his alien lover. Bizarre, beautiful, unsettling, and sublime, *The Drowned Life* showcases the exceptional talents of one of contemporary fiction's most original artists.

"The 16 stories in this collection are a perfect introduction to Ford's work and illustrate the vast range of his imagination. . . . If you haven't discovered Ford, it's time you did. His carefully crafted novels and short stories are all top-notch. Grade: A."
—*Rocky Mountain News* ▶

Have You Read? *(continued)*

THE GIRL IN THE GLASS
(EDGAR AWARD WINNER)

The Great Depression has bound a nation in despair—and only a privileged few have risen above it: the exorbitantly wealthy . . . and the hucksters who feed upon them. Diego, a seventeen-year-old undocumented Mexican immigrant, owes his salvation to master grifter Thomas Schell. Together with Schell's gruff and powerful partner, they sail comfortably through hard times, scamming New York's grieving rich with elaborate, ingeniously staged séances—until an impossible occurrence changes everything.

While "communing with spirits," Schell sees an image of a young girl in a pane of glass, silently entreating the con man for help. Though well aware that his otherworldly "powers" are a sham, Schell inexplicably offers his services to help find the lost child—drawing Diego along with him into a tangled maze of deadly secrets and terrible experimentation.

At once a hypnotically compelling mystery and a stunningly evocative portrait of Depression-era New York, *The Girl in the Glass* is a masterly literary adventure from a writer of exemplary vision and skill.

"Ford has written a book that features a dog man who impersonates a dog and a snake that dies of a broken heart. That, for the record, is a winning combination."
—Chelsea Cain, *New York Times*

A mysterious and richly evocative novel, *The Portrait of Mrs. Charbuque* tells the story of portraitist Piero Piambo, who is offered a commission unlike any other. The client is Mrs. Charbuque, a wealthy and elusive woman who asks Piambo to paint her portrait, though with one bizarre twist: he may question her at length on any topic, but he may not, under any circumstances, see her. So begins an astonishing journey into Mrs. Charbuque's world and the world of 1893 New York society in this hypnotically compelling literary thriller.

"A strange and affecting tale of obsession, inspiration, and the supernatural, with a dash of murder thrown in. . . . The twists and turns of Mrs. Charbuque's commission keep the pages turning."
—*New York Times Book Review*

"Art history, Hitchcockian suspense, and Pynchonesque augury."
—*Baltimore Sun*

Discover great authors, exclusive offers, and more at hc.com.